IGNITE

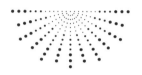

JOCELYNN DRAKE
RINDA ELLIOTT

Cover art by Stephen Drake of Design by Drake.

Copyedited and proofed by Flat Earth Editing.

❀ Created with Vellum

Jocelynn: For the Drakes and their love of explosions.

Rinda: To May Archer. It was so fun meeting you at the retreat. Thanks for your help with the plotting of this book.

ACKNOWLEDGMENTS

Jocelynn: I'd like to give Robert with Fight Write consulting a big thanks for giving me a crash course in grenades, explosives, and other things that have likely put me on the NSA's watch lists.

And a big sloppy wet kiss for the NSA for not kicking down my door for researching the stuff I'm putting in these books.

Rinda: Thanks to Flat Earth Editing for their eagle eyes.

CHAPTER ONE

*R*owe Ward took a drink of the beer in front of him and cleared his throat for the second time. It still didn't dislodge the lump that had swelled in his throat. He'd known this was going to be a difficult day. Not like he didn't have ample warning and time to prepare. But even with time and warning, emotions rose and swirled in his chest, making it difficult to breathe.

This should have been easier.

Lucas Vallois stood, his muscular frame expertly wrapped in a black tux. He slipped his free hand casually into one pocket, looking for all the world like he was gracing the cover of some men's magazine. The room went quiet as Lucas stared down at Ian Pierce, now Banner, giving him a genuine smile that held all the warmth of what he felt for the man. Lucas loved him, just as they all did. It was impossible not to love Ian.

"When Ian came into my life, everything changed for the better. Not a day goes by where I don't think about how lucky I am to have met him. He took a ragtag group of friends and turned us into a real family. And when I say real family, I mean the group of people you would do anything for. The group of people you can't live without. Ian came into our world and rounded us out in ways we didn't even

1

know we needed. Our lives are blessed with his presence, and I truly enjoy all the time spent with him." He paused and Ian gave him a radiant smile.

"One thing I cherish most is our weekly breakfasts. As some of you know, Ian lived with me in the penthouse for a time. Though, I'm pretty sure Rowe and Snow lived there as well, considering the amount of time they spent there."

"It's the one place we could always find a free meal," Snow shouted back at him. A ripple of laughter floated around the room, and Lucas shook his head with a smile.

Rowe had to agree, but the four of them knew Lucas's well-stocked fridge was not the reason for their nearly constant appearances at the penthouse. It was so much about the family Lucas was talking about.

When the room was quiet, Lucas continued his story. "Too soon, Ian wanted to move out and get his own place. Now, some people call me a controlling man." Lucas paused again for the low laughter that filled the reception hall.

Controlling was putting it lightly, but Rowe was pleased to see that Lucas's husband, Andrei, had helped to mellow those instincts a bit.

"Controlling or not, I thought it was too soon for Ian to leave. To get me to be more reasonable, he promised to come over twice a week and cook breakfast at the penthouse. He said it was his way to make sure I was eating properly. It was my way of checking up on him. We both knew that no matter how amazing Ian's cooking was, it was never about the food. It was about touching base with those you love.

"Years have passed since we first made that agreement. We both now have new families. He still comes to my place and spoils me as he has from the very beginning. And now he spoils my daughter just as much. Ian is a warm and caring man, who loves with everything he is. Hollis, you're a lucky guy."

Hollis, looking fine in his black tux, raised his glass and nodded his head.

"Finding true love is one of the greatest gifts we can receive," Lucas continued. "I couldn't be happier that Ian and Hollis have found theirs and I wish them many, many wonderful years together."

Ian stood and hugged Lucas, joyful tears on his cheeks.

A hand touched Rowe's and he turned to find his partner, Noah Keegan, watching him. As it always did when he looked at the man, his heart gave a little excited patter. Noah had left his wavy, brownish-blond hair loose, and he looked fantastic in his suit. Rowe himself might have complained about putting on his penguin suit—neither of them was the suit type—but his dressed-up surfer man looked pretty damn sexy tonight. He winked at him and threaded their fingers together.

The Ault Park Pavilion was the perfect spot for Ian's wedding and reception. The location was one of the most sought after in all the city, a small oasis away from downtown with its lush rose garden and old trees providing a green wall against the city and residential neighborhoods.

But for all the exquisitely landscaped gardens, the real jewel of the park was the white-pillared hall at the top of the hill. Two sets of wide steps led up to it, and in the middle was a tiered fountain that glowed in the evening, lit by warm, yellow lights.

More golden lights had been set around the hall and in the bushes, twinkling in the waning spring light. Blue and white flowers graced the tables, all covered in pristine white tablecloths.

Ian had been planning his wedding for a long time, and Rowe secretly believed he'd put it off because he enjoyed the planning part of it so much. That and he wanted to be married on the perfect date. No anniversary for anything, just a day of their very own to celebrate. He'd picked May for that reason.

And now he was already heavily involved in planning their friend Snow's wedding.

Snow and Jude sat next to them, and Rowe noticed their hands were under the table—probably entwined as well. Their whole group had turned into a bunch of lovesick fools—and he couldn't be happier about it.

He had never expected to find love again after the loss of his wife more than three years before. On the drive to the wedding, he and Noah had taken a short detour. The house he bought with Mel was only a few short blocks from the park. Since the fire, the old house had been torn down and a new one that looked nothing like his old home had sprung up in its place. There was a twinge of sadness that the house she'd loved was gone, but he knew she was still with him.

And she'd be happy that he'd found Noah.

Noah had swept back into his life and shown him it was good to live again. God, he thanked the stars daily for the man.

"So, when are you two tying the knot?" Snow asked Rowe, his usual smirk in place. The music had started again, and people were milling about or dancing.

Rowe felt Noah flinch, and his gut clenched. *What was that about?*

Did Noah want to get married? They'd never talked about it before. And until this moment, not one of his friends had been insane enough to broach the topic.

Marriage was not on Rowe's list of things to do. He didn't feel they needed it. Rowe had already been married, and he'd loved having that with Mel. But then, once he'd decided that he wanted to be with her forever, marriage had felt like a natural step. He knew he wanted to be with Noah forever, but for some reason marriage wasn't necessary.

But he didn't know how Noah felt. Not really. The man had worried in the past that Rowe would want to go back to a woman, and he couldn't be more wrong. He loved Noah with a fierce passion that would last for the rest of his life. That was never going to change. They didn't need marriage to prove their love was strong and real.

Of course, Noah had never been married before. Maybe it was something he wanted. Something he needed to feel complete. And would he want kids to go along with that marriage? Lucas had an adorable little girl. Snow was starting to talk adoption with Jude. Ian was going to have a herd of kids, no doubt. For most people, the natural progression of a relationship was marriage and kids. It was normal to want those things.

A growing uneasiness churned in Rowe's stomach. He didn't want those things at all. What if Noah did? What would happen to them?

He realized Snow was still waiting on an answer, and he forced a laugh. "Our knot is pretty damn tied already."

Noah grinned and tightened his fingers on Rowe's.

Ian and Hollis got up to dance and Ian looked so dazzlingly happy, Rowe felt the prick of tears behind his eyes. He blinked them away. Only Ian could bring up this kind of emotion. If anyone deserved happiness, it was Ian. He'd had a horrible time as a teenager and young adult, and it was only because Rowe and his friends had become attached to him so fast that they were able to get him out of the life he'd been sold into. Yeah, *sold.*

His parents had been the worst sort of losers imaginable. Now, he looked up at his much bigger husband with so much love, Rowe felt it from across the room. And Hollis was looking right back at him the same way. Like he cherished the man. He should. Ian was pretty damned special.

"I didn't like Hollis at first, but he's turned out to be a stand-up guy," Snow said.

"None of us liked him at first because he was so obviously interested in Ian, but it turned out great. Ian couldn't have found a guy more perfect for him." Rowe lifted Noah's hand and kissed his knuckles, telling him silently that he felt the same about them. He glanced up to find Noah's blue eyes watching him closely. He stared back, wondering how Noah felt about the marriage conversation. Had he hurt the man by brushing it off?

Would Noah feel he loved him less because he'd been married to Mel?

Fuck, just the thought gutted him. He didn't want Noah to ever feel vulnerable, yet the thought of his wife made his heart turn over. It didn't slice through him as it once had. His grief would always be a part of him—he'd always miss her—but some of that pain had finally reached a tolerable point. And he felt completely blessed when it came to Noah.

It also helped to know that Mel would have been nuts about Noah. Everyone who met him liked him. He had one of those easygoing personalities that drew people to him. He also had an ornery streak that reeled Rowe in like he couldn't believe. The things that man could get him to do...he shifted in his seat and willed his dick back down.

But marriage...it just didn't feel necessary when it came to them. He already felt just as much, if not more, of a connection to Noah than he had Mel. And a part of that was because after suffering that loss, their relationship felt even sweeter.

Others joined Ian and Hollis on the dance floor. Rowe stood and tugged Noah up with him. He didn't enjoy dancing, but he did enjoy holding Noah. Any excuse to do that was okay with him. Noah pulled him close to his taller body and they swayed to the slow song together. He wrapped his arms tightly around him, loving the slide of hard muscles against him.

It still surprised him to this day how much he loved Noah Keegan. They'd had a brief one-night stand years before, when they'd both served in the Army, and it had freaked Rowe out. But now, he couldn't imagine his life without him. So between Noah, his dogs, and his friends, Rowe's life felt complete.

Fuck, apparently weddings made him sappy.

He tucked his face into Noah's neck, dropping a light kiss on his warm skin. Noah tightened his arms. Two and a half years together and it was still as exciting as it had been in the beginning. Maybe even more so because now there was the warmth of familiarity. The tight bond they'd created. And the sex...well, the sex was unbelievable. He felt like he'd never get enough of Noah. He moved closer and felt the telltale swell of Noah's dick against him. Seemed his man was enjoying the wedding, or dancing, just as much.

The music changed to a fast number and they left the dance floor and returned to the table where Andrei had stopped to talk to Snow, his baby daughter, Daciana, in his arms. She looked around with wide brown eyes that lit on her daddy every so often. Andrei stroked a hand over her hair, and she gave one of those baby smiles that made everyone around her melt. Even Rowe, who didn't want children of his own, wasn't immune to that little smile. Just like her fathers, he was ready to hand her the world. He was happy as an uncle, though. One who planned to babysit when she was a little bigger.

Noah leaned over to touch her cheek, and she gave him another smile. Noah turned into a puddle of goo and in the next moment, he was holding her and smiling down at her. Did Noah want children? He looked as if he'd be great with kids. A natural. Adding children to their lives wasn't something they'd talked about. From Rowe's point of view, their life together was already perfect. The two of them against the world.

Ian came to the table and hugged Snow, who reached up to pull him in close. He had been hugging them all a lot today, basking in the joy of the day. Rowe wasn't surprised he'd taken Hollis's name—it wasn't as if his own last name carried any sentimentality. Ian was starting a completely new chapter in his life, and his happiness was stamped on his face like he exuded sunshine.

He turned and hugged Rowe, who laughed and hugged him back.

"I can't help it. I'm so happy you're all here with me today," Ian said.

"Where else would we be? Wouldn't miss this for the world." Rowe clapped him on the shoulder. "It was a beautiful ceremony."

"It was, wasn't it? It's hard to believe it's finally here."

"You did put this off longer than any of us expected."

"I wanted it to be perfect, and it has been." He looked around, his gaze stopping on his new husband. Hollis started walking toward them.

"When do you leave for the honeymoon?" Rowe asked, knowing they were going to the French countryside for some kind of food and wine tour.

Hollis joined them, sliding an arm around Ian and kissing his temple. "Tomorrow."

"He's looking forward to the medieval castles," Ian said.

"The food, too," Hollis said. "Though I'm already spoiled in that department."

Ian grinned and leaned up to kiss him.

Damn, it was good seeing him so happy. "Sounds like a fun vacation. Noah and I have a vacation planned, but we're just going camping."

Ian shuddered and Rowe burst out laughing, thinking about the last time he'd taken Ian camping. The man had been sure they were going to be attacked by bears. That had been a fun trip—mostly. Up until they'd gone on a search for a missing five-year-old boy. But luckily, they'd found him.

He thought about their upcoming camping trip. Just Noah and a tent with all the sex they liked to have out in the woods. He couldn't wait.

～

*N*oah smiled to himself as he watched Rowe drive them home. His hands slid easily along the leather wheel. Soon those strong hands would be stroking down his body. The way the man kept looking at him during the wedding had him half-hard all evening. He knew it was the wedding—all the romance in the air.

A lingering worry had nipped at him earlier in the day that Ian's wedding would bring back painful memories of Rowe's own wedding, but he seemed fine and Noah couldn't be more thankful.

So, he watched those hands. Being touched by Rowe was like nothing else in this world. The man worshiped his body with an all-in intensity that frankly awed Noah. And he knew that wouldn't change, no matter how long they were together. He took in his dark-red hair, lit by moonlight, disheveled as usual, and his ripped shoulders and arms. The man filled out a suit well, but he couldn't wait to peel him out of it.

"Keep staring at me like that, and I'll be finding a secluded spot to pull over," Rowe murmured, giving him a steamy look.

"That'd be fine with me. Did I tell you how hot you are today? You should wear suits more often."

"Soon as we get home, I'll show you my birthday suit."

"That's my favorite suit of all." Noah grinned.

Rowe pulled to a stop at a red light and turned toward him, his green-eyed gaze hotter than the sun. "You clean up nice yourself. Come here."

Noah leaned over to kiss him. Brakes squealed sharply. Noah jerked his lips away from Rowe's before they could touch. A car had pulled up, perpendicular to theirs, in the middle of the intersection. A loud bang quickly followed and the ping of glass breaking. Startled, he looked at the windshield to find a small hole in it.

"Shit, get down!" Rowe grabbed him and shoved him into the seat, covering him with his body just as another shot broke through the windshield.

"Someone is fucking shooting at us!" Rowe stretched over him to reach the glove box where he kept his gun. He yanked it out but stayed down. "Are you hurt?"

Noah couldn't believe the man covered him, but that was Rowe. "No, I'm fine. You?"

"I'm good."

Tires squealed again and the roar of the car engine grew softer. A knock on the driver's window had them both jerking upright. Rowe aimed the gun in that direction, ready to put two in whoever was stupid enough to be standing there. Noah rose, ready to jump out of their truck and attack.

The woman outside screamed and ducked away from the window. "I was just making sure you were all right!" she yelled, and Rowe immediately lowered his gun. "The person shooting drove off, but I got a good look at the car. I'm beside you at the stoplight. The driver just pulled right into the intersection and someone shot out of the front passenger window. Is everyone okay? I called 9-1-1."

Noah looked out the windshield to find the first hole directly in front of him. He turned and found a matching bullet hole in the seat. It would have pierced his heart. Whoever shot at them had one hell of an aim. Or at least, they would have if Noah hadn't leaned over to kiss Rowe at that moment. *Holy fuck, that was close!*

His stomach was in knots as he met his boyfriend's gaze. "What the hell?"

Rowe rolled down his window, apologizing to the woman for scaring her. "What kind of car was it?"

"A black Volkswagen hatchback."

"Did you see anyone in the car? Could you tell if either person was a man or woman?"

"The passenger looked like a man. I'm sorry, I didn't get a good look at the person's face."

Sirens sounded in the distance, getting steadily closer. Rowe put his gun back into the glovebox and they both got out of the truck to look at the damage. Two police cars arrived with a roar of engines. The first cop opened his door and stood with his gun at the ready.

"The shooter drove away," the woman yelled. She was certainly helpful and brave to have gotten out of her car at all. Her red Honda was still parked at the light beside them with several more cars stalled there as well. None of those people had gotten out of their vehicles, but now they did as the police gathered.

Rowe and Noah answered questions but because they'd ducked, they had less to offer by way of explanation than the woman who'd witnessed the whole thing.

"Was more than likely a drive-by," one of the cops said as he made a few notes in his little notepad. "We've had a few of them recently. I'm glad nobody was hurt this time. The others weren't so lucky."

But Noah had a feeling it wasn't some random drive-by. He couldn't explain it; he just felt there was more to the story. His gut was screaming at him that it felt personal. He'd only aimed at Noah instead of emptying a clip into the both of them.

They drove home in silence, the warm afterglow from the wedding ruined. Now he watched the cars rather than the twinkling city lights, his whole body tense with worry and suspicion.

When they pulled up to the house, Rowe hit the garage door opener and Noah pulled out the gun again, keeping a close watch on their surroundings. After Rowe shut the garage door, they sat staring at each other before Rowe grabbed him and yanked him across the seat. He wrapped tight arms around him.

"That was so damn close," he murmured against Noah's neck.

"I'm fine, babe. You can see that I am." Noah set the gun down.

"If I lost you, I wouldn't survive," Rowe whispered.

"You would, but nothing happened other than the damage to the truck."

"I don't give a fuck about that. Just you." He pulled away and cupped the sides of Noah's face, then kissed him. It was a slow kiss full of love and it made desire curl into Noah's body as he tightened his hands on Rowe's muscular arms. Noah deepened the kiss, loving the low groan that rumbled from Rowe's throat. He twined his tongue with his lover's and felt the answering shudder in Rowe's body. He leaned back and looked at him, meeting those worried green eyes.

"Come on, let's go greet our dogs and go to bed."

"After we check the house."

"After we check the house," he agreed.

Inside, Igor, Vlad, and Daisy ran to them, letting them know all was right in the house. Two Rottweilers and a German shepherd were a pretty big deterrent to anyone thinking of breaking into their place, but they still checked every room and the security system. Now that he was safe, Noah was shaking a little on the inside at just how close he'd come to losing his life. And after such a wonderful day.

When they stood in the bedroom, undressing, Rowe stood beside the bed, frowning at Noah, worry still darkening his gaze. "I don't feel like that was a random drive-by," he said quietly.

"I don't think so either," Noah admitted.

CHAPTER TWO

*N*oah stood with his hands folded on the top of his head as he watched Garrett hit Dom with a leg sweep, knocking him onto his back. A loud, sweaty *thwack* echoed above the uproar as he hit the vinyl mat. Surrounding him were the sounds of men shouting at one another through training sessions, cheers, and fists hitting heavy bags.

On the second floor, he could easily imagine Quinn, Gidget, and Cole quietly arguing over some technical wizardry he couldn't begin to comprehend. He'd been pretty handy with all things tech about ten years ago, but now the kind of stuff the triplets were dealing with just shot straight over his head.

Something settled and gave a happy sigh deep in his chest. He was wrapped up in the day-to-day chaos that was Ward Security. He'd found a home with Rowe Ward and his dogs, but Ward Security and the men who worked there were proving to be an amazing second home. He fit among these people, the sounds, and the insanity that seemed to lurk around every corner.

"Hey, Noah!"

Noah dropped his hands and turned around as Dom picked himself up off the mat, looking for who had called out his name.

Jackson Kent jogged across the main floor toward him with an easy smile, his blond hair disheveled and sweaty. Rowe had managed to recruit him from another security firm on the West Coast, and he'd proved to be an amazing asset over the past several months.

It should have been a sign that he'd be a great fit when he promptly started dating his first client after the case had been closed. Last Noah had heard, Jackson and Wade were still an item and starting to talk about moving in together.

Noah stepped away from the small group watching Dom and Garrett spar so he could talk to Jackson without needing to shout.

"What's up?"

"I heard about the shooting this weekend when you were leaving the wedding."

Noah scratched his jaw, forcing a bit of a smile. He hated that something so horrible was now forever linked to such a perfect event. "You know Rowe and I don't believe in a normal, quiet day," he joked.

Jackson crossed his arms over his chest and frowned at Noah. "Seriously, you okay? How close of a call was it?"

He liked that about Jackson. He was damn perceptive. The man wouldn't be distracted by Noah's attempt at humor. "I'm fine. We're both fine. It was closer than either of us would have liked it to have been, but we're safe."

"Do you have any guesses as to why you were targeted?"

Noah shook his head. "The cops said there's been an increase in drive-by shootings and carjackings. It could have been an attempted theft. Or maybe mistaken identity. Thought we were some gang members targeted for a hit."

"You don't think it was possibly related to any other activities?"

Noah couldn't help but smirk. It was no great secret that the Ward Security boys occasionally took matters into their own hands to protect their people. "We've been good recently." Well, except for that little job to rescue Snow and take down the man who'd hurt Jude's brother.

Jackson took a half-step forward and lowered his voice a little. "I want to make sure you and Rowe know you can rely on me for the more unusual jobs if something comes up. I know I haven't been here as long as some of the other guys…"

Noah clapped his hand on Jackson's broad shoulder and squeezed. His heart warmed just a little bit more. Jackson was one of the newest security agents to join the team, and he supported the men and women he worked beside without question. "Don't worry. We know you've got the backs of your brothers and sisters at Ward, regardless of the job."

Jackson's face lit up with a mix of joy and relief. "Good. I know I dragged my feet about accepting Rowe's offer to join the company, but I didn't want him to think that I wasn't all in. This place—"

Noah frowned as Jackson stopped midsentence. His face turned pale and all the joy drained from his expression as he stared at a point over Noah's shoulder. Noah quickly turned around, trying to spot what had crushed the man's mood so fast.

A stranger was briskly walking down the stairs from the second floor. He had broad shoulders and thick, muscular arms that stretched the sleeves of his black button-down shirt. He wasn't wearing a jacket or a tie, but Noah guessed that this person had just come from Rowe's office. The boss man had been complaining that morning that he had yet another interview to conduct, and this guy looked like a bodyguard.

As he reached the bottom couple of steps, the man spotted Jackson. He grinned and winked at him before heading straight for the lobby.

"What's Dale Carson doing here?" Jackson demanded in a low voice.

"I think he was interviewing with Rowe for the open agent position. Do you know him?"

"I gotta talk to Rowe," Jackson muttered, not seeming to hear Noah's question. Without looking back at Noah, Jackson hurried up the stairs toward Rowe's office.

Curious, Noah followed him. Prior to coming to Ward Security, Jackson had spent five years working for another amazing security company that provided services to billionaires, rock stars, and celebrities. The man knew his shit. But it also meant he knew a lot of other bodyguards. Apparently, this stranger was someone he'd encountered before.

They reached Rowe's office just as Andrei was stepping out into the hall. The COO smiled at them as he tucked his tablet under his arm and headed toward his office down the hall. People around the building had started to call him "Poppa Andrei" now that he'd finally brought his sweet daughter to meet everyone. Noah couldn't recall ever seeing such a large group of sweaty, grumpy alpha males turn into gooey, cooing puddles so fast as when they set eyes on that dark-haired angel dressed in her tiny Ward Security T-shirt.

Jackson briefly knocked on the doorframe of Rowe's office and stepped inside, with Noah following on his heels. Rowe was sitting at his desk, frowning at his computer screen like it was denying him access to something once again. Fuck, Noah felt sorry for Gidget at times. The guy was just horrible with computers, and despite all the amazing work that Gidget did, Rowe couldn't stop himself from relying on the poor woman to get his shit to work each day. But he had a feeling Gidget secretly enjoyed taking care of her boss. She was a bundle of maternal instincts, and she took care of all of them.

"What's up, boys?" Rowe said, finally looking up.

"What was Dale Carson doing here?" Jackson demanded.

Rowe's brow crinkled a little at Jackson's tone, but the man wasn't one to beat around the bush about something. "Job interview for security agent. You know him?"

"Yeah, we worked together at Sanctuary in LA. You can't hire him."

Noah silently shut the door to Rowe's office and leaned against the wall beside it. Rowe sat back in his chair, crossing his arms over his chest. While Rowe and Andrei oversaw the day-to-day operations and handled the scheduling, Noah had taken over the training of all the agents. If Rowe decided to offer this Dale guy a job against Jackson's wishes, he wanted to know what he could potentially be up against when it came to either man.

"Why's that?" Rowe asked.

"Dale Carson is a fucking cancer. He thinks he's God's gift to the world and that he knows better than everyone else. While on jobs, he lets his ego get in the way of keeping clients safe. He won't listen to anyone placed in a position of authority over him, and he won't listen to a client. I've seen him speak abusively to clients, and I've seen him put clients in danger as a way of getting even or punishing them for not giving him preferential treatment."

"And this was at Sanctuary?" Noah asked. "That place has a killer reputation. You'd think that would take a hit with a guy like that."

Jackson turned sideways so he could more easily face both Rowe and Noah. "They learned quickly that they couldn't put him on smaller or personal details. He had to be part of a larger group that didn't have direct contact with the client." He turned his head to look back at Rowe. "I'm not saying he's not good. He is. He's got skills. He knows how to use a weapon and has good instincts, but he lets his fucking ego get in the way. I don't actually see him risking his own life and health to protect someone."

Rowe sat forward in his chair, placing his folded hands on the top of his desk. Noah hated to see the lines of fatigue deepening around Rowe's tired green eyes or the lines around his mouth. Stress was weighing down on his lover's shoulders.

"Anything else?"

Jackson took a deep breath, his hands fisting at his sides for a moment before he opened them again. There was a sadness in his voice, a worry, that Noah had never heard from him before. "Since coming to Ward Security, I've found a family here that I never had at Sanctuary. It was a job. A good one, but just a job. But here, everyone is close. When shit goes down—whether it's Dom being hunted by his brother or helping Quinn move in with Shane or planning Ian's bachelor party—everyone jumps in to help. No questions asked. I don't want to see Dale Carson tear apart this family, and I feel like that's exactly what he'd do."

"I'm not hiring him," Rowe said firmly.

Jackson sighed so heavily with relief that he almost seemed to sway on his feet.

A little smile toyed with Rowe's mouth, and Noah felt himself relax as well. "He was a cocky son of a bitch and walked in like he knew he already had the job. Like meeting me and Andrei was just a formality." Rowe snorted. "Fucker even talked down to Andrei once. I thought Andrei was going to challenge him to a few rounds on the mats."

"That would have taken him down a peg or two," Noah said.

Jackson shook his head. "You would think so, but not Dale."

Rowe's expression grew serious. "You should know that he mentioned you as a reference. Obviously, we're not going to tell him that you didn't endorse him when we call him to say that we've passed."

Jackson nodded. "Thanks. I didn't tell you anything I wouldn't say to the man's face, but I'm not looking for trouble with him."

"And if you happen to have any friends who would fit in at Ward, I'd appreciate it if you gave them a nudge in our direction," Rowe prodded.

Jackson flashed Rowe a wide smile and nodded. "Yeah, I'll keep that in mind. There might be a few people I wouldn't mind working with here."

Noah stepped away from the door, patting Jackson once on the shoulder as the man left, and then closed the door again behind him. When he turned toward Rowe, the man loudly sighed and slouched deep in his chair.

"That was my fourth fucking interview in the past two weeks and nothing!" He dropped his arms over the back of his chair and glared at his computer screen. "I feel like I'm just spinning my wheels while I've got more clients coming on every day with all these high-maintenance needs. I've got guys wanting to actually take a little vacation time because they've got these fucking boyfriends all of a sudden. It's clear that Sanctuary is struggling out on the West Coast, and Andrei is giving me that same fucking Lucas look."

"What 'Lucas look'?"

"The one that says I need to get off my ass and expand to the West Coast so we can soak up all the clients that Sanctuary is losing. But neither one of us has any interest in moving out to LA, even temporarily, so that means finding someone we trust to set up and run the West Coast branch."

Noah smiled at his lover, his heart going out to him. Rowe was not the kind of guy who sat behind a desk all day and thought of ways to expand his empire so he could take over the world. That was a Lucas thing. Rowe just had this idea of starting a little security company to keep some local people safe.

But his good idea grew into a great business filled with amazing people dedicated to protection, honesty, and justice. As a result, Ward Security was growing into something far bigger than Rowe ever dreamed, and he was struggling to meet everyone's needs.

"And then there's that damn shooting I can't get out of my head. I don't believe for a second that it was random. I don't care what the cops say."

Noah arched an eyebrow at him. "Then what shit have you been into that has followed you home?"

Rowe sat up and pointed at Noah. "I haven't been into any Black Ops or secret shit in yea—" He caught himself at the last second and cleared his throat. He had his teeth clenched together so tightly that Noah could see the muscle jumping in his jaw. "It's been a really fucking long time. What about you? The bastard shot at you."

"And we both know that it doesn't mean I was necessarily the target. The fact is, we don't have any information to go off yet. It could be nothing or something."

"That doesn't help in the least."

He had just the thing to help Rowe relax. Before pushing away from the door, Noah turned the little lock in the doorknob, keeping anyone from accidentally walking into the office when they didn't want to be disturbed.

As he crossed the room, Rowe glared at him. "Go unlock the door. We can't do this now."

Noah stepped around the desk and placed one hand on Rowe's chair, pushing him backward. "Do what?"

"No fucking around during business hours."

"That's never stopped us before. Think of it as a nooner."

"It's four in the afternoon."

"Yeah, but a four-er doesn't sound as good."

Rowe cleared his throat like he was trying to keep from laughing and sat up a little in his chair. "I'm the boss, Noah. I've told them no fucking around in the office, and that goes for me too."

Noah paused, eyes narrowed on Rowe for a second, before a wicked thought came to him. Bending down, he pulled open the bottom drawer of Rowe's desk and started to dig around while still holding Rowe's eyes. There was no missing the way his breathing ticked up just a little bit, and his lovely green eyes dilated. There was only one thing Noah would be looking for in that drawer.

"Noah," Rowe said in a warning voice that had also become warm and husky.

He smiled when his fingers wrapped around the bottle of lube. He straightened and smiled at Rowe. "If you don't want to relieve a little stress, then I'm going to go into your private bathroom and think about how good your cock is going to taste when I go down on you tonight."

He strolled into the small private bathroom in Rowe's office. He left the door open, listening for some sign that Rowe had moved. There was nothing for several seconds but the pounding of his own heart.

Reaching down, he unfastened his pants and shoved his hand inside to quickly stroke his dick. He'd gotten hard the moment he thought of kneeling in front of Rowe's chair and sucking him down his throat, the office building still buzzing with employees all around them. Or Rowe ripping his pants off, bending him over the desk, and plunging deep in his ass.

They'd done that more than once in the office, but they'd always tried to limit it to after hours, when the place was empty. This was a business, and at least one of them needed to be responsible. Rowe just fucking scrambled his brain. He wanted to be sucked, fucked, filled, and then cuddled by his man all the time.

"Fuck," Rowe snarled before he heard muffled footsteps across the carpet. When he appeared in the doorway, he was already unbuckling his belt and attacking the button and zipper on his jeans. "Get on your knees. You're getting an early taste."

Noah happily backed up a step and dropped to his knees, mentally thanking who the fuck ever put a little rug on the tile floor. Rowe slammed the door shut behind him and stepped up to Noah.

Grinning like a madman, Noah shoved Rowe's hands away and attacked his pants, getting his hard cock free. A wonderful hint of musk and sweat hit his nose. Leaning forward, he buried his face in his crotch, breathing him in. God, he could just spend his day wrapped in this man's scent.

"You missed," Rowe growled. "I don't know how you fucking missed, but you did."

"I want to eat all of you up," Noah murmured against his skin. He swiped his tongue slowly along the inside of his hip, enjoying the little shiver from Rowe, who promptly shut his mouth. He jerked Rowe's pants down to his knees and licked lower, circling his dick. Rowe said nothing other than to moan softly, obviously enjoying every touch of Noah's tongue. He loved that about Rowe. The man would just lie there and wallow in sensations whenever Noah wanted to explore his body. There was no tugging or demanding that he hurry up. He just reveled in the fact that Noah wanted—no, *needed*—to touch him.

"Fuck, babe. We should have just gone home," Rowe sighed over his head.

"Couldn't. We have to pick up dog food on the way home tonight," Noah replied, kissing around the base of his cock.

Rowe started to make a whiny noise, but it was instantly cut off by Noah sliding Rowe's hard cock all the way to the back of his throat. Noah could completely agree. He'd much rather be stretched out in bed, naked with Rowe as they fucked each other's brains out, but he could make this good too. Enough to hold them over until they were finally home again.

He flattened his tongue, sliding it along that silky shaft, loving the feel and weight of Rowe in his mouth. Fingers tangled in his long, curly hair. They tightened, holding him in place so Rowe could shove his cock deeper. Noah relaxed his jaw, taking him down until he could feel the rough, curly hairs brushing against his lips. Rowe's breathing picked up and he started making shallow thrusts, nearly gagging him, but instantly backing off again so he could breathe. Fuck, he loved when Rowe got lost in the moment, taking his pleasure. Noah would gladly give up breathing and hand himself over to Rowe to be used however he wanted if it meant Rowe was happy.

Noah's dick throbbed in his open pants, demanding attention. But not yet. He wanted to feel and hear Rowe come first.

His hands fisted and he suddenly remembered that he was holding the bottle of lube in his right. Still sliding up and down Rowe's cock, he opened the bottle and squirted some lube on his fingers, not caring what kind of a mess he might be making. Lifting his slicked fingers, he reached behind Rowe and pressed them between his ass cheeks, carefully massaging his hole. Rowe's thrusts increased and he swore loudly. Rowe loved ass play. His dick swelled in his mouth, becoming even harder. Noah pressed two fingers inside of Rowe, stretching him while swirling his tongue around the head of his cock.

Rowe shouted almost instantly, coming hard down Noah's throat. Noah got a hint of the salty flavor on his tongue before he swallowed it, loving the way Rowe's entire body trembled against him.

With a loud grunt, Rowe pulled out of Noah's mouth. "Stand up," Rowe ordered, his voice low and rough. "Your turn."

Noah didn't question it. He carefully pulled his fingers free of Rowe's body and pushed to his feet, ignoring the protest of his knees, while Rowe dropped to his knees in front of him. He watched while Rowe ripped his T-shirt over his head and tossed it aside. The stunning redhead stared up at him with lazy, blissed-out green eyes and Noah took in his wide, muscled chest. Across one pec and along his shoulder was a swirling black tattoo.

Noah grabbed his dick with lube still on his hand and stroked himself, admiring the man's flat stomach and the thick cock that was softer now in the cradle of his open jeans. Everything about the man kneeling before him was so fucking sexy and perfect. Rowe was made for him.

"Come on, babe. I wanna see it. Wanna feel it."

Rowe's low, guttural tone went straight to his fucking balls. There was no stopping the orgasm. He'd been close already, but Rowe shoved him straight over the edge. He gasped as he came hard, shooting across his lover's chest and face. Marking. Claiming him all over again.

Pleasure streaked through Noah's body, leaving him swaying on his feet. He carefully kneeled down and kissed Rowe hard, tasting himself and the man he loved so much together on his tongue. So fucking perfect.

Rowe hummed softly against his lips. "I think we somehow did this wrong."

"Feels pretty damn right to me."

"Yeah, but you sucked me off, and I'm the one who needs a shower."

Noah pulled back a little to look in Rowe's eyes. The lines of worry and fatigue he'd seen there earlier were completely gone. He once again looked as if he was happy. At peace. That was what Noah worked so hard to maintain in Rowe's life. Through all the chaos and insanity, he wanted to offer Rowe that little center of peace and joy.

"Just a couple more hours and then we'll be home. We can keep trying this until we get it right."

"That's a date."

CHAPTER THREE

*N*oah stretched. Bones creaked and muscles burned. There was a wonderful tissue-deep ache that reached straight down to his soul. And it was fucking fantastic.

He lay with his head at the foot of the bed and his toes tucked under the pillows. Goose bumps broke out across his skin as the sweat started to cool under the breeze created by the lazy spin of the ceiling fan. There was still a throb from the deep bite Rowe had taken on his shoulder, and he smiled at the idea of the bruise that would likely form.

Rowe had been waiting for him when he stepped out of the shower after dinner. What had started as sweet and tender quickly turned to voracious need. But that was par for the course with them. They'd been together for more than two years, and they still couldn't get enough of each other. Probably never would. And Noah didn't have a single problem with it.

He was perfectly happy with their life as it was. Work, the dogs, their unique and growing family, and their private time together. He didn't need anything else.

But was it enough for Rowe?

The wedding had started to dredge up old doubts and concerns that he'd thought he'd put to rest long ago. Before Noah showed up on his doorstep, Rowe had enjoyed an entire life with another person. Melissa Ward was a tough act to follow, not that he saw himself in competition with her memory. She'd actually become a guardian angel of sorts for him. When Rowe wasn't around, he'd sometimes find himself standing in front of one of the many pictures of her around the house and talking to her. And it was always about Rowe. If anyone understood the complicated man and what Noah was struggling with, it was Mel.

But the truth of the matter was that Rowe had felt so strongly about his love for Mel that he'd married her. Gotten that damn piece of paper that bound them together in the eyes of the world. He heard about the "pregnancy scare" at Mel's last Thanksgiving with the family. Ian had told them that it had been a wake-up call that got them at least thinking about kids and long-term dreams.

Mel's time was cut short.

Noah picked up the baton in a way. He was there to love and protect Rowe. To give him joy and peace.

But Noah didn't want to get married.

He understood and respected the need of their family members to get married. For Lucas and Andrei, it seemed natural. Same for Ian and Hollis. Snow and Jude were a bit of a surprise, but Noah had a feeling that something had changed a little in both men, or at least they'd both had some hard realizations after Snow had been kidnapped.

Marriage wasn't for him. It felt like a dog that was tethered to a post in the center of a yard, the chain too short to run and play. He didn't want anyone else but Rowe in his life. He'd never want anyone besides Rowe. But he wanted to keep the free feeling he had with Rowe. That they could run together, go on any crazy adventure that caught their attention, and then stumble home battered and exhausted, happiness overflowing from their hearts, when it was all over.

Kids didn't feel like a good fit either. He loved Daciana Vallois with all his heart. She melted something deep inside of him every time he saw her. He could spend hours with her in his arms, and he was looking forward to babysitting, introducing her to the dogs, teaching her so many different things. He looked forward to the kids that Ian and Snow would add to their respective families.

But at the end of the day, they'd go back to their fathers, and he and Rowe would go back to their happy life. Ward Security was their baby. All the employees at Ward were their other family and Noah loved it. He loved running off on one adventure or another when trouble arose. They didn't have to worry about endangering the life of a child. There was no having to choose one over the other.

Their life made sense to him. It was perfect exactly as it was.

But is it enough for Rowe?

That one nagging thought kept tearing at his brain since Ian's wedding. He and Rowe were the only ones left who hadn't announced an impending wedding or plans for kids. Did Rowe want those things? Did he wonder if Noah didn't love him as much as Mel had loved him because he wasn't rushing for the altar or a list of surrogates?

And if Rowe wanted those things, where did it leave Noah?

If he said he didn't want to get married, would he lose Rowe? Or if he admitted that he didn't want to have kids?

Life and relationships were all about compromise, but this was a damn big compromise for one of them. What would happen to the happiness they'd achieved over the past couple of years? Would it wither away under the weight of bitterness and frustration?

If they had kids, Noah had no doubt that he'd love them with all his heart, but would he find himself missing their old life?

And if they didn't get married and have kids, would the rest of their family understand and respect their decision? Would they think that Noah didn't love Rowe enough?

Noah clenched his eyes shut against the tangled questions. He didn't like the answers he was coming up with, because they all seemed to take him a step away from Rowe. And the idea of losing Rowe stole his breath away. He couldn't lose Rowe, so until he came up with a better solution, he was keeping his fucking mouth shut.

A low groan rose from the other side of the bed, and some of the growing panic eased in his chest so he could draw in a deep breath. He turned his head toward the sound and brushed some curls from his face. Rowe's feet weren't too far from his nose. Looking over his shoulder, Noah found his lover sprawled naked across the bed, a light sheen of sweat glistening on his skin, drawing his eyes up to his black tattoo. Fuck, Rowe was sexy. If he could find the energy, he'd crawl up the man and start sucking the sweat off his skin, working back down to that lovely cock and balls until Rowe was shouting his name.

Later.

He'd rest for a few more minutes. Get some water. Maybe a snack. Then he'd fuck Rowe until his voice was hoarse from shouting.

"Whatever wicked thing you're planning, just remember we've got to work tomorrow," Rowe warned in a rough voice.

Noah felt his grin shift, growing even wider. He hadn't even real-ized he'd been giving Rowe a wicked look. "Aren't you the boss? You can come in late tomorrow."

"It's not the coming I'm worried about. It's the walking funny."

Noah chuckled and flopped onto the bed again. At that moment, he felt he'd be lucky if he ever walked again. A strong, rough hand dropped down on his ankle and started to rub the back of his calf. The last of the tension and worry that hummed through his frame instantly dissolved under Rowe's touch.

From the moment they'd started dating, Rowe never hesitated to reach out to touch him. The only place he restrained himself was in the office, and there were plenty of times that he couldn't stop himself there. Sometimes it was only a hand on his shoulder, the nape of his neck, a touch to his lower back. Didn't matter. If Rowe could reach out and touch Noah, he did. He needed that almost constant contact like it was as critical to his survival as oxygen. Like it centered him. And Noah soaked it up. He never wanted to be out of reach of Rowe again.

A muffled chiming slowly drew his attention from where his brain lazily drifted. He didn't want to move. He was too damn comfortable.

"Is that your phone?" Rowe asked.

"I was hoping it was yours," Noah mumbled into the rumpled comforter.

"Nope. Mine's on the nightstand beside me. Sounds like it's coming from your side of the bed."

Noah groaned. The ringing stopped and he sighed. He'd check the caller ID later. But before he could settle, his phone started ringing again. If there was a problem on a job, the person would be calling Rowe. This had to be something else. And likely important if the person was immediately calling again.

Grumbling to himself, he pulled his torso across the bed so he could reach the pile of clothes on the floor. His phone was still in his back pants pocket. As he grabbed the phone, his heart gave an uneven thump in his chest when he saw JB's name flash across the screen. He hadn't talked to his old Army buddy in...*fuck*...it had been at least a couple of years.

Jumping to his feet, Noah answered the call. "JB! What the hell, man. I haven't heard—"

"Oh, thank God!" the familiar voice said in a rush, cutting off Noah's warm greeting. There was a shaky mix of fear and relief rising through those three words. "I was afraid I was too late."

"Too late? What's going on? What's wrong?"

"Can you meet me? Alone?"

"Where are you?"

"I just got to Cincinnati. You're still with that Ward Security, right?"

Noah turned back to the bed to find Rowe sitting up, a look of concern twisting his once-relaxed features. "Yeah," he said slowly.

He couldn't believe JB was in town. He hadn't seen him in a long time. Not since he'd left the military roughly three years ago. They'd been...complicated. Fuck, no...it hadn't been complicated at the time. But it suddenly felt complicated as Noah stood there looking at Rowe.

"Are you on a job? Can you meet me?"

There was a frantic urgency to JB's voice that Noah swore he'd never heard before, and they had been through some pretty hairy shit overseas. "Yes, I can meet you, but what's going on? Why are you in town? What happened?"

"Chris and Paul are dead."

"What?" he asked, his voice soft. It felt like JB had knocked the wind out of him. His knees wobbled and he just barely managed to get to the bed before they gave out. As it was, he sat down on the edge, heavier than he'd meant. Chris and Paul had been part of the team he headed up during his final two years in the Army. It had been just the four of them—Noah, JB, Chris, and Paul.

"They're dead and I think we're going to be next. We've got to talk. Can you meet me?"

"Yeah," he said absently and then repeated it in a stronger voice. He jumped to his feet, quickly searching for a pen and a scrap of paper. His brain was scattered. He was afraid he'd forget anything JB told him before he could reach him. "Where are you?"

"You know the Fairmont in Florence, Kentucky? Off...fuck, what highway—"

"I know where you're at," Noah quickly said. "What room?"

"247."

"I'll be there in twenty-five to thirty minutes."

There was a soft sigh of relief, and Noah's worry grew for his friend and former comrade in arms. "Be careful. Watch your six. And come alone."

JB ended the call and Noah stared at his silent phone for a couple of seconds, his brain utterly confounded by what had just happened. He hadn't heard from JB since he'd told him he was retiring from the Army. His friend hadn't taken it well, accused him of abandoning the team, of abandoning him. He'd later apologized in an email and wished him the best, but Noah had never really felt like the friendship had fully mended.

At the time, Noah had needed to get away from the Army. That life had begun to feel empty, and he'd witnessed too many years of death. He'd needed something more. His heart had known at the time that he'd needed Rowe Ward, but his brain had been unwilling to stake too many hopes on what seemed to be a highly unlikely thing.

"Who's JB?" Rowe asked, drawing his thoughts away from a younger man with a quick and easy smile.

His head snapped up and he stared at his lover's worried expression. "JB...he was on my final team. Ranger. Or maybe former Ranger now." He gave his head a hard shake and snatched up the pants that were on the floor. He should probably take a shower, but it sounded critical that he reach JB as soon as possible. "He's in town. The other two members of our team have turned up dead and he wants to meet. I don't know what's going on, but I need to talk to him."

With his pants on, he grabbed up the T-shirt he'd thrown on the floor. He gave it a quick sniff and jerked back. Okay, that wasn't good to wear again. Dropping it on the floor, he darted over to the closet and grabbed the first shirt he saw. He wasn't even sure if it was his or Rowe's.

Rowe hopped out of the bed and pulled on the pants lying on the floor on his side of the bed. "I'll make sure the dogs are settled and be right behind you."

"No." Noah stood in the center of the room, a pair of folded socks in his hand. "He said to come alone."

"Are you fucking kidding me? After you were nearly shot? Not a chance," Rowe said with a snort.

"I'm serious."

"So am I. You just told me that two other members of your team are dead. There's no fucking way I'm letting you meet this guy alone."

"JB would never hurt me!" Noah said.

"Don't give a shit." The look Rowe gave him reminded him of a bulldog sinking his teeth in and preparing for a fight.

Noah bristled at Rowe's dictatorial tone. The bastard had a way about him when he tapped his fucking inner alpha and just expected everyone to follow behind him. It was like he was spending too much damn time with Lucas. In the bedroom, it never failed to make Noah hard. Outside the bedroom, he ached to punch Rowe in the mouth.

"You don't know him."

"Exactly. I don't. What I do know is that two men you served with are dead, you've been shot at once already, and this guy just suddenly shows up in town. No fucking way you're leaving this house alone!"

Noah glared at his lover for a couple of seconds. As much as he hated to admit it, Rowe was right. Not about JB. He was positive JB wasn't behind their friends' deaths or the recent shooting. If something bigger was going on, then he wanted Rowe right there with him. The man had been through more squirrely and insane situations than he thought possible for a single human being. If anyone could help, it was Rowe.

"We're out the door in five minutes," he growled.

～

*J*f Noah thought he was going to meet this guy alone, he was out of his fucking mind. Rowe was still simmering in the passenger seat as Noah drove them south to the motel where this JB was hiding. His lover had already been shot at. They never got a look at the shooter. It could just as easily have been this asshole. And since he'd failed once, why not just call Noah in and shoot him when his guard was dropped?

To hell with that.

Of course, if Rowe was being honest with himself, it wasn't just that Noah wanted to meet this guy alone. Noah had never mentioned him before. Not that they spoke a lot about what happened after Rowe had left the Army. His years had been largely filled with getting into trouble with Lucas and Snow, rescuing Ian—not a topic that anyone wanted to rehash—and then Mel. It was a fucking minefield.

Rowe didn't feel like Noah's time was going to be much better. Sure, he would have had a team that he worked with, but Rowe had spent plenty of time in the field. He knew what it was like. The fighting, death, uncertainty, and bad intel. He had no desire to bring up those memories for Noah. Not when he could fill their time together with happiness and good memories.

Noah pulled into the dimly lit parking lot of the no-star, two-story motel. All the doors opened directly to the parking lot, making for a quick and easy escape. Noah backed his truck into a spot facing JB's room and cut the engine. There were only about half a dozen other cars in the lot, and they were all parked close to the motel. Lights filled three of the windows. The other guests must have called it a night. Not surprising since it was nearly midnight.

Out of habit, Rowe pulled out his gun, popped the magazine, and checked that it was fully loaded before slamming it home again. He chambered a round. No one was going to steal Noah away from him.

"You feelin' ready over there, Rambo?" Noah drawled.

"We get a call from some guy you haven't heard from in years, demanding that you come *alone* to this nowhere motel, and this is all after you've been shot at once. You really think I was going to come to this unarmed? You're lucky I didn't call in for more backup."

Noah snorted. "The only ones off tonight are Sven and Royce. I'd rather not drag Sven out from under Geoffrey and then deal with little G-man's wrath."

Rowe pursed his lips so he couldn't see his smirk. Geoffrey Ralse was a former client, friend, and now boyfriend of one of his employees. The little guy might be short, slender, and look incredibly delicate, but the kid had surprising skills and he could get vicious when someone tried to pull his Sven away from him. Naturally, the mountain of man just smiled and took it all in stride.

Despite all his talk, Noah still used the key on his ring to open the console between them and pull out his own gun. He went through the same checks as Rowe, helping to ease a little of the anxiety eating away at Rowe's sanity.

"This is not because I don't trust JB. If someone killed Paul and Chris, then they could also be on JB's trail." He narrowed his eyes on Rowe. "I'm not stupid."

Rowe flashed him his best innocent look. "I never said you were stupid."

Noah made a little growl as he grabbed a holster and clipped it to his belt. He shoved the gun inside and pulled his T-shirt down to cover it. Yeah, he was definitely pushing all Noah's buttons and not in a good way, but if they survived this, Rowe would make it up to his lover. He soothed his own conscience with the idea that he couldn't make Noah happy if he wasn't alive.

"I'm still not convinced that the drive-by after Ian's wedding wasn't random or at the very least tied to you."

"Me?"

"Yeah, you," Noah snapped. "You've had way more time and chances to make enemies than me."

Rowe's mouth hung open for a moment in surprise, Noah's words cutting across his heart. Yeah, Jagger had been his fault. The fucker had been after all of them at one time and that put Noah in his sights. He hated that Noah had ever been in danger because of him. Could his actions have put Noah in danger all over again? He'd already lost Mel because he'd not taken more precautions. He couldn't lose Noah too.

"Whoa. Whoa. Whoa...babe." Noah leaned across the cab, his hand sliding up to cup his cheek. He pressed soft kisses to the corner of his mouth and along his lower lip. He was nearly across to the other corner before Rowe could even respond and gently kiss him back. "Regardless of who the bastard is and why he was shooting, it's not your fault. I wouldn't change a thing. Don't want to be anywhere else but right here with you."

"But—"

"No buts except your sexy one," Noah murmured, cutting him off. "Not going to lose me."

Rowe closed his eyes and pressed his forehead against Noah's. He took a deep breath, filling his lungs with the scent of Noah. Hints of his cologne, sex, sweat, and just the wonderfulness of his lover. Noah centered him. Knew his brain better than any other person. Possibly even better than Mel ever did. The growing panic ebbed and rational thought crept in, grabbing control of the reins again.

"Sorry," he mumbled before sitting up.

Noah smiled at him. "Nothing to be sorry about."

They both climbed out of the truck and silently closed the doors. Rowe kept his gun in his hand as they hurried across the open lot, his eyes sweeping back and forth for hidden assailants. He had no clue as to who they were up against. Nothing moved.

In the distance, he could hear the steady whoosh of traffic as it rushed down the expressway. The crickets were noisy and there was a faint dance of lightning bugs in what looked to be a thin band of trees and bushes toward the rear of the lot. If he remembered the area correctly, the other side of those trees opened onto a residential street. The afternoon heat had completely dissipated, and there was a chill that had Rowe wishing he'd grabbed a jacket.

They climbed the exterior concrete steps, taking them two at a time. The white paint was chipped and peeling. Trash and leaves littered the stairs. It was definitely not the type of place you came to if you had a choice. And Rowe was willing to guess that this JB had been looking for a place where he could simply disappear. Just pay a wad of cash and not sign any paperwork. Maybe even give the front desk clerk a little bonus to forget his face.

He could so easily see the sneer on Lucas's face if he were walking around there. The man had become a pampered princess who needed his high-thread-count sheets and room service at all times. Not that Vallois hadn't stayed in places just like this when he'd sneaked away for his secret hookups before he found Andrei. Or before he made his first million. They'd all stayed in places like this during their darker days.

Not a sound was made as they walked down the narrow path. At the room JB had indicated, they found the hotel lock flipped out, holding the door partially open. Noah pressed his shoulder to the wall and reached back with his right hand, wrapping his fingers around the grip of the gun. He looked at Rowe, who nodded, his gun already raised and ready.

Rowe's heart pounded a fast, steady rhythm in his chest as Noah reached out with his left hand and knocked loudly on the door a couple of times. "JB? It's Noah," he called out.

There was soft sound inside the room. Movement of some kind. "Yes! Noah! Come in!"

With one last nod, Noah pushed the door open and stepped inside the brightly lit room. Rowe followed on his heels a second later. His gaze flew over the room, taking in the empty double beds with ugly floral-patterned comforters, the bland beige walls, heavy burgundy curtains pulled over the one window, and the even uglier green carpet.

The gun snapped up at the man who rushed across the room toward Noah, his arms open and his hands empty. That was the only thing that kept Rowe from putting one in the asshole's shoulder.

And then the guy was hugging Noah tightly as if his life depended on it. Rowe was pretty sure the man hadn't even noticed that Rowe was standing there, pointing a gun in his direction. He definitely didn't notice Rowe when he pulled back and kissed Noah hard on the lips.

Hell. Fucking. No.

CHAPTER FOUR

*N*oah froze. He'd hugged JB back out of habit, but when the man kissed him, he fucking froze. He could feel his lips soften and there was some part of him that wanted to kiss him back, but again, out of habit. But there was a much louder voice screaming in his head to pull away, this was wrong. So damn wrong.

Chaos exploded in the room. "What the fuck?" Rowe snarled.

Noah could only think that Rowe was armed—this was not going to end well.

JB reacted before Noah could. His Army friend grabbed the back of Noah's shirt tightly and slung him roughly behind his slightly smaller frame while pulling a gun that had been hidden somewhere on his person. He pointed the barrel directly at Rowe's face, and Noah swore that his heart stopped.

"Who the hell are you? What are you doing here?" JB shouted. With a flick of his thumb, the safety was off.

When Noah saw Rowe do the same, he found his voice again.

"Wait! He's with me! He's with me," he spit out.

Tension still tightened JB's shoulders and the hard fist holding the gun. He didn't lower the weapon, but he at least moved his finger out to the trigger guard.

"I told you to come alone."

"Not a fucking chance, kid," Rowe snarled. His boyfriend looked like he was still deciding whether to shoot him, and Noah had a feeling a lot of it had to do with the kiss. Rowe was incredibly possessive and territorial with what and who he considered his. Most of the time Noah found it to be an incredible turn-on. At that moment, he was more concerned with Rowe overreacting and shooting JB before they could find out what was going on.

"JB, this is Rowe Ward. My boyfriend. I've already been shot at once. He's here to cover my back." He wanted to reach out and force JB to lower his weapon, but he didn't want Rowe to accidentally get shot. "Rowe, put your damn gun down."

A second ticked by. And then another, before JB slowly lowered his gun. Rowe hesitated another second before doing the same. But he didn't put it away as he continued to glare at JB.

Sighing loudly, Noah pulled free of JB's hold and stepped around his friend to cross the room. He roughly brushed past Rowe and flipped the lock back into the room so he could close the door and secure it. No need to make it so easy for someone else to follow them into the room.

"Boyfriend, huh?" JB said. There was a lightness to his voice that had Noah inwardly cringing. Fuck, he did not need JB throwing more fuel on the fire. "Sorry about the kiss. You didn't mention a boyfriend."

Noah turned and glared at JB. It was still hard to stay mad at him. The kid, though it was hard to call him that when he had to be at least thirty-three or thirty-four by now, had the sweetest face and an adorable smile on just-fuck-me lips. And yeah, Noah knew firsthand exactly how fuckable those lips were, which he'd have to hash out with Rowe. Not that it should matter. That past had happened while Rowe was married to Melissa, but he was pretty damn confident that Rowe would have a problem with it.

"That call was the first time we've talked in years. When you told me that Paul and Chris were dead, I didn't think it was a good time to give you an update on my love life," Noah snapped, wiping the smile from his handsome face.

JB seemed to deflate right in front of them, his shoulders slumping. He shoved his gun into the holster on his hip and his hands hung empty at his sides.

Noah stepped up and slapped Rowe's shoulder, nodding toward the gun he still held. Rowe glared wordlessly at him for a second, but he tucked his own gun away and crossed his arms over his chest. Oh yeah, they were gonna have words. Angry ones.

"JB, this is my boyfriend, Rowe Ward," he formally introduced. "Rowe, this is JB Alexander. We served together. Former Ranger and hell of a good soldier. And a good friend."

JB extended his hand and Rowe took it.

"What? I don't get a kiss hello too?" Rowe sneered.

JB opened his mouth and Noah was sure that he was going to apologize again, but Rowe didn't deserve another one. JB hadn't known. It wasn't his fault. Noah smacked Rowe's shoulder again.

"Ignore him. He's being an ass." Rowe released the bear grip Noah was sure he had on JB's hand, not that the younger man was showing any discomfort, and at least had the good sense to look slightly chastened. "Why don't you tell us what's going on?"

JB paced a short distance away from them toward the bathroom, shoving both hands into his soft, dark-blond hair. "I don't know. I wish I did, but I don't."

"JB—"

"Jesus, fuck, Noah. They're dead. Chris and Paul are both dead. Chris hadn't been home for more than six months, I think. Paul was home maybe a year." He paced back and there was no missing the fresh tears that glistened unshed in his pale blue eyes. "We're home. We all thought we'd be safe here. Sleep in a bed without having a sidearm under your pillow."

Noah looked over at Rowe and whatever anger had cut lines across his face had instantly been replaced with worry and compassion for JB. Noah was sure he'd not let go of the kiss yet, but he could at least put it aside in the face of JB's pain.

Stepping forward, Rowe moved directly into JB's path and placed a firm hand on his shoulder. "Sit down. Tell us what you know. We'll get this figured out. No one is going to touch you or Noah."

JB's worried gaze jumped to Noah's face just over Rowe's shoulder and Noah nodded, giving him a reassuring smile. That same question had crossed Noah's mind once a few years ago. What could a civilian do when a murderer was hunting them down? When it came to Rowe Ward, the answer was a lot.

JB sat on the edge of one bed, while Rowe sat on the edge of the opposite bed. Noah stepped over and grabbed a chair that had been placed next to a battered old dresser, putting himself between the two men and the door.

Running his hand through his hair again, JB left it sticking up in different directions. Now that Noah wasn't worried about friendly fire, it was easy to see the dark circles under JB's eyes and the lines of stress and fatigue around his mouth. The guy looked dead on his feet.

"Start from the beginning," Rowe said with a gentleness that surprised Noah.

JB took a deep breath, held it for a second, and slowly released it. "Chris Perkins and Paul Grimes were part of the team that Noah headed up. After Noah retired from the Army, the three of us kept in contact." JB's eyes darted over to Noah, and there was no stopping the stab of guilt.

No, he hadn't tried to keep in contact with anyone from his Army days. At the end of his career, his head had been a mess. He wanted to block it all out and then shortly after he got out, he discovered that Rowe's wife died. His thoughts had been a black quagmire, and he didn't feel good about reaching out to former friends who were still stuck in dangerous war zones.

He should have done so later, and there was no excuse for it.

"I got out almost two years ago. Then Chris and Paul followed not long after. We didn't talk a lot. Mostly emails and some texts here and there. Less than a week ago, I got a weird email from Chris. He'd just gotten a job at a security company in Alexandria, Virginia. He was asking about Dave Johnson. He was sure that Dave was one of the guys that got killed in the Afghanistan ambush. He was asking for one of us to see if he was listed among those killed or captured. Wanted us to send him a pic of the guy."

Noah straightened in the chair he'd been sitting in, a chill running down his back. The cold streak hit him anytime anyone mentioned the Afghanistan ambush. It had been a terrifying close call for his team. At least twenty-seven lives were lost that night, not counting the three men who had been taken prisoner. Last Noah had heard, their bodies were never recovered, but it was widely believed that the men were dead.

"I replied that it was likely that the guy just looked similar. Paul said that he'd dig around and see what he could turn up." JB paused and pressed the heel of his palm into one eye, rubbing it. "I'll admit that I didn't give it much thought. Every time I think of that damn ambush, I keep thinking that it could have been us. I didn't want to dig into it. Two nights ago, I got a call from Paul. It went to voice mail. I was out and didn't have the ringer turned up loud enough." Noah swore he could see a light blush steal across the man's cheeks. He had no doubt that JB had been out having a drink and trying to get laid. Nothing wrong with that. With a face like his, Noah was confident that he didn't have to work too hard.

Reaching over to the nightstand between the two beds, he picked up his phone and pulled up the voice mail. He turned up the volume and Noah stepped closer as he pressed play. Paul's terrified voice filled the silent room.

"Fuck! JB, pick up! You gotta run, man. Grab your bugout bag and go dark. Chris is dead. Three are after me. You need to find Keegan before it's too late. Warn—"

There was a loud shot and then the phone clattered. Noah's knees gave out at the sound of Paul's low, pained moan and the rasp of fabric rubbing against grass. He found himself sitting on the end of the bed. Rowe's strong hand wrapped around the nape of his neck, and Noah could finally breathe again. He reached up and gripped Rowe's wrist, using it to keep him grounded as he listened to two more shots. The sound of gravel crunching under booted feet whispered across the line. The recording stopped as if someone had hung up the call.

JB put his phone on the nightstand, his hand now shaking, while Noah roughly wiped the tears burning his eyes. Chris and Paul had been damn good men. They'd never hesitated to jump into a fight and they'd always had his back.

Clearing his throat a couple of times, JB continued. "I tried calling Chris but got no answer. Yesterday, I actually managed to talk to his wife. She said he died in a car accident. The day after he sent the email."

Rowe's hand tightened reflexively on the back of Noah's neck, and he instantly wanted to pull Rowe into his arms. The man had already lost Mel in a so-called accident.

"After listening to the voice mail and not being able to reach Chris, I did what Paul said. I grabbed my bugout bag and just started driving. That first day, I didn't even have a plan. Last I heard you were in Cincinnati, but I wasn't sure if I should reach out to you. If this was about that stupid email, then you were safe because Chris didn't include you on the original email. But if this person was taking out the old team, then you were a target too. I didn't want to bring these fuckers to you, but if you needed to watch your back and didn't know…"

Rowe released Noah and reached across the open space between the two beds, grabbing JB's forearm. "You did the right thing by coming here."

The relief on JB's face nearly broke Noah's heart, but Rowe seemed to mend it in an instant. He didn't think it was possible to love the redhead beside him more than he already did, but Rowe proved him wrong time and again. Noah wasn't foolish enough to think that Rowe was at all comfortable with JB or Noah's unknown past with the man, but Rowe undoubtedly saw someone who was hurting, scared, and only trying to keep Noah safe. All things Rowe could understand all too easily.

"Someone shot at us when we were leaving a wedding."

"Someone shot at you," Rowe corrected as he released JB and straightened.

"We thought it was just a random drive-by shooting," Noah continued, giving Rowe a little side eye, but Rowe just puffed up his chest. Obviously Rowe had been right, and Noah had been the intended target.

Oh yeah, let's just add this to the list of things I'm going to hear about later. God, it's going to be a long fucking night.

"What about this 'Afghanistan ambush' you mentioned?" Rowe asked, dropping the topic of his victory for later.

"We were on deployment in Afghanistan. It was 2014, I think," Noah started.

"Late 2014. Almost winter," JB added.

"It was one of our last missions before we were going to be rotated out. We were accompanying a weapons delivery, acting as added protection. We stayed with them for three days. Slow moving through some bad terrain. We reached the temporary base, no problems. The escort team replacing us was already there. We completed the hand-off, ate some chow, caught a few hours of sleep, and then left, heading back to HQ. It was only when we reached HQ that we found out the base had been hit hours later, probably about 0300. Never really got a clear answer on the how, but everyone was killed."

"Except for the men who went missing," JB said.

"Missing? AWOL?" Rowe asked.

Noah shook his head. "They think three of the men were taken captive, possibly to torture for information. I never heard that their bodies were recovered, but that wasn't uncommon, unfortunately."

Rowe roughly rubbed his hand over his face. "Except that Chris thinks he spotted one of the captives working at this security company in Virginia. He tells his two good friends, and now two of the four men in your team are dead. To quote Mark Twain, something smells fishy to me."

Noah smiled broadly at Rowe. "Mark Twain never said that."

Rowe smiled back at him, and Noah's heart melted a little more. "According to the internet, Mark Twain said everything."

"I think you're confusing Mark Twain and Scooby-Doo."

" 'Jinkies, gang. I think we've got another mystery on our hands,' " JB quoted.

Noah fell on the bed, laughing. Rowe shot to his feet, groaning, which only made Noah laugh harder.

"Aren't you a little young to remember Scooby-Doo?"

"First, I'm thirty-four, old man. Not eight. And second, everyone knows Scooby-Doo."

Noah jumped to his feet and inserted himself between a glaring Rowe and a smug JB. "Grab your bag. You can follow us to our house."

"*What?*" Rowe and JB demanded in unison. *Lovely.*

But where JB just sounded surprised, Rowe sounded resistant.

Noah looked over at his boyfriend, placing his hand over his heart. "We're far better armed at the house. Plus, there's the security systems and the kids. We both know that JB isn't safe here on his own and we need to give Gidget a little time to start her digging."

"You've got kids?"

Noah smiled over his shoulder at JB. "Just three adorable little puppies." Which was a massive understatement when it came to the more than three hundred pounds of slobber, fur, and teeth charging through the house anytime the doorbell rang.

"Bite your fucking balls off," Rowe grumbled under his breath.

"It might be better—"

"No," Rowe said with a heavy sigh. "Noah's right. Our place is safer. We can at least get some sleep and try to come up with a plan of attack tomorrow." Rowe then directed his narrowed gaze up at Noah. "And we're going to be having a long chat too."

Noah had no doubt as to exactly what they'd talk about. He wasn't going to hide or sugarcoat his past for Rowe. He'd been single and alone. They'd made no promises to each other. No talk about a tomorrow, because Rowe had run from their one intimate encounter.

But the important thing was that they had been given a second chance, and nothing was going to take that from them. Whatever was said between them, Noah's only goal was to make it clear to Rowe that he was the only person in the world for him.

CHAPTER FIVE

*R*owe leaned back in the passenger seat and watched the city lights reflecting off Noah's face as he drove home with JB following. Rowe took note of his tight hands on the wheel, the way he kept glancing at Rowe as if he was waiting for the grilling to begin.

And he was sorely tempted. The sight of anyone kissing Noah had switched off all rational thought in his brain, turning him into a caveman with a handgun. Not the best combination. He'd ached to put a couple of bullets into JB's sweet, handsome face. No one was allowed to touch his Noah, to come between him and the man he loved.

But rational thought finally started to kick in while he listened to JB tell his story. In 2014, Rowe had been married to Melissa. He went to bed every night with a woman he loved more than life. He could reach out and touch her, kiss her whenever he wanted.

What had Noah had during that time? Cold, rocks, bullets, and some shitty rations. Was it so wrong that Noah had someone to make his life a little easier while he was fighting overseas? *Fuck, no!* He hated the idea of Noah being alone. No one there to hold him, to rub his back, or tease him on those rare times when he got too serious. If

Rowe couldn't be there, he was glad that Noah had found some comfort with JB.

But all that old shit stayed in the past. Rowe had set his claim on Noah, and no one was taking his place.

"So...JB, huh?" Rowe asked, inwardly proud of himself for sounding so damned civilized.

"I didn't expect him to kiss me."

He couldn't stop his amused grin at Noah's defensive tone even as inside, Rowe was still kind of simmering over the whole thing. "You slept with him." It wasn't a question because it had been damned obvious he had.

Noah nodded. "It was after you and me. Scratched an itch, that's all."

"It was just once?"

Noah glanced at him again. "No, it was more than once. I broke things off because I was in love with you, and it wasn't fair to him."

"He wanted more." Again, it wasn't a question. Of course the guy wanted more. Anyone would want more with Noah Keegan. He'd had Noah for *one night* in Prague so many years ago and had definitely wanted more, but the idea of it had scared the shit out of him.

"Yes, he did. But like I said, my feelings were firmly with someone else. You." Noah hit the blinker and slid into the right lane. "You have nothing to worry about. It was just fucking for me."

It might have been just fucking to Noah, but Rowe had picked up something entirely different from JB, and the knowledge sat like a heavy lump in his stomach. The guy was going to be staying with them. A guy Noah knew intimately. An extremely good-looking guy...

He had to bite back a growl because a part of him wanted to beat his fists on his chest and declare Noah his. He wasn't proud of that. He knew Noah loved him and he didn't have anything to be concerned about, but it still felt like he'd eaten something bad. His rational brain and inner caveman were not liking this arrangement at all.

They reached the house and JB pulled in behind them, his head-lights sweeping across the brick. Knowing both Noah and JB were in danger had Rowe extra vigilant as he looked over the quiet house and neighborhood. All he saw were well-maintained homes and well-manicured lawns. It was a quiet area with mostly older couples and families with children. A kid's bike was parked right outside his next-door neighbor's house in plain sight and would still be there in the morning. Seeing nothing out of the ordinary, Rowe got out and opened the garage door into the house. Three happy dogs immediately assaulted him. Vlad, Igor, and Daisy greeted Rowe as if he'd been gone for days and not a couple of hours.

JB dropped to his knees, chuckling when he got a tongue in his face. "You've got your home well-guarded."

Rowe disengaged the security system as he nodded. "I don't know what's better—the system or the dogs. Together, they keep the place secure. You'll be safe here." He watched as Noah kneeled beside his friend and loved on their dogs, his smile easy and happy. The two together made an attractive picture. Rowe fought back a scowl.

JB stood and walked farther into the room, stopping at the wall of photographs. They stretched across the wall leading into the hallway from the kitchen. Rowe looked at them, realizing there were far more images of him and Mel than him and Noah. How had he not noticed that imbalance until right at that moment?

After the home he and Mel created together went up in flames, Noah had reached out to his friends and collected dozens of pictures of Rowe and his wife. Noah had always made sure Mel was still part of their lives. That Rowe never had to choose between them.

But there should be more images of them as a couple. They'd been together for more than two years, building a life and memories.

Noah had hung a lot of the pictures of Mel, so they obviously didn't bother him, but still…did they make Noah feel like he came in second to Mel? Rowe needed to fix this.

JB didn't say anything. He turned and slid his hands into the pockets of his jeans, still looking around. Rowe and Noah recently had the kitchen remodeled, and it looked nice with the dark cabinetry and granite countertops. Rowe had bought the house after his wife's death, and Noah had moved in here with him. This three-bedroom house had all they needed, especially since it had a large backyard for the dogs, which Noah took advantage of then, leading the reluctant trio out when they were much more interested in checking out the newcomer.

"Thanks for letting me stay here," JB said once Noah was outside, his voice low as he looked at Rowe.

He wanted to say it hadn't been his idea, but the man *was* safer here. Instead, he found his tongue getting away from him. "You and Noah have a past."

JB's mouth twisted up in one corner. "Not much of one, so don't worry. I'll respect what he has with you. I can tell you've made a nice home here together." His gaze strayed again to the picture of Rowe with Mel. This one showed Mel in her usual state—head back and laughing. The woman had spent the majority of her time laughing. He still missed her. Always would.

"She was my wife," Rowe said. "She died three years ago."

"I'm sorry for your loss."

"I'm sorry for yours," he answered, speaking of Chris and Paul.

JB's lips tightened, but he didn't say anything else as Noah came inside with the slobbering trio. Daisy, the German shepherd, ran up to Rowe and stuck her nose in his hand. He stroked her soft fur, wondering if she felt the awkwardness that filled the room like a thick fog.

"Come on," Noah said as he hefted up JB's bag. "I'll show you to the spare bedroom."

Rowe watched the two leave and headed for the cabinet where they kept the hard liquor. He didn't know how to feel when faced with someone Noah had been intimate with. The shot of whiskey did little to help, though it did burn in his stomach and make him feel a bit more grounded.

JB was a very attractive man with his tight, lean build and dirty-blond hair. He could definitely see why Noah had been interested in him. He frowned and poured himself another shot, his mind going to their story about the ambush in Afghanistan. At least they had a little to go on. He'd put Gidget on it in the morning.

46

Noah strolled into the kitchen and lifted an eyebrow at the shot in Rowe's hand.

"Want one?" Rowe asked, nodding toward the bottle.

"Nah. JB is going to shower and hit the bed. Why don't we head that way ourselves, see if we can make heads or tails of what's going on in the morning?"

He eyed his boyfriend, seeing the welcome in his gaze and had to smile. Yeah, he'd be taking Noah up on that invitation.

They reset the security system, made sure the dogs had everything they needed, and shut off all the lights. He followed Noah. Hearing the shower running in the guest bathroom, Rowe was brought back to when Noah had arrived years ago and the night when they'd talked in that bathroom. So much time had passed and now, they were a tight unit that meant the world to him.

Noah tugged off his T-shirt when they got to their bedroom and turned to face Rowe.

Rowe shut the door behind him, then backed Noah into the wall and leaned into his body, loving the delicious slide of all those hard muscles against him. Noah was built big and tall, his shoulders wide, his waist narrow. Soft, crinkly hair covered his pecs and narrowed into a silky trail under his belly button. Rowe ran the backs of his fingers over that hair, stroking down to the low waist of Noah's jeans. He dipped his fingers behind the material and butted them into the head of Noah's cock.

Noah sucked in a breath, blue eyes glittering down at Rowe. "You really don't have anything to worry about," Noah whispered.

"I know. Just want you."

"Then have me."

Fuck, the man made him crazy with lust. He could feel it ramping up in his body, making every nerve tingle to life with anticipation. The tip of Noah's erection was already wet, and he smoothed his fingers through it, touching around the soft head. He slowly unzipped Noah's fly with his other hand and wrapped his hand around that gorgeous cock.

Noah never took his eyes off Rowe, and the pure eroticism of the moment made Rowe's knees feel weak. His heart swelled in his chest, and he leaned up on his toes to press his mouth to Noah's. The man opened for him and he took the kiss deep. He could never get enough of Noah's mouth or the way his hands came up to cradle the sides of his face. He stroked his tongue into Noah's mouth, loving Noah's fingers on his cheeks. His touch stoked a fire deep in Rowe's bones as it always did.

He couldn't get enough of the man, period.

Pulling away, he tugged his T-shirt over his head and came back to Noah's body. Chest hair rasped over his nipples and he rubbed against Noah, sucking his lower lip into his mouth. A low, rumbling moan left Noah's throat.

"Want you," Noah whispered, leaning down to kiss his shoulder. "Want you so badly."

Rowe tugged him toward the bed and pushed him down onto it. He stood over him and unbuckled his belt, tugging it out slowly. He undid his pants and pulled them and his boxers off.

"I could look at you all night and it wouldn't be long enough," Noah said.

Rowe leaned over him and peeled off his jeans and underwear. "I could look at you my whole life and it wouldn't be long enough."

And he meant it. Noah, stretched out on their bed, was a thing of utter beauty with his long body. Thigh muscles quivered when Rowe ran his hands over them, then stretched out on top of Noah. Fuck, he felt good against him. Noah spread his legs and Rowe fell between them as they kissed.

Noah ran his hands down Rowe's back and grabbed both cheeks of his ass in his big palms. He ground their lower bodies together, causing Rowe to gasp. Soon, they were rubbing against each other until that wasn't enough.

Rowe crawled off Noah to get the lube off the bedside table. "How do you want me?"

Noah promptly rolled over and shoved a pillow under his hips, making his stunning ass stick up in the air. Rowe groaned and stroked his hands over it.

"Oh yeah," he breathed. "Better grab on to the headboard."

"It's that kind of night, is it?"

"I'm fucking you through this mattress, so you need to hold on."

"Yes!"

Rowe had a moment to wonder if JB could hear them, then didn't give a shit. Let him hear. Rowe lubed his fingers and pressed them to Noah's hole. He hoped Noah wasn't sore from earlier, but Noah promptly moaned and shoved his ass back toward him. That tight hole around his finger felt so damn good, he knew he wouldn't last long once he got his cock in there. Not with the way he was feeling— still kind of off-kilter from meeting JB. So, he wanted to make it good for Noah. He slowly fucked his fingers into him, stretching him and making sure to brush over that spot that turned Noah into liquid sex. He used his other hand to reach underneath and stroke Noah's cock, the pillow soft against his knuckles.

This time, Noah's groan was louder as he writhed under Rowe's ministrations. Soon, Rowe had him gasping and rocking his hips into the pillow.

"Now! Fuck me now!"

He couldn't resist that plea and he hurriedly coated himself in lube and brought his cock to Noah's entrance. He slowly pushed inside his body, gritting his teeth at the tight, hot clasp around him. He meant to take it slow, but with the way Noah was letting out hoarse cries and grabbing on to the sheets, he was soon pounding into him hard. So hard, the headboard banged into the wall with loud booms. He gave brief thought to their guest before letting it go. Noah felt too damn good wrapped around him and under him.

He leaned over and kissed Noah's sweaty back, running his lips down his spine and anywhere he could reach. "You feel so damn good," he breathed into his skin. "So damn good wrapped around my dick."

"Harder," Noah panted.

Rowe came up and grabbed his hips to better ram into him. The headboard hit the wall again and this time, he felt a fierce joy in the loudness of the sound. Noah was his to fuck. His to love. Faced with a lover from his past had unnerved him in a way he didn't like. Made him feel the need to prove the man was his. It was a primal, raw sort of feeling he'd never had before. "Mine," he growled.

"Yours." Noah shoved his hips back into him. "All yours. Forever."

He dug fingers into Noah's hips and drove into him, the pleasure so acute, his toes curled. His orgasm built until it crashed through him and he held on to his man hard as he came into his body. He came so hard, he moaned and fell on top of Noah. Noah still moved underneath him, and he slowly pulled out and turned him over, falling onto him with deep kisses before he kissed down his sweaty body and pulled his cock into his mouth. He sucked him in as far as he could, and Noah bucked up off the bed.

"Yeah," he grunted. "Take it deep."

He was so fucking hot, he stole Rowe's breath. But so did his cock. He loved the slick, satiny skin, the way the soft head bumped into his throat. He rubbed the flat of his tongue along it as he pulled it deep as Noah asked.

When Noah shouted and grabbed his head, bowing up off the bed, his eyes rolled back into his head and he thought of coming again, but his body was too sated. Instead, he reveled in Noah's pleasure, loving that he'd given him this. He drank him down and slowly pulled off, then rested his head on Noah's leg as the man panted above him.

"Felt the need to make a little noise there?" Noah asked softly.

"Maybe just a little."

Noah reached down and stroked his fingers through his hair. "You, Rowan Ward, are my life. It's you I've always wanted."

He turned and dropped a light kiss on Noah's inner thigh. "I know. But now he knows, too." He peeked up at Noah, who grinned at his sheepish expression.

"Come up here, crazy man." Noah tugged on his shoulder.

Rowe lay down on top of Noah, falling between his legs. He crossed his arms on Noah's chest and propped his chin on them to stare down at the man who was his everything. "First time I've been faced with someone you've been with. A little jealousy is called for."

"I seem to remember you being jealous another time."

Rowe had to think a moment. "You mean the date with Ian?" Heat crept up his neck, and he knew his smile was slightly guilty. "That one scared me to death. It's impossible not to love Ian, and you and I weren't together."

"We were after that." Noah chuckled. "But damn, were you jealous. That gave me my first glimmer of hope." He sighed and touched Rowe's cheek. "There is no reason to worry about JB."

"He still cares about you."

"Of course he does. I'm irresistible." A dimple popped in Noah's cheek.

"That you are." Rowe leaned up to kiss him. "That you are."

CHAPTER SIX

"I think we should go to Alexandria, Virginia, and talk to Chris's wife," Rowe announced when JB entered the kitchen the next morning.

Noah was busy making pancakes and bacon, his favorite breakfast, and instead of doing it half-naked as usual, he was dressed in sweats and a blue T-shirt that matched his eyes. His tousled, shoulder-length hair lay in a mess around his face. Sunlight streamed in through the windows, making the blond streaks shine. Rowe couldn't help but touch his hip as he placed a stack of pancakes onto the table. He kneaded that spot, enjoying the hard muscle under his fingertips. He knew Noah had put the shirt on because of JB and he appreciated it.

"Dig in," Noah told JB, pointing the spatula at the syrup. "Real maple syrup."

"I feel spoiled," JB said with a grin as he sat at the table in front of an empty plate. He forked a couple of pancakes onto it. He was wearing a loose red T-shirt and a pair of khaki shorts that showed off muscular legs. He also had a pillow crease on one cheek. The dark shadows under his eyes didn't seem as heavy, and the anxiety that had tightened every muscle last night was largely missing. If his loud performance with Noah had disturbed JB in any way, the man wasn't showing it. Rowe was willing to guess that he'd finally gotten some solid sleep for the first time since Paul's phone call.

"I think going to Alexandria is an excellent idea," JB continued. "Sally didn't seem too keen on talking on the phone. Not that I blame her—her husband just died."

"I'll put Gidget—our resident computer genius at work—on what we have already, and we'll start out this afternoon. It's not that long a drive—about eight hours. If we drive, we can take plenty of toys." Rowe got some pancakes and covered them in maple syrup. "Maybe we can get the name of the company Chris joined."

Noah set a plate of bacon down, then sat next to him and grabbed the butter. "I'll call Sven and get him to cover the job I had lined up this week. We can reschedule his classes. Oh, and I'll call the dog sitter."

Rowe reached for a slice of bacon and bit into the crispy strip. Flavor exploded on his tongue. There was nothing like bacon with the rich sweetness of maple syrup.

They ate quietly for a few moments, JB giving them both looks and when Rowe met his gaze, a slight flush filled his cheeks. So, he had heard them last night. Good. He placed his hand on Noah's thigh under the table and squeezed it. He knew his feelings about JB were uncalled for, but every time he looked at him, he imagined the two of them fucking, and it was driving him crazy. He couldn't help but wonder if JB was the sort for marriage and kids, because he still didn't know if that was what Noah wanted.

Noah put his hand on top of Rowe's, shooting him a wry look.

Yeah, he was being a little possessive. So what?

They finished their breakfast and JB got up to help with the dishes. He really was an attractive man with his long, slim and tight body, and Rowe felt that knot forming in his belly again. Daisy ran up and stuck her nose in his lap, her dark eyes looking up at him. He rubbed her head, knowing she was picking up on his uneasy feelings. She'd always been a sensitive dog. He didn't know why he was letting JB bug him so much. He knew how Noah felt about him, knew their bond was stronger than ever. He was being an ass.

With that in mind, he stood and opened the back door to let all three dogs out. He stepped outside and lifted his face into the morning breeze. He needed to just let this go.

When Noah joined him, he gave him a pointed stare. "You're worrying for nothing."

"I know," he answered softly.

"It's good to know you care so much, but your trust means a lot to me, too." Admonishment laced his tone.

"Oh, I trust you," Rowe insisted. "Please don't think I don't."

"Then why is he bothering you so much?"

"I think it's just being faced with someone you've...been with."

Rowe looked over to see Noah frown as he stared out at the back of the yard. "We've never talked about people from our pasts," Noah said, his voice low.

That was a nice way of putting one-night stands.

"Never wanted to know," Rowe replied.

"But I never questioned that there were others for you after you left...the Army."

A little pain shot through Rowe's heart. He had a feeling that Noah had nearly said "left me," which was sort of true. He might have gotten shot, ending his career, but he'd run from Noah first.

"There were others between your time in the Army and finding Mel," Noah continued.

"True." There had been a few women after he left the Army before he found Mel. Just faceless bodies to help pass the time. But no men. After his one night with Noah, there had been no other men. He hadn't even considered it.

"Did you think that I was celibate after you returned home?"

Rowe sighed loudly and shifted from one foot to the other. Now he definitely felt like an ass. "No. I just...I just never thought about it. Didn't want to think about it. From the moment you came back into my life, you were mine. That's all that mattered to me. To hell with our pasts."

Except that Rowe's past covered their walls. Fuck, did Noah feel like this every day because of Mel? That was a rabbit hole he wasn't prepared to jump down so early in the morning.

"Sorry. This just has me off my game."

"Well, get back on it. What I had with him never would have gone anywhere, and you know the reason why."

Rowe felt heat creeping up his neck. Noah was right. "Just ignore me. We'll go to Alexandria and talk to Chris's wife. See if we can figure out why someone is after you two. God, if something happened to you, Noah, I couldn't handle it."

"Nothing is going to happen to me." Noah pulled him close and kissed him. "My life is exactly where I want it now, and nothing will take that from us."

～

That evening, they arrived in Alexandria. Dusk was settling over the city, and they found a motel not too far from where Chris's wife lived off Richmond Highway. Even at this later hour, the traffic was intense. Trees filled the landscape in between apartment and office buildings, and when they passed a Mexican restaurant, Rowe's stomach growled. This city bordered Washington DC, so he knew there were a lot of professionals here who worked for the federal government and U.S. Military. Which would explain the heavy traffic. Still, he was surprised at how long they sat still on Route 1.

The motel had a huge moon on the sign and looked decent, so they got a couple of rooms before scouting out Sally Perkins's home. Rowe figured it might be a good idea to do a drive-by to make sure everything looked okay.

She lived in a small house sitting far off the street with a large front yard. Sad-looking flower beds bordered the home, and Rowe imagined they hadn't seen water since before Chris's death. Rowe took note of a black sedan parked several houses down with two men sitting inside. Nothing about the car or the men really stood out, but he was feeling overly cautious. Otherwise, everything looked normal and quiet.

With his stomach still growling, Rowe easily convinced his companions to turn back to the Mexican food they'd passed on their way to the motel. It was too late in the day to spring a surprise meeting on the grieving woman. It would be better to start earlier in the day. Both Noah and JB had met Sally before, but it had been years since Noah had seen her. JB had seen her a year ago when Chris returned from his last overseas tour.

Bellies full, they wandered out of the restaurant and toward Noah's Jeep. Rowe looked over to see JB sigh as he stretched his arms over his head. The man had listened with rapt attention as Rowe and Noah had told one insane story after another about either their unique family or strange things that happened at Ward Security. Rowe had to admit that whether he was talking about his brothers or his Ward Security family, he was always surrounded by crazy people looking to do crazy things. And he felt so damn lucky to have them.

"What do we do now? It's only"—JB paused and lowered his arm to glance at his watch—"eight o'clock. Still early."

"Go back to the motel and sleep," Noah grumbled. "Some of us spent the bulk of the day driving, while others slept."

"Hey, I didn't sleep that much. I would have slept more if Rowe hadn't snored so loud," JB said.

Rowe turned and took a playful swipe at JB, but the younger man jumped away, laughing. Even Noah chuckled at their antics.

"Besides, you guys just want to head back to the room for noisy sex. You've gotta take it easy on us single guys," JB continued. "We're sharing a freaking wall."

"Are we shredding your fragile innocence, kid?" Rowe teased.

"Nah, just give a guy some warning. I can take a cab, grab a drink out somewhere."

"No," Noah said sharply. "We don't know who knows we're in town. We're sticking together until we get to the bottom of what happened to Chris and Paul."

JB leaned against the rear passenger door and crossed one ankle over the other. "Come on. Just an hour out. Grab a beer. Something. I've spent way too much time in motels and cars recently. I don't want to waste another hour starting at the damn TV."

Rowe rested his hands on his hips as he stood opposite JB, gazing around the parking lot for some idea to spark. He didn't mind going back to the motel and stretching out in bed with Noah. Even if they didn't have sex, he enjoyed just lounging in bed watching some mindless TV for an hour or two. But JB had lost two people important to him already. He didn't want to be alone, and he could do with some kind of entertainment. Noah would probably also like to spend a little time with JB. Something they could all do would mean Rowe could keep his jealousy and insecurity under control.

"How about that?" Rowe said, pointing at a big flashing neon sign across the street. It looked like a retro arcade, offering pinball machines and video games straight out of the eighties.

"That looks cool," Noah said. "I haven't played pinball in years."

Loading up in the Jeep, they drove the short distance over. They were pleasantly surprised to find that the place catered as much to adults as to kids, with a fully stocked bar and a nice offering of food. Rather than coins and tokens, they received wristbands indicating how many hours they paid for. All the games were already open, ready for an endless stream of players.

The two-story building was a cacophony of flashing lights, buzzers, ringing bells, and computerized beeps from all the games. There was a medium-sized crowd for a Tuesday night, leaving most of the games free. At Noah's nudging, JB and Rowe each grabbed a beer, while Noah grabbed an iced tea before they wandered around the place.

For the next two hours, they worked their way through old-fashioned pinball machines, some of them more than fifty years old. They played their favorite arcade video games from their childhoods. They cheered each other on and talked epic amounts of trash, which was ridiculous because not one of them was good enough to make a single leaderboard. It didn't matter. They were laughing. Rowe could forget for a time that JB and Noah had a past. And it looked like both Noah and JB managed to forget about the grim reason they were in town in the first place.

They finished the night with a Skee-Ball tournament. JB won the first game, Rowe won the second, and Noah won the third. Of course, they had to play a fourth game to break the three-way tie. When Noah threw his last ball, inching just ten points ahead of Rowe, JB shouted and hugged his old friend in celebration. The moment JB caught sight of Rowe, he flushed and took a step back, but Rowe gave him a reassuring little nod. He knew the guy hadn't meant anything by the hug.

Walking to the car, they were all still buzzing on two hours of laughter and gaming adrenaline. Rowe noticed that JB and Noah seemed to be talking more easily now, as if they'd found an old familiarity they hadn't enjoyed in so many years. A niggling worry nagged at the back of Rowe's brain. It wasn't jealousy, really. Or even that old insecurity. This was the Noah Rowe was accustomed to seeing when he was talking to Jude and Andrei at the last dinner they had over at the penthouse. All easy grins and big laughs.

Everyone Rowe saw Noah acting that way with were people he counted as his family first. And a few people at Ward Security. But JB was different. He was a friend Noah made outside of Rowe. Was there a reason Noah didn't contact old friends? Rowe didn't think he was keeping Noah away from his friends, but it did strike him as odd.

"You've been quiet," Noah said later that night when they were stretched out on the lumpy motel mattress. *Gah!* He missed their bed already. "That black sedan outside of Sally's house bothering you?"

"Not really," Rowe replied and yawned. He rolled over and wrapped his arm across Noah's waist, snuggling closer. The air conditioner was cranked up, and there was only a thin blanket on the bed. He was going to take advantage of Noah's body heat. "I kind of figured she might be watched by whoever is behind Chris's death. We'll get another look at them tomorrow when we talk to her. Maybe catch a plate number off the car."

"Then what? JB's not still bothering you? Not that hug?"

"What? No!" Rowe said, sounding offended. "That's ridiculous."

"Thanks for tonight. We both appreciated it. Good distraction. I don't know how many people he's close to back home. I'm glad he kept in contact with Chris and Paul after leaving the Army, but it's not the same as having someone you can talk to and hang out with in person."

Rowe turned his head, brushing his lips against Noah's shoulder. "Is there a reason you didn't when you left? I mean, I get you ending things with JB on the physical side, but you look like you were pretty good friends. Why not keep in contact?" Rowe knew his voice sounded hesitant. He and Noah didn't talk about his time in the Army after Rowe was forced to retire early. Rowe had been there. He knew how bad it could get. There was no reason to drag up those ugly memories if he didn't have to, but there had to have been a few good ones in there too.

Noah sighed, but he didn't tense under Rowe's touch. "At the end, I was in a really unhealthy headspace. I didn't have a home to go to when I got out. You were the last friend I had that was a civilian, and your wife had just been killed. I wandered for a while, which just put me in a darker place."

"But those men were your friends…"

"And I couldn't burden them with my problems. They were still stuck in war zones, worrying about whether they were going to get blown up or shot. They didn't need the added stress of my problems. And I damn well didn't want them worrying about having my same problems when they finally got out. It wasn't fair to them."

"What about later? When you got your head on straight?"

Noah chuckled. "Later, when? You mean when we were taking down Jagger? Or helping Royce out with his unique family issues? Or even Dom's brother problems? Or how about that impromptu trip to Oklahoma that ended in our best explosion yet?"

"And then Snow's little kidnapping," Rowe added with a little groan.

"In between all that, I've been helping you build up Ward Security and spending time with our Cincinnati family. Life has been busy." Noah paused and bit his lip. Rowe lifted up on one elbow so he could more clearly see Noah's thoughtful expression. "But I should have made the time. I regret not reaching out to Chris, Paul, and JB. You would have really liked Chris and Paul. They aren't quite as rowdy as your brothers, but they were good men with just the right amount of crazy."

"I'm sorry," Rowe murmured.

Noah gave him a sad, uneven smile. "You've got nothing to be sorry about. I told myself there wasn't time. Too busy. But I was making excuses and I was wrong. I should have made time. I'd like to make time now...for JB. Just friends."

"I think that's a good idea. And I can always use another friend too."

Noah's grin became absolutely huge. He lunged forward and sealed his soft lips over Rowe's in a warm, tender kiss that wrapped right around Rowe's heart. Fuck, this man was his everything.

"You're a saint, Rowe Ward."

Groaning, Rowe rolled to his side and flipped off the light on the nightstand closest to him. "You're damn right I am." He wished he didn't still hate JB a little bit for knowing what it was like to be touched by Noah. Not quite a saint. But he'd try...for Noah.

CHAPTER SEVEN

The next morning, a woman in her early thirties in jeans and a yellow sweater answered the door of that cute little house, her eyes red and swollen. Rowe's heart turned over for her because he knew all too well how she was feeling. Losing his Mel had left him a shambling disaster for too many months. He'd finally had to escape, run away to the Colorado cabin he'd inherited from his grandfather, so he could get some breathing room. He couldn't imagine how she was dealing with staying in the same house that held all the memories of her husband.

She was a tiny thing, standing no more than five feet. Slim and pretty with bright-blonde hair. The three men seemed to dwarf her the moment they stepped into her home.

She led them to the couch in her living room, flushing when she had to move aside a pile of clothes so they could sit. The house was overly warm, and Rowe tugged at the neck of his T-shirt. He wondered if she was still in shock with the sweater and the heat. There were several planters overflowing with waxy green plants that looked brand new. A stack of cards was placed in the center of the coffee table. Some even looked unopened.

"It's good to see you, JB, Noah," she said as she dumped the clothes on a small table by the door. "I'm sorry you missed the funeral. Chris hated those damn things. Told me years ago he didn't want one, but his family needed to say their good-byes." They'd missed the funeral by two days, according to the obituary they found in the local newspaper.

"I'm sorry we weren't here." JB pulled Sally in for a quick, gentle hug. "It just happened so fast."

Sally stepped back from JB and gave a jerky little nod. "Chris still had all the funeral arrangements in place from his last deployment. I think he was sure he was going to die in the service. Said the odds just weren't in his favor." She paused for a moment, seeming to get lost in thought, and then suddenly turned overly bright eyes on Rowe. "It's nice to meet you, Rowe. Did you know Chris, too?"

"No, I never had the pleasure. We are so sorry for your loss," Rowe said, his voice low as he sat on one end of the couch. Noah sat between him and JB.

"Can I get you anything? Coffee maybe?"

"No, Sally. We're good," Noah said with a smile. "Thank you."

She sat in a chair across from them, wringing her hands together as if she suddenly didn't know what to do with them. Rowe understood that restlessness too. After Mel's death, he'd hated sitting still. Sitting meant there was time for thinking, which only led to horrible thoughts about what if and what could have been done differently. It was a horrible cycle that seemed to be stopped only when he was doing something, anything.

"There are a few things that have happened recently that have us concerned," Rowe carefully started. He shifted on the couch, moving toward the edge of the cushion. "That's why we're here. We're trying to find out about the car accident that Chris was involved in and what was going on in his life before he died."

For the first time since they entered the house, some of the pain that was drawing lines in her face was erased by confusion. "What sort of things?"

JB leaned forward, his elbows on his knees. "Sally, did you know that Paul was killed too?"

She gasped and covered her mouth. "What? No! Not Paul. How…"

"He was shot." JB paused and licked his lips, glancing over at Noah before he continued. "And someone shot at Noah as well."

Sally's wide eyes immediately jumped to Noah in shock and worry.

Noah flashed her a reassuring smile. "I'm fine, I swear. The person was a horrible shot. Totally missed me."

Rowe wanted to throw Noah a look because it had been sheer luck Noah hadn't been hit that night, but he didn't want to upset Sally more than she already was.

"So, you're thinking Chris's accident wasn't an accident at all…" Agony and building anger burned in her blue eyes. "Oh, my God!"

"We don't know," Noah said. "But with everything else, we have our suspicions. Was he upset about anything before his death? JB mentioned getting an email from Chris."

Sally nodded and tucked a strand of hair behind her ear with a shaking hand. "He was going on about a man he'd seen in the company. One he thought was dead. Dave something or other. I'm sorry, I can't remember his last name."

JB cleared his throat. "We have the name. Can you tell us anything else? Do you know if he talked to this guy before he died?"

Sally shook her head. "They didn't talk. He said it was little more than a glimpse of the guy, but it was driving him crazy. Like he'd seen a ghost." Sally pursed her lips together for a moment, frowning at the three men. "I know how that comes off, but Chris was of sound mind when he came back from service. He was going to talk therapy once a month, but it was more about adjusting to civilian life again after so long. He was eating right and wasn't suffering from nightmares. He was excited to start a new job and for us to finally build a life together."

"I know," JB said firmly. "Chris, Paul, and I all talked regularly. He was so happy to be home with you again."

Sally nodded, giving him a teary smile.

"Do you happen to remember the name of the company Chris was working for?" Rowe inquired.

"Sure. I have a card, too. Hold on." She got up and went into the kitchen, coming back with the card in hand. "It's Clayborne Security." She handed it to JB. "Chris was really upset about this guy, but he didn't tell me why other than he was sure he'd seen him before overseas. I wish I could help more."

"Do you know how Chris heard about this job opening?"

She shook her head. "No clue. I just assumed he found it online. He'd applied for a few government jobs, but he was looking more for something in the private sector."

"Did he talk about anyone else at the company? Give you the name of his boss or any other coworkers?" Noah asked.

"No, I'm sorry. The job was new and he was excited about it. Said that he'd be working with a lot of people who were ex-military, but he never gave any other names besides this Dave person. He was just sort of obsessed with him."

"What did the police say about the accident?"

"Just that it was a hit-and-run." Her voice hitched and she hugged herself. "Someone slammed into his SUV and left him there to die. He'd gone out for ice cream I asked for. If I hadn't wanted that damn ice cream." Her eyes filled with tears. "He'd been spoiling me since he got out of the service. And he was so happy to have that new job. We'd planned to start a family. But if what you think is true…" Her shoulders sagged. "I don't know what to think."

God, Rowe's heart ached for her. He looked around the room, taking in the pictures of her with her husband and was taken back to the days of his own loss. That pain had been like nothing he'd felt before, and he could see that same suffering in her face. Noah reached out and took his hand, squeezing it. He threaded their fingers together and held on tight.

"I don't know anymore," Sally said. "Do you really think his death wasn't an accident? What's going on?"

"We don't know, but we'll figure it out."

"Well, if you find anything out, let me know. I want to see the asshole who hit him pay." She tightened her lips.

"We will." Rowe stood and offered his hand. "Thanks for talking to us. And again, I'm sorry for your loss."

She offered a tremulous smile as she stood and shook his hand.

They walked outside into the bright sunlight and Rowe fought to take a deep, cleansing breath. He didn't mean to be rude to her suffering, but the pall of death over that house brought back too many of his own ugly memories and emotions. He couldn't risk letting himself fall into that old, tangled knot and getting distracted when Noah's and JB's lives were on the line.

Standing on the sidewalk, he closed his eyes and tilted his head up to the sun, leaving its warmth soaking into him. The house had been stifling hot, but Sally's suffering had chilled him down to the bone. Behind him, he could hear both Noah and JB checking to make sure that she didn't need anything and that she knew how to contact them if she had problems of any kind.

With his soul warmed again, he glanced down the street and immediately noticed the same black sedan from the night before parked a few houses down, under a low-hanging tree. He slipped his sunglasses off his head and stared at the car. There were once again two people inside, but it was too shadowed to see much more. Definitely not enough light to tell if they were the same two people, but they definitely had a clear view of Sally's house and anyone who came and went.

Once Sally shut the door behind JB, Rowe pulled out his phone and called Gidget. "You in the mood to do something sneaky like in the old days?" he asked.

"Always. Shoot," she replied with her usual bubbly enthusiasm.

"I need you to look up Clayborne Security. Get pictures and names of all the employees."

She made a little dismissive sound in the back of her throat. "Is that all?" They both knew Rowe had asked for far sneakier from her over the past several years.

"Take down this license plate number." Squinting, he read off the letters and numbers from the plate affixed to the front of the sedan. "See what you can find on it and anything you can find on the company. Anything in the news—just any information you can find."

"Got it."

He hung up, got into Noah's Jeep, and started it, waiting until Noah and JB were in the car before nodding toward the sedan. "Same car as last night."

"Saw that," Noah said. "Let's see if they follow us."

Rowe pulled out and sure enough, the sedan started after them. "Let's give them something to worry about. What's that address on the card? I'll key it into the GPS and we'll drive by."

Noah grinned at him. "Nothing like a little live bait."

"Aren't you ballsy?" JB laughed from the back seat, then read off the address.

It took them thirty minutes in traffic to reach Clayborne Security. They kept their tail the entire way, not that Rowe had tried anything fancy to lose them. No, he wanted to see if he could rattle their cages a little bit. Get these assholes to put their full attention on them rather than Sally. The poor woman had already been through enough.

Rowe stopped the car across from the building. It was nothing special—an old box of a three-story brick with a sign out front. There weren't even that many windows, so he could only imagine how stifling and dark it was inside. A few men milled near the front door. He glanced in the rearview mirror to find the sedan behind them.

"Whoever is following us isn't even trying to be subtle. I don't know whether they're cocky or just idiots."

"Probably both," Noah muttered.

JB leaned between the seats. "If our suspicions are correct, they probably work for this company, and now they know we're on to them. I expect they'll bump up their attempts to get rid of us."

"I'd like to see them try," Noah said with a wicked glee in his voice. He rubbed his hands together. "So, what should we do next?"

"Go to the motel and wait for Gidget to work her magic. We need more info."

JB flopped back in the seat. "Boring."

"But first, we lose this tail." Rowe pulled into traffic and proceeded to do just that.

CHAPTER EIGHT

The motel they'd settled in was only a couple of small steps above the motel they'd found JB in two nights earlier. Noah frowned at the single double bed with faded blue comforter and ridiculously flat pillows. He tried to remind himself that he'd survived worse conditions. That he'd slept on the cold ground with only his arm for a pillow and a gun clutched to his chest. But this…this somehow felt just as bad.

And just one double bed. He would have preferred a king or at least two queens. But last night hadn't been too bad. He'd fallen asleep with Rowe wrapped around him, the covers mostly kicked down to their feet. He was also lucky Rowe had been worn out. The fucker liked to kick in his sleep, and Noah wasn't fond of being woken in the middle of the night by taking a knee to the balls.

Standing in the center of the room, he rubbed his hands over his face and shoved them through his hair. "I think Lucas has been a bad influence on me. I'm turning into a hotel snob."

Rowe hissed at Noah, ducking his head down to his shoulders as if to protect himself. "Don't say his name!"

"Whose? Lucas?" Noah asked with a chuckle.

"He's like fucking Candyman."

"You're ridiculous."

"Who's Lucas?" JB said.

"Come on! I'm serious. It's like he can sense it," Rowe said in a near whine. He glanced around the room like he expected Lucas to step out of the mirror and start berating him for not reporting his most recent adventure to the rest of the family.

Noah looked over to find JB leaning against the doorjamb in the opening that connected their rooms. His arms were loosely folded over his chest and he was grinning at Rowe like he was a lunatic, which was kind of true.

"He's a good friend."

Rowe snorted. "Billionaire, property mogul, philanthropist, reformed playboy, and nosy motherfucker."

"Who loves you like a brother," Noah firmly added.

Rowe's expression softened and he looked up at Noah. "Loves you too."

Noah found himself smiling at Rowe, the thought warming some dark part of Noah's soul. Rowe's words shouldn't have surprised him. He did love Lucas like a brother. He loved Andrei, Snow, Jude, Ian, and Hollis as well. Adored the beautiful Daciana too.

But he hadn't thought much about it. Hadn't thought that the love he felt for those men, his family, flowed both ways. But it did.

He couldn't believe how lucky he was. When he'd hoped and prayed for a second chance with Rowe, he'd never expected that he'd also be welcomed into an incredibly tight-knit family. That he'd find a home he'd been longing for his entire life.

"Doesn't change that he's a nosy, bossy ass who likes to micromanage everyone's life," Rowe grumbled as he went back to cleaning the gun in his hand.

"I think he's going to do that less now that he's got Daci." Noah reached into his pocket and pulled out his cell phone. He stepped over to JB while flipping through the pictures to his favorites from Ian's wedding. Yeah, he was *that* uncle and he didn't give a shit. He was going to show off his perfect niece to everyone smart enough to let him. "Daciana Vallois. She's about six months old and so damn smart already. Got her poppa's smarts and looks," he added when he got to a picture of Andrei holding the little girl. "But I'm sure her other daddy will help her with her plans for taking over the world."

"She's gorgeous, but it looks like she comes from a very gorgeous family," JB said.

"Oh yeah," Rowe murmured.

Noah shook his head as he started to search for a picture he'd taken of Daciana at Ward Security with several of the bodyguards. Those huge guys doted on her.

"Are you guys planning to have kids too?" JB asked and Noah's finger froze on the screen of his phone. He swallowed hard and glanced over at Rowe to see the same "deer in the headlights" expression he'd seen when Snow teased them about getting married.

In the two years they'd been together, they'd never once discussed it. They'd lain in bed and talked about getting llamas, moving to Colorado, expanding Ward Security, closing Ward Security, and a hundred other insane and mostly stupid ideas. But the concepts of marriage and kids had never crossed their lips. Outside of one joke about a skydiving wedding in Vegas...

"Right now, I think we're good with the three oversized babies we've got at the house," Noah said, hating how uneven his voice sounded after too much silence.

"Plus we tend to travel a lot. Things randomly blowing up on us," Rowe added, helping to smooth over the awkward moment. "Have you heard anything from Gidget yet?"

"It's only been a few hours," Noah said. He tucked his phone away as he strode across the room. He was trying like hell not to pace because there just wasn't a whole lot of room to move around. And if he started getting twitchy, Rowe would get twitchy. "Give the poor woman some time."

After losing the two men in the sedan and driving around the city for a while just so they wouldn't have to return to the motel, they'd found a small diner to grab a bite to eat. They'd checked over the car to make sure they hadn't picked up a tracking device while they were in talking to Sally. Noah's Jeep was clean...in a manner of speaking.

With nothing but time on their hands until Gidget came back with something useful, they decided to drive into DC for a little sightseeing. Noah had never been to the nation's capital. They found a spot and wandered along the national mall and ducked inside the Smithsonian National Museum of Natural History. Noah was a closet history nut. He loved wandering through the exhibit on the evolution of man and then getting to see the Hope Diamond on display.

And since Noah had started it, both Rowe and JB voted for a visit to the Smithsonian National Air and Space Museum. Noah had to chuckle at the two of them going ape over the Spirit of Saint Louis and the war gear and aircraft on display from World War II. Noah had been more interested in the space race.

A good, happy exhaustion was wearing on them when they finally shuffled back to Alexandria and their motel. With their tail missing and no tracking device, they felt fairly certain that they'd be able to get a good night's sleep. But Noah was starting to feel very skeptical over how any of them were going to be able to sleep. Gidget hadn't sent over any information yet. Other than to knock on the front door of Clayborne and demand answers, they didn't have a next step, and that didn't sit well with Noah.

Chris was dead.

Paul was dead.

Dave, who was supposed to be dead, was somehow alive?

They'd been in town for a day, and they already had people following them.

"Can either of you tell me anything about this Dave guy Chris saw?" Rowe said.

Noah glanced over at JB, who frowned at him. "I don't remember meeting him personally," Noah said. "When we arrived at the temporary base, I immediately met with the captain overseeing the camp and platoon. Officially handed over our charge to the next team. We were dismissed to return to our base of operations. I chatted with a sergeant major as I was heading to the chow line about recent reconnaissance and activity in the area."

"I remember you saying that no one was asking us to stick around, so we might as well head back," JB chimed in.

Rowe glared at him. "You were looking for a fight?"

JB shrugged. "This was our first mission in almost two months. It had been too quiet, and we weren't trained to sit on our asses. It was like they were telling us we weren't needed in Afghanistan. Fine, then send us somewhere we could be of use."

"It's not like I can recall you ever sitting still all that well," Noah teased.

Rowe had been pretty intolerable between missions when they were in the Army together. His superiors had quickly learned to keep Rowe in the field and occupied or else he was going to end up in jail for some kind of disorderly conduct. His favorite target was the press, and they'd learned to run from Rowe on sight. From what he'd heard from Snow and Lucas, Rowe had been the same when they were serving together.

Rowe nodded, lines cutting around his brow as he frowned. He looked up at JB. "Do you remember him?"

"Nope. I popped by the supply tent with Paul. We were low on some field dressings, and I needed a new first aid kit. We hit some minor trouble and had to restock if we could."

"What about Chris?"

This time, it was Noah's turn to shrug. "He could have. Of our team, he was the more personable one. He liked to talk to the other teams and get the gossip. He usually got more interesting dirt than the official intel I could pull out of the officers."

"He didn't trust that we were getting the full scoop when Noah got the latest report." JB straightened and shifted to his other foot. "Liked to chat up the other men. It's very likely that he could have talked to this dead guy. I don't recall him mentioning anyone in particular when we met up again."

Groaning, Rowe stood and looked around for a second before flopping back down on the edge of the bed with a frustrated huff. "Looks like there's not much we can do until Gidget gets her hands on the official report of the attack or at least the lowdown on this Clayborne Security."

"You know, I gotta say that I'm kind of surprised." JB paused and scratched his jaw. "When I heard that Noah had taken a job with a security company, I thought it was just some protection gigs. Keeping celebrities and rich people safe. This...this strikes me as a little more than protection, and you guys don't seem to have missed a step."

"We've..." Noah started and then paused, looking over at Rowe who was grinning at him like a fool. Yeah, there were way too many things Ward Security did that were outside of the norm for a security company and a whole mess of it wasn't legal, but it was their way of making sure the clients stayed safe and the good guys won.

"We've got a team dedicated to making sure our family, friends, and clients remain safe," Rowe filled in, and Noah was happy to leave it at that. It wasn't that he thought JB would have a problem with them bending the rules. He just didn't want to get into a discussion about where that line was, because even Noah wasn't one hundred percent sure any longer.

"Well, I guess we're probably not going to get a lot more done tonight." JB stretched his arms over his head and Noah was quick to glance down at the ground. There was no denying that JB was a handsome man with his hard, lean body, but he didn't need to give Rowe any more reasons to be uneasy about his friend or to question where Noah's interest lay. For now he was willing to give Rowe some room and be understanding of his insecurity. The trip to the museum and the arcade the night before made him think that Rowe was at least trying to pull his head out of his ass.

"Get some sleep. We'll knock if we hear from Gidget," Rowe said.

"Night," JB called, waving at Rowe and then Noah.

With a grunt and a nod, Noah watched as JB pulled the door between their rooms closed, but there was no click of the lock sliding into place. That would allow them to easily get into his room if there was a problem.

When they checked in, Noah had been the one to ask Rowe to get adjoining rooms. There was no way in hell Rowe was going to sleep soundly with JB in their room and Noah didn't like the idea of not being able to hear if there was a problem should someone attack JB in the night.

"Does he snore?" Rowe asked out of the blue in a low voice.

"What?"

"Does he piss on the seat and never clean it up? Does he pick his nose and wipe it on his clothes? Does he—"

"What are you going on about?" Noah walked over to stand right in front of his lover.

Rowe sat up and turned his head so he could comfortably meet Noah's eyes. "I can't believe it, but I'm starting to like the guy and I really need you to give me a reason not to. Anything, Noah. Is he a fucking slob?"

Grinning, Noah placed his left knee next to Rowe's hip and crawled into his lap so that he was straddling the man. "No more than the man that I'm currently living with."

Rowe pulled him in tighter. "I'm only a slob when it comes to laundry." He paused and gave a little groan. "And the dishes."

Leaning down, Noah nipped at Rowe's lips until they softened from their frown and he opened, letting Noah slip his tongue inside. They kissed slowly, each kiss becoming deeper than the last until Rowe dug his fingers into Noah's back and moaned. That wonderful sound reverberated through Noah's chest and he lived for that feeling. The knowledge that he created that bone-deep pleasure in Rowe.

He broke off the kiss and smiled. "JB is a nice guy. Raised by an incredibly nice family. When he came out as bi, his mom immediately started trying to set him up with cute guys as well as girls."

"Probably raises orphan bunnies and takes little old ladies shopping on the weekends," Rowe grumbled.

"Don't know. Maybe," Noah teased. Rowe growled and released him, starting to move like he was going to push Noah away, but Noah grabbed a fistful of Rowe's hair, forcing him to look up at Noah. "I don't care. I just know that JB isn't the soft-hearted, stubborn, dirty, evil fucker beneath me right now."

One of Rowe's eyebrows came up. "Soft-hearted, evil fucker? You're not making any sense."

"You don't make sense on your best day, but I still love everything about you. You're the one I want. Always have been."

Rowe relaxed under him and his hands returned to his waist, tenderly massaging muscles. "I don't deserve you."

"Nope, but—"

Whatever Noah had been about to say was cut off by a thunderous crash from the next room. Using Rowe's shoulders as leverage, he shoved to his feet. He raced to the dresser where he'd set his bag and weapons when their own motel door exploded inward. He barely managed to grab his gun before shots were fired through the opening. This was definitely not the cops. They would have been shouting that they were the police. Noah managed to get off a couple of shots before diving into the little niche for the bathroom.

"Rowe?" Noah shouted. He hadn't seen what had happened to his lover. Rowe's gun had been closer at hand on the nightstand.

"I'm good. We need to get to JB."

There was so much noise in their motel room that he wasn't sure what was happening in JB's. Unfortunately, they were pinned down in the room with no clue as to how many people were outside.

How the hell had they been found so fast?

Gunfire slowed as magazines were emptied. They needed to make a move while the men were changing out. But what? There was only one way out of the motel room and that was currently under fire.

The door that led into JB's room exploded open. Noah raised his gun and started to take aim at the figure who flew horizontally into the room but stopped himself at the last second as he realized it was his Army friend.

"Frag!" JB shouted as he flew through the air.

Noah had a second of denial, confident that there was no way these fuckers had gotten their hands on a fragmentation grenade. But the near-deafening explosion in the next room had Noah hunching down. The worst of the bomb wasn't the explosive force, but the little metal shrapnel that was sent in every direction. He could hear it pounding against the drywall and embedding in the concrete outer walls of the building.

"We are getting the fuck out of here," Rowe snarled. Noah had to agree. They couldn't wait around for these assholes to throw another grenade in their direction now that they were all gathered in one room.

"Lead!" JB called out as he rolled to his feet. He fired twice, taking out one guy who'd been peeking into the doorway.

Noah took a second to secure his bag on his shoulder and shove a fresh magazine into his front pocket. Rowe followed quickly on JB's heels, adding to the suppressing fire that was backing up their attackers. With those two pushing back the enemy, Noah rushed forward and grabbed Rowe's bag from beside the bed and car keys off the nightstand.

Stepping out onto the narrow walkway of the second floor of the motel, Noah quickly counted two dead bodies outside their door and one outside of JB's. They wore nondescript jeans and black T-shirts, but gloves on their hands as if they didn't want to risk leaving behind prints.

Moving around the bodies, Noah quickly crept down the walkway, his gun at the ready, while Rowe and JB provided cover. He caught glimpses of two other similarly dressed men running for a dark SUV idling in the parking lot.

"Move your ass, Keegan!" Rowe roared.

Noah glanced over his shoulder to find both Rowe and JB heading down the concrete stairs to the ground floor. Noah's Jeep was less than a hundred feet away. Reaching into his pocket, he tossed the keys to Rowe and hurried to the stairs. Their booted feet thumped loudly on the concrete as they raced to their vehicle.

In the distance, they could hear police sirens growing closer with each passing second. They needed to get gone before the cops arrived. He wasn't too worried about going to jail since they were the ones who'd been attacked, but the police would only slow down their investigation into what happened to Chris and Paul. And Rowe had proved to him more than once that they worked so much better without the police meddling in their business.

Braced against a pillar, Noah stopped long enough to fire a couple of rounds into the SUV's front passenger tire before racing after Rowe and JB to the Jeep. He could hear the other men shouting to hurry, and Noah could only hope that they were looking to make a quick escape from the law as well. The men had attacked, relying on the element of surprise to take down Rowe, JB, and himself, but three former Rangers weren't that easy to kill. At least, not with a sloppy frontal assault.

The truck engine roared to life as Noah jumped into the passenger seat and slammed the door shut behind him.

"Slow ass," Rowe muttered as he shoved the car into drive.

From the back seat, JB chuckled between pants. Noah glanced over at his friend and except for a few scrapes and cuts on his face, he looked fine. He'd even managed to grab his own bugout bag in the chaos. There wasn't any blood on Rowe either, so the man appeared to be fine as well.

"Get us the fuck out of here," Noah said, flopping back against his seat.

His heart was hammering so hard in his chest, he was sure it was going to give out at any second. It had been a while since he'd been in an insane situation like that. There was a little voice screaming in his head for him to reach over to Rowe and run his hands along his man, checking to make sure that he was truly safe and well. Touching him was the only way he was going to be positive Rowe was unharmed.

"Is that your phone?" JB asked.

Noah looked around at him, brow furrowed. He wanted to ask what he was talking about when the muffled theme song to the 1970s TV show, *Wonder Woman* finally reached his ears.

"Gidget!" he shouted before scrambling to pull his phone from his pocket. He'd assigned that ring tone to her cell phone number.

"Thank God," Rowe sighed as he raced out into the quiet street and away from the police sirens. "Maybe she can finally give us some useful info."

"Gidget! Tell me something good!" Noah said into the phone.

"What's going on, Noah?" growled a cold, hard voice that had Noah wincing.

"Lucas! Heeeyyyy…" Noah drawled out. "What are you doing on Gidget's phone?"

"I told you! I fucking told you! He's like Candyman!" Rowe shouted beside him, pointing with his right hand at Noah's phone. "He can sense when you say his name. Now he's going to claw your face off with his hook and eat your soul!"

Noah smacked his hand away. "Shut up, you lunatic!"

"Guys, we've got a tail," JB announced the moment Rowe grew quiet again.

Noah swung around to look out the rear window, his mouth hanging open. "Are you shitting me?" It took only a second to spot the car that hurried away from the side of the road and was quickly closing the distance between them. It looked to be the same dark sedan that had followed them earlier in the day.

"Noah!" Lucas snapped. "Where are you? What's going on?"

"A friend from the Army passed away. Me, Rowe, and another Army friend popped out to Alexandria to pay our respects." Which was totally not a lie.

"I stopped by the office with Andrei after our date so he could pick up a contract. We ran into Gidget, who told us you two were in Virginia stirring up trouble with another security company."

"We did *not* start this. They started shoot—no! Stay on the side streets! The side streets!" Noah directed when it looked like Rowe was about to get on the highway. "It'll be easier to lose them on the side streets."

"I'm calling my pilot. Andrei and I can be there in three hours," Lucas announced.

"No! We're fine. It was just a little shooting. Daciana—"

"Andrei's parents are in town still. They can keep her."

This time Noah growled at Lucas. "We're fine. We've got this under control, bossy asshole!"

Rowe cackled, slapping his hand on the steering wheel, while it sounded like JB snorted behind him. Noah was accustomed to watching Lucas get high-handed with Snow and Ian, but he'd never had it directed at him. No wonder Rowe wanted to strangle the man most of the time.

Taking a deep breath, he said more calmly, "We're still doing some digging, trying to get to the bottom of why two Army friends were murdered and why JB and I might be next on that list." He grabbed the handle on the door as Rowe took a hard left into traffic, causing the tires to squeal while other cars blasted their horns. "We'll call if we get in over our heads."

Lucas was silent for several seconds, and Noah checked to make sure the line hadn't gone dead.

"Call before it gets to that point," Lucas grumbled.

Noah sighed with relief. "I will. We wouldn't dare leave you boys out of the fun."

"And I'm calling Snow to give him a heads up."

"Tattletale."

"Keep us in the loop," Lucas pressed on one last time and then ended the call.

Noah dropped the phone in his lap and closed his eyes. He loved Lucas and the rest of the gang. Loved when they all worked together on something sneaky, but there was no way in hell he was going to let Lucas and Andrei in on this mess when they had a little girl waiting for them at home. It was just another reason why Noah didn't want kids. He loved this wild and crazy life he had with Rowe. He didn't want to slow down or stop because they had to worry about a little one depending on them at home.

"I told you not to say his name," Rowe muttered, and Noah couldn't help but chuckle. His lover really was insane.

"Nothing from Gidget," Noah said. "Just the-man-who-can't-be-named checking in."

"I think we lost them," JB announced into the growing quiet of the car. He grabbed the front seats and pulled himself forward so that he was between Rowe and Noah. "Where do we go now?"

Noah's phone vibrated in his hand, and he looked down at a series of texts that Lucas had sent. His laughter filled the vehicle.

"Lucas says that Garrett and Royce are on standby if we need them," Noah read aloud.

"Bossy fucker," Rowe said, but he was also grinning.

"And he says there's a spare set of keys waiting for us at the security desk."

"What security desk?" JB asked.

Rowe laughed before Noah could answer. "I totally forgot he's got a penthouse in DC. Bought it years ago, before he met Andrei, but he's never used it much."

"If it belongs to Lucas, I'm sure it's posh," Noah murmured.

"Definitely. It'll give us a place to hide out and safely catch some sleep for a few days before we might have to move again," Rowe said.

Noah turned his head to look over at Rowe as they sat at a red light. "How did he know? I didn't say we needed a place to crash."

Rowe just shrugged. "He's just like that. Bossy as hell, but always thinking ten steps ahead of the rest of us. Always has a plan. Always ready to take care of his family even if he can't be there to do it in person."

It was a family Noah had never expected to find, but he was damn glad to have it.

CHAPTER NINE

"This place is nuts," Rowe breathed as they stood in the foyer of the luxurious penthouse apartment. White porcelain floors and dark millwork stretched out in a living room that rivaled Rowe's entire house for space. Soft blue sofas sat perpendicular to a long gas fireplace with a white, marble coffee table in between. Like the penthouse in Cincinnati, this place had floor-to-ceiling windows, this one with a view of the Washington Monument. Rowe wouldn't be able to stand all the open windows. It was like living in a fishbowl.

He strode through the room to the kitchen where there was more white in the countertops and cabinets. A massive island took up half the kitchen, and stainless-steel appliances gave the only color outside of the silver backsplash. The whole apartment looked like it was ready for a spread in a magazine for the rich and famous.

"Sheesh, Lucas," he muttered, turning a circle.

"You haven't been here before?" Noah asked as he opened the refrigerator. "Holy shit, there's food. Good, I'm starving."

"He probably had a delivery placed ahead before he even called us." Rowe set his satchel on the countertop and frowned. "There is way too much fucking white in this place. I feel like I'll get it dirty if I breathe on it."

"What kind of friend is this?" JB asked as he strolled into the kitchen.

"A ridiculously rich one."

"I like the way he spoils you. There's a bottle of Johnnie Walker Blue Label in here with a ribbon around it." JB winked and strode back out of the room, his head moving right and left as he took everything in.

Rowe looked up at the cathedral ceilings and whistled. "Why the hell would he need a place like this when he's hardly ever in DC?"

"You know Lucas." Noah pulled a bag of grapes out and started hunting through the cabinets. Probably for a colander. "Likes to have the best of everything. Sees it as a smart investment. How many condos do you think he has?"

"Who the fuck knows?" Rowe opened the refrigerator and grabbed a beer. "Even the booze is already cold." He chuckled. "Sweet asshole."

JB returned, his blue eyes blinking wide. "There are four big bedrooms, five bathrooms, and an upstairs living room in addition to this one. Plus, a study. How big is his family?"

"Depends on how you count. Three who live in his house, but with all his friends, it's pretty big. But he likes his space, that's for sure." Rowe offered JB a beer, and he took it with a nod of thanks.

Noah found the colander and rinsed the grapes under the faucet. The man was a fruit junkie and Lucas knew it. Rowe felt a pang of affection for Lucas for paying attention and caring so much for his boyfriend. There were also apples and oranges in a bowl on the counter. He looked at JB. "You should probably clean up all the scratches."

JB looked at his hands and arms, which were covered in cuts, but it was his face that had gotten most of the damage. Both cheeks held dots of blood and he had a large slash over his lip. "First, does anyone wanna tell me why we aren't going to the police with this? We were the ones being attacked."

Rowe looked at Noah, who grinned and motioned for Rowe to answer the question. Yeah, a smart man, a sane man, would be on the phone with the police the moment they noticed the tail, but Rowe never once claimed to be a sane person.

"Police just complicate things," he muttered.

"But isn't that their job? To serve and protect. I think we could use a little protecting about now. Particularly when these lunatics are tossing frag grenades into freaking motel rooms."

Okay, JB had a point. The grenade was extreme, but that was something they'd have to talk about later. For now, he needed to settle JB's worries, because he didn't want the guy sneaking off and involving the cops behind their backs in an effort to keep them all safe. Rowe wouldn't blame him...but...he'd probably hit him for making their lives more difficult.

Leaning his forearms on the center island, Rowe met JB's blue eyes and gave him a reassuring smile. "Look, I know calling the cops seems like the smart thing, but what's going to happen if we involve them? We're all going to get hauled into the police station for a hell of a lot of questioning and finger-pointing. They're going to take our weapons and possibly even hold us as they sort out the dead bodies we left in our rooms, regardless of the fact that it was obviously self-defense. They're going to haul in poor Sally Perkins for questioning, upsetting her more. Then after losing a lot of time we don't have, they're going to dump us on the street, *without* our weapons, and tell us to go home. I don't know about you, but I like my gun."

"You've got plenty of other guns at home," Noah teased.

Rowe held up one finger at Noah. "Not the point." He then directed his comments at JB. "They're going to tell us to let them handle the Chris investigation, assuming they even reopen the investigation into his death. Do you want to risk going home knowing that Paul and Chris were killed at home?"

"No," JB said sharply.

Rowe continued before he could add any other comments. "And do you want to leave the investigation over to the cops when they were so quick to call it a simple hit and run?"

"No."

"Calling the cops in means that they're digging around in this investigation, putting up potential roadblocks for us, and generally making our lives hell. We're going to have enough trouble trying to dissect this group of killers and tracking down all the hows and whys. I personally don't want the cops making it even harder."

JB frowned at Rowe for a second and then looked over at Noah. "Do you ever feel like you're dating the devil? Because I'm pretty sure that calling the cops is the right thing to do, but he makes it sound so much more logical and saner to simply keep the cops out of it."

Noah huffed a laugh. "Yeah, Rowe could probably seduce a nun if he wanted, but I think he's right about this. I want to handle this personally. I owe it to Paul and Chris. I should have kept in better contact with all of you. I might not have been able to stop this, but they deserve to have their killers brought to justice." Noah's hand came to rest on Rowe's shoulder. He squeezed and Rowe shifted his weight so that he was leaning ever so slightly against Noah. Just that little bit of contact breathed new life into him. "If you're not comfortable with that, you can walk away. Rowe and I will take care of this. No hard feelings. I get it. Respect it. When this is over, we'll fly out to see you and tell you everything if you want."

"No, you're right," JB said firmly. He placed both of his balled fists on the countertop. "I want to handle this personally too. I want to do this for Chris and Paul. I don't want to worry about the cops botching the investigation or not taking it seriously. Our friends deserve justice."

"And we'll get it for them," Rowe said.

"But what about the motel? Can't the cops just pull the credit card information for the rooms? We'll be wanted for questioning."

Rowe grinned. "Paid in cash. Slipped the night clerk a little something extra to forget our faces."

"Any security cameras in the lobby?" Noah asked.

Rowe made a motion like he was grabbing the bill of a baseball cap and straightening it. "Wore a hat into the lobby. They never got a good look at my face or hair. All the cops have is the description of a white male, medium height and build." He snorted. "Good luck with that."

Noah chuckled and JB shook his head while sighing. They were right. He could be quite sneaky and devious when he wanted. It was a good thing that he liked to protect and help the little guy.

"We've still got to talk about what we think is going on, but JB needs to take care of his face first." He motioned toward the half bath. "Rowe, can you see if Lucas has a first aid kit in there?"

Rowe nodded and searched the bathroom. Sure enough, there was a kit under the sink. He handed it to JB, who disappeared into the bathroom. When he came out, he'd cleaned up the cuts. The one over his lip looked swollen and painful, but it still didn't detract from his good looks. He had a sort of western Brad Pitt vibe to him that got on Rowe's nerves. But it was hard not to like the guy, who kind of reminded him of Noah with his easygoing personality. He also showed real skills in the way he'd handled himself back at the motel.

They took their time picking through the contents of the kitchen for some food. There was a current of dread filling the penthouse. Shadowy ideas were starting to coalesce in Rowe's brain, and they pointed at some damn ugly truths.

Pain was starting to beat against Rowe's temples. He wanted to do nothing but curl up with his boyfriend and sleep, but they had to get the ugliness said before any of them could rest for the night. He settled on one of the blue couches and yanked Noah down beside him. JB took one of the two striped chairs. He lifted his beer to his lips and winced.

Rowe cleared his throat. "So, we obviously forced them into upping their hand after our visit to their headquarters today. It's too much of a coincidence that our fucking motel got hit hard afterward. I mean, why go straight to fucking grenades and big hit squad?"

Noah scrubbed a hand over his face and dropped it into his lap. "Yeah, it's like this guy has never heard of a measured response. He jumped like five steps by chucking that frag into JB's room."

"The guy behind it could be insane," JB suggested.

"Or scared shitless. But why? We don't know anything."

"We know about Dave," Rowe said. "And we knew to come here. We could have gone to...where was Paul killed?"

"Casper, Wyoming," JB answered.

"We have to figure out what they're hiding, and it has to be about this Dave guy that Chris saw at Clayborne."

"If it is indeed Dave, then he never went missing in the first place," JB said. "I don't even want to contemplate what that would mean."

Rowe gripped Noah's thigh. "It means inside knowledge. If he survived the ambush and popped up with a new identity, then it's likely he knew exactly who hit that base. He was in on it. None of us wants to think one of our own would do such a thing, but it's the only thing that makes sense."

Noah shook his head. "It was just dumb luck Chris went to work for the same company this guy works for."

"Yeah," Rowe agreed. "And because it's more than one person after us, that means a lot were involved. We need numbers for what we're up against."

They were all quiet, then. The ramifications of this train of thought were hard to swallow.

"We don't have nearly enough information," JB said. He crossed an ankle over his knee and ran a hand through his hair. "What do we do now?"

"Lay low until Gidget can get us the pictures. Maybe drive out to the scene of the accident to see if we can find anything. Do you think you can recognize the guy that went missing?"

Noah shook his head. "Probably not. I don't think I ever met him. Chris would have been the one who could ID the guy easily."

"Well hopefully, there's enough security in this building to warn us should anyone show up." Rowe grimaced. "I didn't install the security system in this place, so God only knows what we've got watching over us."

"There are other good security systems," Noah teased.

"No one is as good as Ward Security," Rowe replied with a smirk. But the look died away and he turned serious again. "We should probably sleep in shifts just in case, though."

"I'll take the first," Noah said. He stood and stretched. "Why don't you two hit the hay."

"Wake me in three hours," Rowe said as he stood next to him. JB wandered off in the direction of the guest bedrooms and Rowe wrapped his arms around Noah. "I'm going to miss you in what is surely a huge bed in Lucas's room."

"After this long day, you'll be asleep in minutes," Noah scoffed but wrapped Rowe up tight in his embrace. "That was a close one tonight."

"We're lucky we came out of it unscathed. These guys mean business."

Noah cupped his face and stared into his eyes before kissing him gently. "Get some sleep. I'll make sure no bad guys come through this door."

"There is one other thing that's bothering me," Rowe admitted as Noah lifted his lips from Rowe's.

"What?"

"What if they're not insane or scared?"

Noah cocked his head to the side, his brow furrowing slightly as he looked at Rowe. "What are you thinking?"

"What if they chucked that frag into the room because they knew they could get away with something like that? We're just outside of freaking Washington DC. We're in the center of law enforcement and intelligence for the entire country, and this shady guy and his team set up a security firm here to potentially act as a shell company for illegal activities. That takes either big, steely balls…"

"Or someone is protecting them," Noah whispered in a horrified voice.

"And if that's true, the cops aren't likely to do us any favors."

"Fuck, that's just a lovely thought to try and fall asleep to tonight." Noah's hands tightened on Rowe, holding him closer as if he was unconsciously trying to shield Rowe's body with his.

"I could be wrong, but it's an idea. If Gidget can't turn up anything useful, I've still got a few contacts in DC that might help."

"You're such a sneaky bitch," Noah teased, his voice full of love and warmth.

Rowe smiled and kissed him before heading to where he assumed the master bedroom was. Rowe knew he found it when he spotted the king-sized bed set on a raised platform—next to another floor-to-ceiling window. He shook his head and grinned. Lucas liked to be the king of the city, no matter what city it was. He grabbed a quick shower to get the motel grime off and crawled into the massive bed. Like Noah predicted, he was out soon after that.

~

*T*hree hours later, Noah searched out the master bedroom and had to chuckle when he saw how over-the-top it was. It was the size of their living room and kitchen at home combined, with stately looking furniture surrounding the platform bed. Moonlight spilled over the massive bed with its white comforter and Rowe actually looked small in the thing. He was also really out with his mouth hanging open and soft snores spilling from his lips. Noah stood by the bed, smiling with fondness. His heart swelled in his chest as he looked at this man who was his everything. He decided not to wake him and left him sleeping peacefully.

Back in the living room, he settled into one of the chairs and stared at the door. He could probably nap on the couch—he was a light sleeper when he needed to be. He didn't expect anyone to show up at the penthouse and try to take them out, but these guys had proved to be one step ahead, so anything could happen. Shadows filled the corners of the penthouse, which was bright due to the city lights coming through the windows. There weren't even curtains to pull closed here. He got up and snatched an apple out of the bowl on the kitchen island before returning to the chair.

"Why don't you let me take a shift?"

JB's quiet voice made Noah turn his head as the man walked into the room. "I've got this. I wasn't hurt like you were."

"I can't sleep anyway." JB sat on the couch, keeping his tone low. "I'm not really hurt, just scratched up a bit. Decide not to wake the boyfriend?"

Noah sat back in the chair. "He looked too peaceful. I didn't have the heart." He took a bite of his apple.

JB's grin shone white in the moonlight. "You sure are gone over him."

"I've been gone over him for more years than I can count." He leaned forward in the seat, the darkness of the early morning hour making him decide to be painfully honest. "It's why I broke things off with you all those years ago. Wasn't fair to you that my heart was so taken."

"I always knew your heart was with the guy you talked about. At the time, I was pretty upset. Liked you an awful lot, Noah Keegan." He drew his name out in his soft, southern, Texas drawl.

"I liked you, too. You've always been a good friend." He smiled because he had truly liked the man. If he hadn't already been in love with Rowe, JB would have been someone he could see spending more time with. He was fun, responsible and really, really easy on the eyes. They'd had fun together even if it had all been only casual for Noah. "So, what have you been doing since you've been out?"

"I went back to my family's ranch in Texas. It's a big spread just outside Austin."

Noah could feel his brow furrow as he frowned at JB. "I remember that was something you didn't want."

JB shrugged. "Changed my mind. The Army cured my wanderlust, and it's been nice getting to know my sister's kids." He gave Noah a little smirk as he grabbed his phone so similar to how Noah did when he was talking about his "niece" Daciana. Leaning closer, he showed Noah a picture of an adorable little girl who looked to be about three years old. In the next picture was a woman with blonde hair like JB's, holding a dirty, laughing little boy who couldn't be more than one year old.

"Adorable," Noah murmured as JB sat back again, setting his phone on the arm.

"It's good to be home. The work is hard, but I like it. Keeps me in shape." He was silent a moment. "It was lonely after you left the service."

"I wasn't in a good place then."

"I haven't been either. Feels strange to be out—like I don't really fit in. I think it shows, too, because my mother keeps trying to set me up with both men and women since I've been back. Cracks me up how well they accepted my bisexuality, because there have been more men than women with her."

"Nobody caught your interest?"

"Nah, but I wish that weren't true. I want something like you've got with Rowe. I know it's the very thing I said I didn't want nothing to do with years ago when we met, but the whole marriage and kids thing is sounding pretty damn good now. Build a home and a life with someone."

He didn't say it, but Noah knew he'd wanted something like that with him. He shifted on the seat, suddenly uncomfortable. To cover up his discomfort, he took a healthy bite of the apple. He'd known how JB had felt back then, and it had broken his heart to hurt him. He could only hope he still wasn't nursing those old feelings. Particularly since the "marriage and kids" thing didn't appeal to him in the least, even with Rowe.

Would he be sitting there if he and Rowe had a little one at home? Adding a kid or two to the mix would change everything. It wasn't a bad thing. Just that Noah loved the life he already had with Rowe. A kid wouldn't give him a feeling of completion like it did for his friends.

And marriage? That was an uneasiness he wasn't sure he could explain to anyone.

He swallowed the apple, gaze going back to JB, who watched him quietly. "So, that's your plan? Take over the family business?"

JB nodded. "I like it there. Feels good to be home. I'm in the right frame of mind for it now because you're right, it wasn't what I wanted when I was younger. But there's a sort of...I don't know...beauty in the hard work. And the spread my parents have is gorgeous. At the end of the day, I can ride out and the whole world is spread before you. Big sky and the earth just stretching on forever. No one shooting at you. Just the wind and the prairie dogs. You and Rowe should come out there and visit sometime."

Noah snorted. "I don't think Rowe's comfortable enough with you for something like that."

"Not yet. When he sees I don't have designs on you, he'll thaw. Man is nuts about you, Noah."

"I'm thankful for that every single day."

They were both quiet then, and Noah stood. "If you're going to be awake, I'm going to grab a few hours."

"Go ahead. I'll keep watch."

He nodded and made his way to the master bedroom where Rowe lay exactly as he had before. Noah stripped off his dirty clothes and crawled into the bed. Rowe immediately rolled over and wrapped himself around Noah. "My shift now?" he whispered, voice raspy with sleep.

"Nah, JB took it. Go back to sleep."

" 'Kay." And like that, he was out.

Noah snorted into the pillow and snuggled against Rowe, who tightened his arms. Noah didn't worry with JB on the watch. He'd watched his back often when they'd been in the service. JB was a good guy. He thought back to when they'd been together. He *had* had a lot of fun with the man; their relationship had been easy. Almost too easy. But it had never been anything more than a temporary thing for Noah. He ran his hand over Rowe's arm, loving the rasp of hair under his palm. Unfortunately for JB, nobody could compare to Rowan Ward.

CHAPTER TEN

*N*oah patted his complaining belly as he stood in the bright sunlight. The apple and orange he'd scrounged for a quick breakfast weren't going to be enough. The sun was already set high in the sky, beating down on his head, promising to make it a hot one.

He stretched, feeling like he hadn't gotten enough sleep, his body screaming with exhaustion. Rowe was the only one who looked wide awake as he crawled over every inch of the scene of Chris's accident.

Noah couldn't help but worry that this accident brought up memories of Mel. Hers had been the same—a fatal hit-and-run but in the winter. Rowe had been the actual target, and that knowledge probably sat heavy on his boyfriend at all times. While hers had been on the highway, this one was in a neighborhood, so they could get out and look around.

It was a quiet street not too far from Chris's home, someplace his wife probably had to pass whenever she drove anywhere. Noah's heart ached for her because it was obvious this had been where Chris died, due to the mangled stop sign that hadn't yet been replaced.

All the houses sat far off the street like hers, their yards full of well-manicured landscaping. Colorful May flowers dotted the area, and one of the houses had a family of happy gnomes that looked like they were frolicking in the garden.

"Any clues there, Scooby-Doo?" JB asked Rowe as he kneeled on the street and looked at a skid mark. Rowe threw JB a dark, warning look over his shoulder before turning his attention back to the road. "What exactly are you expecting to find?"

"I didn't really expect to find anything." Rowe stood, plopped his hands on his hips, and turned a full circle before facing west. "From the angle of the stop sign, it looks like Chris was hit on the driver's side and pushed off the road. The person driving had to have run their sign and been going fast."

"Sounds deliberate to me," Noah said, still remembering that someone had *deliberately* run into Rowe's wife. Her hit-and-run had nearly taken one of their close friends with her. Noah still hated to think about what that must have been like for both Rowe and Ian.

Rowe seemed to be handling this okay, though. He was busy playing detective and was sexy as fuck doing so. He wore jeans and a black polo shirt, his red hair bright in the sunlight. It was kind of surprising that Rowe hadn't considered becoming a cop or a detective. But then again, the man hated doing things the legal way.

"Somebody here had to have seen the driver." Rowe eyed the closest house and stalked toward it. Guess he was taking the detective thing further.

He knocked on the door, and a scowling elderly woman answered. She had on a pair of blue jean overalls that had dirt on the knees. From her yard, it was easy for Noah to guess how that happened. She had a showcase of flowers, shrubs, and trees on her property.

"Hello ma'am," Rowe said, smiling and turning on the charm. "We're sorry to bother you, but we were wondering if you happened to see the accident that occurred right outside your house one week ago?"

Her scowl deepened. "You cops? Because I already talked to the cops."

Rowe's voice took on a sad cast. "No, we're actually friends of the man who was killed, and we're trying to find out what happened."

She stared at all three of them for long moments before her expression softened in sympathy. "I saw it. Was tending my rhododendrons and azaleas." She pointed to the bright pink and red flowers that took up the majority of her yard. "Takes a lot of love to grow those."

"I bet it does," Rowe said, giving the flowers a look she had to appreciate. "And they are beautiful. My grandma used to grow azaleas." He cleared his throat. "What did you see exactly?"

"I saw the man pull out at the stop sign—he had the right of way—and the other car came out of nowhere, sped up, and rammed him. Actually sped up! I heard his engine kind of growl. Just like I told the police. Was no damn accident."

"What kind of car hit him?" Noah asked.

She looked at him. "One of those big yellow things. A hummer. The guy in the little car didn't stand a chance. He was run right into the sign, and the hummer drove off. I called 9-1-1 myself, but it was too late for that fella." She shook her head, gray curls bobbing. She opened the door farther and a wave of cool air came out. With it, came the scent of fresh-baked bread. Noah's stomach rumbled.

"Did you see the driver of the hummer?" Rowe asked.

"Just a pair of shiny sunglasses," she answered. "You know the ones that look kind of orange? I remember because the sun was shining off them and he looked ridiculous in them."

"I do know that kind of sunglasses. Is there anything else you can tell us?"

"No. That's what I told the police, too. That hummer shouldn't be hard to find. I hope they catch that guy." She scowled and crossed her arms. "Shame that woman lost her husband. I used to see them working in their yard. It was beautiful."

"You sure it was a man driving?" This came from JB.

She nodded. "That I do know." She tilted her head and squinted off into space a moment. "Had dark hair. Cut short. Like one of them military dos. Does that help?"

"Everything you told us helps more than you know," Rowe answered her. "Thank you for talking to us."

"I'm sorry about your friend."

"Thank you."

Technically, Chris wasn't Rowe's friend, but Noah knew it had been easier to get the woman to talk this way. Rowe hit up two more houses. One man hadn't seen anything, and the other woman had a similar story to the first lady's.

They got back into Noah's Jeep, Rowe once again taking the wheel. The man had a few control issues that yeah, sometimes got on his nerves, but Noah was happy to let him navigate the strange city. The vehicle was hot, so he quickly turned up the air conditioner.

"I think it's safe to say this was no accident," JB said, settling into the back seat with a heavy sigh. "Though I knew that from them coming after us. I hope we hear from your computer guru soon, because I'm not sure what else we can do here."

"I'm not sure where to go from here either." Rowe pulled the vehicle past the accident site and drove out of the neighborhood. He steered onto Richmond Highway and once again hit heavy traffic. This route would drive Noah nuts if he lived here. Wall to wall cars halted on the highway at all times, it seemed. An apartment building was to their right, next to a diner. He eyed the diner, his stomach growling as he thought about stopping for a real breakfast. One with bacon and pancakes.

Rowe shot him a grin, so he must have heard it. "We could stop and eat, but it would be a shame to let all that food Lucas ordered go to waste."

"Just take us back to his condo. We'll scrounge there again. There was plenty of sandwich meat and bread. Chips."

JB leaned between the two seats. "The more I think about this, the more I'm surprised. It's pretty ballsy, ramming Chris's car like that in broad daylight in a neighborhood. Especially with the neighbors outside like they were. And with a yellow hummer? Hard to hide one of those."

Noah turned to look at him. "You know, I can wait on the food. We could drive by the merc's office again. Do either of you remember seeing a big yellow vehicle there?"

"No, but there was a garage. We could try and get a look inside." Rowe growled. "But now we have a tail again. Same black sedan with only one guy in it this time."

Noah turned to find the car a few rows back. "On the plus side, he's just as stuck in this traffic. Isn't wearing orange-colored glasses, so it's probably a different guy."

They inched along what was also known as Route 1, Noah keeping an eye on the car tailing them. He then eyed the bag at his feet and got an idea. It would be risky with all the people in cars around them but they needed answers, and this would be the best way. He bent down and dug around in the bag until he found what he wanted.

"Rowe, follow my lead," Noah announced, putting his hand on the door handle.

"Sure thing!"

Noah climbed out of the Jeep just as JB asked, "Did he take duct tape?"

Keeping low as possible, Noah skirted several cars, running to the sedan and hoping the guy didn't have time to hit the locks before he reached him. Most of the other drivers were staring at their phones since they were stuck in traffic. Just a few noticed him. He winked and smiled, trying to make it look like a big joke.

He got lucky; the driver's window was open. He paused long enough to look around at the other cars, but no one was paying attention to him. Standing suddenly, Noah reached through the open window and slammed his fist hard into the side of the guy's head. The driver gave a sharp cry and fell over into the passenger seat.

Noah didn't give him time to react. Opening the car door, he shoved him into the passenger seat. Climbing in after him, he pressed one foot on the brake to keep the car from rolling. He hauled back and let another punch fly. The big guy's eyes fluttered and he was out, slumped in the seat.

Settling behind the wheel, Noah quickly pulled the car out of traffic, choosing the closest place—the half-empty parking lot of a grocery store. He parked the car.

The guy recovered enough to fight back at this point, and Noah took a punch to the jaw. Pain exploded in his face. Now that he'd lost the element of surprise, he had to use brute force to wrestle the man down until he was on top of him. They scrabbled in the front seat, and Noah pushed open the passenger door and fell out of it, his elbow scraping along the harsh surface of the pavement. He quickly got to his feet and yanked the man out of the car, but the guy came out fighting, slamming Noah into the ground.

He hit with a hard whoosh of air but quickly rolled them until he was on top. He came up to his knees and the guy scrambled away from him. Noah grinned and dove at his legs, using his weight to pin him down. Climbing back up the guy, he smashed his fist into the man's nose, causing him to scream and reach for his face.

Shoving to his feet, Noah kicked him in the side, knocking the wind out of him. He paused for a second and then kicked him in the groin for good measure. The man howled, curling up as he held his wounded dick and balls. Noah hurried into the car for his duct tape.

He stood over the guy for only a second as he pulled a nice, long strip.

By the time he'd disabled the man and wrestled him into the back seat of the car, he was soaked with sweat, and his face and elbow ached. He got into the sedan just as Rowe pulled into the parking lot. He motioned for him to follow.

Now they had to find a quiet spot where they could get some answers.

CHAPTER ELEVEN

"*I* get it now," JB said when he climbed out of the Jeep and came to stand next to Rowe.

Standing with his arms folded over his chest, he waited for Noah to park the sedan in a clear spot near the truck. It felt like the entire world had fallen away as they'd driven for so long in what looked like a whole lot of nowhere. Trees closed in around them, blocking any sight of the road and the darkening sky. The birds had gone quiet with their presence in the area. Other eyes were on them, watching from a safe distance, but he was sure none of them were human. They were safe for now, but it was only a matter of time before the people after them realized their lookout had gone missing.

"Get what?"

JB flashed him a wide grin. "Why you keep an entire box of duct tape in the back of your truck. When did they start making it with so many colors and designs?"

Rowe made a tsking noise as he shook his head. "Kid, you've got so much to learn. They've got glow in the dark tape now."

"And scented tape, like grape and orange cream," Noah called out as he climbed from the sedan.

"Yeah, but I'm not wasting the scented tape on assholes and shit-heads trying to kill me," Rowe called out.

Noah chuckled as he stepped backward to the rear door and pulled it open. "No, the scented tape is for private fun and games."

Rowe glanced over at JB to find that his eyes had widened, and a soft flush was staining his pale cheeks. He could only imagine what thoughts were zooming through his head, and Rowe didn't care so long as all those images of Noah also contained Rowe right there with him.

With a smirk, he walked over to the car and placed a hand on Noah's shoulder. They got up to some strange and kinky things at times, and Rowe was surprised by how freeing it could be. He'd never felt particularly restricted with Mel, but there was something about being with Noah that tapped his adventurous side. But even when they weren't getting their freak on with duct tape and lime Jell-O, he loved putting a look of pure joy on Noah's face.

Unfortunately, their fun was largely put on hold until they could uncover what the fuck was going on and why JB and Noah were now in a killer's sights.

Rowe placed his hand on Noah's chin and gently turned his head to look closer at the dark bruise that was forming on his jaw. There were a few other scrapes, but he'd seen Noah looking far worse. For the most part, he just looked sweaty and hot from his struggle and the drive.

"Trust me, he's far worse than me," Noah said with a cocky grin.

Rowe looked around Noah to find the man with a strip of duct tape over his mouth, his hands bound behind his back, his ankles bound together, and then another piece of tape binding his feet to his hands.

"You hog-tied him?" Rowe asked in surprise.

"I had to make sure he couldn't cause problems while I was driving."

"Yeah, but I watched you. It couldn't have taken you more than a minute. That's damn fast."

Noah's grin grew wide and a little wicked. "I've got skills with tape and rope."

Rowe's eyes narrowed and he tilted his head to the side. "Are you into shibari and not telling me?" he asked in a low voice, referring to the Japanese form of rope play.

"I never said I'm *not* into it." The heat in Noah's gaze shot straight to Rowe's groin and put fire in his veins. The sudden image of Noah tying him up and slowly working him over was melting his brain cells. They'd played with tape and handcuffs a few times, but this…

The man in the back seat of the car made a muffled noise and shifted across the bench seat like he was straining against his bindings, but with little success. Rowe needed to get his head back in the game. JB was likely standing somewhere close by, and he didn't want to think about how much he'd overheard.

"We're gonna put a pin in this and discuss it again at a better time."

"Or I can give a demonstration," Noah suggested. Rowe glared at him for a second, making Noah's shoulders shake with silent laughter. As it was, he needed to freaking adjust himself, but he didn't want to do it with an audience.

"Grab his feet," Rowe directed. "I'll grab one arm and JB can grab the other. We can take him into the woods." The man moaned and stared at them over his shoulder with wide, wild eyes. Rowe gave an evil chuckle. "We're gonna ask you a few questions."

Noah picked up the man's feet and pulled him part of the way out of the car. He started to struggle, but Rowe grabbed his arm and lifted him off the seat. He might have "accidentally" slammed the guy's head into the car door as they pulled him out before JB could move around them to grab his other arm. The asshole settled, moaning again, but this time it was likely from pain. Rowe couldn't feel too bad about it. The man was well over six foot and weighed a fucking ton. Well, not really, but it was enough that he was tempted to just drag him through the woods on his face.

They were lucky in that the area was flat, allowing them to comfortably walk deeper into the woods. Rowe glanced over his shoulder to see the cars almost immediately disappear. The trees closed in and it was like a dome fell over the world, blocking out sounds of human life. There was only the crunch of their feet on broken branches and dead leaves. Wildlife backed off and watched with curious eyes.

Rowe always enjoyed his trips into the woods for hiking and camping. It let him clear his head and push away the worries of work. He could concentrate on one thing and figure out a solution. Or he could think about nothing at all. Just soak in nature around him and let everything fall away.

But this was darker. He didn't know what was going to happen to this man, but he was willing to cross any line he had to. Noah's life had been threatened at least twice by these assholes. Not again. Never again. Rowe didn't want to contemplate a life without Noah. The very idea stole his breath away and erased all rational thought. He'd already lost Mel and it nearly killed him. He couldn't go through that with Noah. The world needed Noah. *He* needed Noah.

After walking nearly a quarter of a mile into the woods, Rowe called a halt and directed them to place their captive down on a fallen log. JB quickly unsheathed a long, wicked looking blade and cut the tape binding the man's feet to his hands so he could sit on the log.

Rowe grabbed his phone and nearly sighed with relief when he saw that he still had two bars. Not great, but it was plenty to put in a call to the office and the triplets—the IT team of Gidget, Quinn, and Cole.

"Remove the tape on his mouth and hold his head up," Rowe said.

Noah held the man's short dark-brown hair in one fist while JB grabbed one corner of the tape. Leaning down in front of the man, Rowe could see JB grinning at him.

"Do you want it fast like a Band-Aid or slow like a bitch?" JB asked.

The man's response was garbled behind the tape, but Rowe was pretty sure it consisted of "Fuck you."

JB looked up at Noah, who grinned at him. "I think he said like a bitch," Noah supplied.

"Oh, he's not a sad, punk-ass bitch," JB mocked. A horrible ripping sound filled the woods, followed by the man's pained shout as JB pulled the tape off from his mouth lightning fast.

Noah chuckled, looking at the man's face. "I think you got some facial hair there."

"You ripped my fucking lips off," the man snarled before pressing his sore lips together with a little whimper.

Rowe held his phone up and snapped a couple of quick, clear pictures of the man's face. He sent the images over to the triplets at Ward Security and then dialed Gidget's number.

"Hey, Boss!" she greeted. "Ooooh…who's the grumpy lump in the pictures?"

"That's what I'd like you to uncover for me. I think he's an employee of Clayborne, but I'm not sure."

"I can run him through the facial recognition software. We're starting to get all the details on Clayborne and its employees. We should have a full report for you in an hour or two."

Rowe grunted. "Email it to me and Noah when you have it compiled. Call me when you get everything on this fucker in the pictures."

"Should I check for a police record too?"

Rowe narrowed his eyes at the man who was glaring right back at him. The muscles in the man's jaw flexed and jumped like he was clenching his teeth, determined not to say another word. Rowe wasn't worried. Noah was pretty good about getting information out of people.

"Everything. I think he was in on the attempt on Noah's life and could have been in on the deaths of Noah's friends."

"We'll get everything," Gidget said, her voice hardening. She was just as protective of Noah and the employees at Ward as Rowe was. These men were her family too. She'd spread the word to her coworkers in the tech room. They'd drop everything to uncover every little scrap of information about this fucker and they'd do it fast. Thanks to the digital age, there was no longer any hiding.

He ended the call and put his phone back into his pocket.

"You might as well let me go. You're not getting anything out of me," the man snarled. "And you don't have the balls for torture."

From a sheath on his belt, Rowe pulled out his black-handled ka-bar with its exquisitely sharp seven-inch blade. It wasn't as flashy as JB's knife, but Rowe could wield it like it was an extension of his own body. He stepped closer to the man and let the edge scrape along the tender flesh under his chin.

"I've already killed the man who murdered my wife," Rowe started in a deceptively low and soft voice, as if he were whispering to him the secret of life. "I've killed to protect a man I see as my brother. I've killed total strangers because it was part of my job. Do you really think I would have any problem slowly gutting you until you're telling me every little secret in your head?" Keeping his gaze locked on the man's wide brown eyes, he lowered the knife until the tip was pressed into his dick. "And I'm more than happy to start with your balls if you doubt me."

"B-bullshit," their captive stammered. His voice had lost most of its heat and strength. Sweat broke out across his pale face, and Rowe was sure it had little to do with the heat in the air.

Straightening, he looked over at Noah, who was standing beside the man. His eyebrows were raised in question, and he looked a little pale. Noah knew the majority of the ghosts that left stains on his soul. He wasn't hiding anything from his lover. Maybe just playing it up a little bit. But only a smidge. Rowe wouldn't hesitate to kill this fucker if it meant keeping Noah safe, and he'd sleep soundly the next night.

"I think we can skip the torture and just kill him," Noah said lightly.

"Really?" Rowe said, one corner of his mouth tilting up.

"Oh yeah, I'm pretty sure I can figure out who he is and what he knows." Noah's voice oozed confidence. "I just need to look at him. Sort of the Sherlock Holmes method."

"Whoa! Who said you get to go first?" JB interjected. "I'm pretty sure that I can figure it out just as easily as you. We were both trained in the same method."

Rowe stepped back farther and put his knife in its sheath before leaning against a large tree to watch the "argument." He knew Noah's method of interrogating, and it was kind of creepy. The way he could simply stare at a person and read the tiny reactions, from a muscle twitch to a hitch in the breathing to a simple eye dilation—all things people could barely control. And now the way JB was talking, he had a feeling that the two of them had worked in tandem on interrogations.

"Then we fight for who goes first," Noah offered.

He placed his fist in front of the man's face and waited. JB did the same. They counted to three, their eyes locked on each other, and they both came up with "rock" on the first go. On the second turn, they both hit "paper." And on the final one, it was a tie of "rock" again.

"I guess we go together," JB said.

The man between them looked up at them, appearing as if he thought they were both insane, and then he looked over at Rowe who flashed him his most wicked grin. He hadn't a fucking clue as to what JB and Noah were up to, but at least it was entertaining.

JB and Noah each kneeled down on one knee in front of the prisoner and stared at him, eyes narrowed and bodies tense. They didn't say a word. Seemed to be barely breathing. Seconds stretched into minutes. The man shifted uncomfortably on the log, looking from one man to the other. He tried ignoring them, but his eyes kept getting drawn back to either JB or Noah. Sweat trickled down the side of his face and along his nose. He tried wiping it away by rubbing his face on his shoulder but couldn't get to the spots near his eyes.

Rowe waited, curious as to their method.

"I'm not telling—" the man started to say, but JB was there, softly shushing him.

"Quiet now," he murmured. "You had your chance to talk. We've got this."

The man looked at him in dumbfounded shock. It was a strange course of action. They had taken him to get information out of him, but they didn't want him talking.

"I know who he is," Noah declared. "But you don't have to tell us if you don't want to tell us."

"I bet I figured it out first," JB jabbed.

The man's face clouded with skepticism, but the anger was gone. He'd become calm watching the duo. His breathing slowed down so that he was almost in rhythm with Noah and JB. He was now watching both men with rapt fascination, as if hypnotized. Rowe had to wonder if maybe he partially was. Both men were talking in monotone but authoritative voices. Steady and firm. It was unsettling. But more unsettling was the way the man was looking at Noah. Like his eyes were trapped.

Was he hypnotized?

"You weren't sent here to kill us. You weren't even tasked to follow us. You didn't talk to anyone about it because it was all your idea," Noah started reciting in the same even tone.

"You're here to help us out. This whole mess has been bothering you from the start," JB added. The man blinked slowly, but he still kept his gaze on Noah even though JB was now talking.

"We're so glad you came to us." Noah extended his hand as if he wanted to shake his hand.

The man shifted, looking as if he was pulling against his bound hands. Before he could blink again, JB slammed his hand into the center of the man's chest. A harsh gasp filled the clearing and the man sat up straight for a second.

"Sleep," Noah commanded in a hard, monotone voice.

The man exhaled and his eyes fell shut. His entire body slumped, forcing JB to quickly catch him, steadying him on the log again.

"Holy shit," Rowe whispered. They fucking hypnotized the guy. Everything about his posture was relaxed, and his breathing had slowed to a steady rhythm. He couldn't believe it.

Noah looked over his shoulder at Rowe and gave him a quick smile before looking at his target.

"We're so glad you came to us. You did come to help today, didn't you?" Noah said.

"I did come to help," the man said.

"What's your name?"

"Jeff Hastings."

"Do you know why Chris Perkins was killed?"

Jeff's brow furrowed for a moment as if he was trying to remember something. "He recognized Dave Johnson from the Army. Dave was afraid that Chris would tell people. Put him in jail."

"Was Paul Grimes killed for the same reason?"

"I...I don't know him."

Noah looked over at JB, who gave a little shrug but kept his mouth shut.

"Did Dave kill Chris?"

"No. He just told Erik about Chris. He was really scared. Panicked. Erik ordered people to get rid of Chris and keep an eye on his widow. Make sure no one came around asking questions."

"What's Erik's last name?"

"Johnson."

"Are Erik and Dave related?"

"Brothers."

That was interesting. Had Erik cooked up some scheme years ago that roped in his brother while he was in the Army? Had Erik been behind the ambush that resulted in deaths and the disappearance of a cache of weapons?

"Has Erik asked you to kill anyone?"

"No, I'm just a lookout. I follow around Sally Perkins. Listen to her phone calls. Make sure she doesn't think there's anything strange about her husband's death. Erik won't tell me what's going on. Don't think he trusts me."

JB's grin grew huge and he nodded at Noah. Rowe couldn't see Noah's expression, just that he nodded to JB.

"Erik doesn't trust you because you didn't join Clayborne to hurt people."

"No. I wanted to help."

"That's why you're leaving Clayborne tonight. You know that something is dirty there."

"Evil," Jeff said, his voice barely more than a whisper.

"That's right. Evil. When you wake up, you're going to feel relieved that you told us the truth. A huge weight has lifted off your shoulders. You're going to drive straight home and pack a bag. You're going to pull out as much cash as you can and then drive south to Alabama. You're going to hide for the next two weeks. Then you're going to find a new job and start a new life. You're going to help people."

"Help people," Jeff murmured.

"I'm going to snap my fingers. When I do you're going to wake up, refreshed and grateful to have told us the truth. You're going to leave here. Pack. Cash. Alabama."

"Gonna leave," Jeff said on a sigh.

"Three…"

As Noah started to count, JB grabbed his knife and motioned like he was cutting through the tape holding Jeff's hands.

"Two…"

JB put his knife away and carefully removed the tape from Jeff's hands, tossing it into the grass behind him. Rowe pulled out his gun but held it behind his back. If something went wrong, he wanted to have it ready to put Jeff down.

"One." Noah snapped his fingers.

Jeff blinked a few times, straightening where he sat on the log. He looked directly at Noah and heaved a heavy sigh as he stuck out his hand.

"Thank you so much for your help," Jeff said with what sounded like genuine sincerity. "This whole thing has been a giant mess."

Noah ripped apart the tape on his ankles, took his hand, and they helped each other to their feet. "We're happy to help. We're going to make sure that no one else gets hurt. Help people."

"Yeah, that's right." He still sounded a little dazed, but he nodded, his smile staying firm.

"But I know that you're in a hurry to get out of here. You mentioned that you're taking a trip to Alabama. I know you want to get on the road."

"Yeah. Yeah, I gotta get out of here." He took a step forward and then stopped as he looked around at the trees surrounding them.

"Here. My friend JB is going to walk you to the car."

JB quickly stepped up to Jeff's elbow and started to lead him through the woods and back to where they'd parked the cars.

As soon as they were several yards away, Noah wandered over to where Rowe was watching JB and Jeff disappear from sight, his gun still at his side.

"Tell me you've never hypnotized me," Rowe said in a low, hard voice. He had no idea that Noah could even do that, and the fact that he'd done it so fast was terrifying. And pretty damn amazing. He was seriously in awe of the man.

Noah's low chuckle wrapped around him. He slid his hand down his back to grab one ass cheek. "No, I've never hypnotized you."

Rowe turned his head and glared at him. "Seriously?"

"Hypnosis is largely about planting an idea or a command in someone's subconscious." Noah pressed his forehead against Rowe's. "You already give me everything I could want. Why would I need to hypnotize you?"

The tension eased in Rowe's chest and he sighed, realizing that he was being silly. Noah would never do something like that to him. "Smooth talker," he murmured. He started to kiss Noah and then jerked away when an evil thought popped into his brain. "Can you hypnotize Snow? Do something like make him meow every time Jude says the word 'lube'?"

Noah stumbled backward a couple of steps, laughing. The mental image was pretty freaking awesome. Snow would probably kill both of them, but it would be so worth it. "I'll think on it."

Rowe started through the woods, motioning for Noah to fall into step with him as they headed to the Jeep. They needed to return to the penthouse. With any luck, the triplets would have some information for them, preferably a face and details to go with the name Jeff handed over.

They didn't get much from Jeff, but at least it was a starting point, and they didn't have to torture a man who was largely innocent of the mess they found themselves entangled in.

CHAPTER TWELVE

oah heaved a happy sigh when he looked over their haul. They had two large pizzas loaded with toppings, beer, and a giant chocolate-chip cookie. No, it wasn't Ian's amazing cooking. It wasn't even some steaks Rowe threw on the grill with vegetables. But sometimes he just wanted a simple, greasy meal that brought back so many good memories.

They'd stopped for the food on their way to the penthouse. After a quick search of the place to make sure no one had been inside, they settled in the living room with the grub. So far, the penthouse was untouched, and they hadn't been followed since sending Jeff on his way. They were safe for at least another night. He was sure that was going to come to an end soon enough, but for now, he was going to enjoy the soft bed and safety.

"I can't believe that worked!" JB crowed for the second time. He tipped his beer to Noah, who clinked his against it. "We haven't done that in years. We're still in sync."

"I guess we haven't lost our touch," Noah said around a mouthful of pizza.

"I've got to know where you learned to do that," Rowe said. "I remember seeing you do something similar with that kid we caught after my house went up in flames."

"Whoa! What?" JB gasped.

Noah shook his head. "Arson case from a few years back," he said quickly, turning his attention to Rowe. He didn't want to go into it. The arsonists that had torched the home Rowe had created with Mel still left Noah feeling uneasy. Shit went south in that house, and no matter what Rowe said, Noah couldn't get rid of a lingering feeling of guilt. If he'd been paying more attention, things could have ended differently. "I used some of what I learned about hypnosis on the kid, but it wasn't true hypnosis. That was more about reading tells. Little facial tics."

"Whatever," Rowe said with a wave of his hand. "I still gotta know. Where did you learn it?"

Noah grinned around the crust of his slice of pizza. Rowe was not one to give up on something when it piqued his curiosity. He was a dog with a bone. "So, a Ranger, a PsyOps, and a CIA agent walk into a bar…"

"Oh, fuck you!" Rowe snarled. He jumped to his feet with his empty beer bottle in hand. He tilted the bottle toward JB, silently asking if he wanted another. JB nodded. "If you don't want to tell me, then don't." Rowe stomped off toward the kitchen to dump his empty into the recycling and grab some fresh from the fridge.

Noah grabbed his napkin and wiped his mouth before turning on the couch toward the kitchen. The open format reminded him of Lucas's penthouse in Cincinnati. "I'm being serious."

Rowe returned with three fresh beer bottles in hand. He set one in front of each of them before flopping back in his chair. "Then go for it, comedian."

Noah smirked at Rowe. He couldn't help teasing him a little bit. Rowe was older and while Noah might have spent more time in the military, Rowe was no slouch. He'd kept up with various techniques and weapons. He maintained a vast array of contacts both in the military and with intelligence agencies. It was all too rare for Noah to learn or know something before his boyfriend.

"I was selected to be a part of a unique team for a special mission. After the mission, we were sitting around a safe house. The PsyOps guy pulls out a bottle of thirty-year-old whiskey. So, we start drinking and swapping random stories. No real details of people and places. Just the crazy shit. Of course, one of us starts talking about the weirdest interrogations. CIA pops in with hypnosis. Psy Ops is laughing his ass off and saying that there's no such thing. That it's just a stupid magic trick. CIA seems to laugh it off. Later, he's acting like he's getting ready to leave. PsyOps puts his hand out to shake CIA's and the CIA dude hits him in the chest. Just a tap. And the guy is out in the blink of an eye. It's a five-second hypnosis trick. CIA gets me to film him clucking like a chicken, then brings PsyOps out of the trance. He doesn't remember a thing, but he freaks when he sees the video."

"Did he kill the CIA guy?" Rowe asked.

"You could tell he was thinking about it. I think it helped when the CIA guy taught us some of the basic tricks. It's all about voice, eye contact, and messing with certain patterns we come to expect. They create openings to speak right to a person's subconscious."

"That's just crazy," Rowe murmured as he grabbed another slice of pizza.

Noah nodded as he picked up his fresh beer. "It was, but I practiced it out of curiosity. Something to do when I had some downtime. Tried it out a few times on JB."

"And seriously pissed me off when I realized what he was doing," JB added.

"So, I taught JB. When we both got good, we started working in tandem with targets. Some people are good at blocking out one person, but it's harder when two people are doing it. They end up locking in on one person's eyes and voice. When that happens, that person takes the lead."

"The same way Jeff focused on you," Rowe said to Noah.

"For interrogation, it's not great. You can get some basic details. The more they have to think and dig around in their memory, the more you risk the person waking up. It's better for implanting commands and ideas. If the command feeds into their own emotions and desires, the better the likelihood it's going to lock in."

"That's some twisted shit," Rowe muttered, but there was an evil twinkle in his green eyes. Noah could almost hear the wheels turning in his head. Noah was not going to teach him, and he wasn't going to use it on their family. He didn't want them worrying about whether they could trust him.

Well, he might do the meowing command with Snow first, but that was it.

"It's just a shame that we couldn't get more out of Jeff," JB said. He tossed an uneaten bit of crust into the box and sank back into the couch, groaning softly like he'd stuffed himself. "We know he wasn't involved in Chris's death and that Dave's brother Erik seems to be the head of what's going on, but we still don't know anything. If Dave is alive, why didn't he come forward? Does it mean that the other two guys who were taken hostage are alive as well? Where are they?"

"I have a feeling we're not going to be able to fit any pieces together until we start getting some data back from Gidget and the rest of the triplets," Rowe said.

JB sat up a little, cocking his head at Rowe. "You've got triplets working for you?" The confusion cleared from his face and he grinned. "Are they hot?"

Rowe snatched up a pillow from the couch and tossed it at JB. "Not that kind of triplets."

Noah laughed. "Ward has a tech team of three people—Quinn, Gidget, and Cole. Two guys and a woman. All brilliant."

"I call them the triplets because they tend to be inseparable."

As if she could sense they were talking about them, Gidget's dedicated ring started rising from Rowe's cell phone. He snatched up his phone from the charger. "Gidget?" he asked. He was wary now that Lucas had called once using her phone. He didn't want to make the mistake of being fooled by the man.

"Hey, Boss! I've got a big chunk of the info that you were looking for. Do you or Noah have your laptop or tablet handy?"

Rowe looked over at Noah and mouthed, *tablet*. His man instantly jumped to his feet and jogged to the bedroom where he'd stashed his bag. One of them always brought a tablet along when traveling not only for work, but for binge-watching some of their favorite shows when they were cuddled in bed at night. Rowe loved lying in bed with Noah, his head on his shoulder, while they watched some movie or TV show before falling asleep. It was their quiet time together, and he treasured it more than Noah probably realized.

"Noah's getting his. How're things in the office?"

"Quiet."

"Too quiet," Quinn added, proving that Gidget had them on speak-erphone. "You gotta get back here soon, Rowe. Dom has been restless and he's been talking about making this crazy obstacle course for the next team-building exercise. He thinks the entire company should do it. *All* of us. You know I don't run, Boss."

"You'll run if you're being chased," Cole muttered in a low voice.

"That's why I like my computer. It doesn't chase me with a paint-ball gun. That shit hurts!"

Rowe looked up when JB made a noise, and the man was covering his mouth with his hand like he was trying to keep from laughing. Cole, Quinn, and Gidget were an interesting bunch. Rowe didn't always understand what they were talking about, but they were incredibly skilled when it came to locating the information he needed.

"A little running is good for you," Rowe said.

"Trust me, I've got ways of getting plenty of cardio," Quinn grumbled.

"Sex doesn't count."

"If you think sex doesn't count, then you're not doing it right."

A loud bark of laughter from Noah filled the main room as he returned just in time to hear Quinn's comment.

"Don't you worry about your boss's sex life," Noah said. "He's doing just fine."

As Noah returned to the couch, they quickly cleared away the mostly empty pizza boxes and beer bottles. Gidget worked her tech magic to take control of Noah's tablet, pulling up the information they needed while Noah set it up in the center of the coffee table for them all to see.

"We're ready, Gidget. What do you have for us?" Rowe said.

"We've uncovered a lot, but I'm not sure how much is actually useful yet. The picture of the man you sent me was Jeff Hastings. He joined Clayborne about a year ago. No criminal record. Not married and no kids."

"He's been handled and should be headed to Alabama as we speak. Keep feelers out for him and alert us if he stays in the DC and Alexandria area or if he gets too close to Cincy," Noah said.

"What about Erik Johnson and Dave Johnson?" JB asked.

"Dave Johnson was listed among the missing for the ambush in Afghanistan in 2014. He is presumed dead, though his body was never recovered," Gidget said. The screen changed to show two pictures of what looked to be the same man, but with different hairstyles and facial hair. "We dug up an old military picture of him and compared it to the staff roster that we found. We found a 97.6 percent match with a guy by the name of Travis Long. Noah, I think this is who your friend Chris saw."

"Dave Johnson definitely did not die in Afghanistan," Quinn said. "He's alive and pretending to be someone else."

"And he's not the only one," Cole said, his voice near a growl.

"Right! Joseph Cates was also listed among the missing after that ambush and was presumed dead," Gidget took up the story, changing the screen to show another man in a neat, formal uniform. "He's also working at Clayborne under the name of Brent Wilder." A new picture appeared on the screen next to the military picture. Again, it was the same man but with a new haircut and beard.

"What the fuck?" JB said under his breath. "I...I don't get it. How are they alive? And living under new identities?"

Rowe had a feeling he knew the reason, and it was an ugly one that made his blood boil. "What about the third guy that was taken prisoner in the Afghanistan ambush?"

"We figured you'd ask that," Gidget murmured. The image on the tablet changed to a military picture of an older man. "He doesn't match anyone we could find associated with Clayborne Security. Cole ran his picture against some other databases. He turned up as a dead John Doe about two years ago in Pensacola, Florida."

Rowe looked over at Noah and JB, who were frowning.

"So, he works with Dave and Joseph, but maybe had a falling out with the other guys?" JB started.

"Or maybe just a falling out with Dave's brother," Noah added. "Erik decides to silence the guy rather than risk him telling the wrong people about what he did."

Rowe grunted. "Seems likely. This group has already killed twice to protect their secret. I wouldn't put it past them to kill one of their own."

"How does Erik figure into all of this?" JB asked. He shifted to the edge of the cushion, leaning closer as if to pick up some extra detail from the tablet. Rowe noticed the man rubbing the fingers of his right hand together as if a growing anxiety were making it hard to sit still. "When we talked to Jeff, he said Erik was the one calling all the shots."

"Erik Johnson is Dave Johnson's older brother. There isn't a lot about him. He was dishonorably discharged from the Marines about fifteen years ago and spent several years working as a mercenary, we think. Spent three years in prison on assault charges. We've got a wide gap of time where we can't find anything on him, but then about three years ago, he started Clayborne Security."

"Can you tell if Clayborne is actually operating as a real company or if it's simply a shell?" Noah asked.

"Not yet," Quinn replied. "We're still digging. The company roster was largely pieced together through a variety of social media, company data, and networking algorithms. Their security looks to be pretty tight."

"Track down Joseph Cates's address," Noah said.

"I also want you to dig deep on Erik. Pull a list of known associates, particularly during his mercenary years. Anyone he was known to work or travel with," Rowe added.

"You want me to also highlight anyone who might be in the Alexandria area today?"

"That's my girl," Rowe said with a grin. Gidget could always read his mind.

"Anything else?"

"I want to know what happened to the weapons taken in the Afghanistan ambush," Noah said, his voice hardening, and something inside of Rowe's chest hurt. His lover's mind was following the same track as Rowe's, and it was leading to a very dark and ugly place. He didn't want to think any soldier was capable of such a betrayal, but the pieces were lining up too neatly for it to mean anything else.

There was silence on the line for a moment, and Rowe could easily imagine the triplets looking at each other, nonverbally communicating in a way that was a little eerie. Though it probably shouldn't have been. Those three had been working closely for months now, and Rowe had seen his own security agents develop the same type of silent communications from years of working together.

"We'll try very hard," Quinn said slowly. "That information is going to be stuff the government has closely guarded."

"Understood," Rowe said. In the back of his mind, he started running through the list of contacts he'd maintained over the years. Which thread could he pull now to quietly get the information that he wanted? It was just lucky they were in DC. He could pay a very personal visit if he needed to. "Keep us posted if you learn anything else. And get some sleep."

"Thanks, Boss," the triplets called out before Noah ended the call.

Rowe looked over at his lover to find his face pale and his hands balled into tight fists in his lap. JB didn't appear to be faring much better. His bright-blue eyes had taken on a dazed cast, and he kept rubbing his mouth as if he couldn't believe what he'd just heard.

"I need a fucking shower," Noah growled before jumping up from the couch and stalking to the bedroom.

"I need a drink," JB murmured and the headed into the kitchen.

Rowe grabbed Noah's tablet and followed him to the bedroom. He needed to help Noah first. Then maybe he'd make sure that JB didn't climb into the bottle of booze he was searching for. They needed to be sharp if they were going to survive their next encounter with Erik's men.

CHAPTER THIRTEEN

*L*ucas's master bath was a thing of beauty with black marble countertops, a deep bathtub, and a black-and-white shower big enough for three. Or four if the participants were particularly close. A large showerhead came down from the ceiling, making it feel like Noah was standing in a waterfall. He stood under the spray, his head back, and let the hot water beat down on his body.

Noah knew a shower wouldn't take away the kind of dirty he felt after hearing what Gidget and her team had found, but it would help. It would also give him a few moments to himself so he could come to terms with what he'd learned. They'd played around with the idea of one bad soldier, but to hear it confirmed? And it wasn't just one. At least two, possibly three, soldiers had committed treason and been responsible for the deaths of a lot of good men. And for what? Weapons. Fucking weapons.

He poured shampoo onto his palm and scrubbed his scalp, trying to rub away the crawling sensation on his skin. He couldn't believe any soldier would kill his brothers like that, but to know that more than one man had turned on his family...his gut knotted sickeningly and he leaned one hand against the tile while he swallowed back the

JOCELYNN DRAKE & RINDA ELLIOTT

bile. He hadn't known the men who'd died in that ambush, but he may as well have. Soldiers like him.

Like the fucking men who'd betrayed them.

Noah finished his shower and when he grabbed a towel, he noticed Rowe leaning against the counter with his arms crossed, an expression of sympathy on his rugged features. He looked good in his loose jeans and tight black shirt. Rowe held his hand out for the towel, and Noah handed it to him. Rowe slowly ran the cloth over his shoulders and chest, his lips tight. When he kneeled to dry Noah's legs, Noah ran his fingers through his hair, loving the soft strands against his skin. He cradled the back of his head and pulled him close for a light hug, his face in Noah's hip.

Rowe dropped a kiss on his hipbone and looked up at him. "You okay?"

"Not really."

He nodded as if he'd already known that. "Hard to believe anyone would betray fellow soldiers that way."

"It is. Sometimes, this world is not a good place."

"There's still a lot of good in this world, Noah." Rowe spent extra time drying his groin and Noah couldn't help but smirk a little as his body hardened in reaction. The grin he got in response lightened his heart. Fuck, he loved this man with every cell in his body.

When Rowe stood, he wrapped his arms loosely around him and pressed their foreheads together. "We're going to expose these guys for what they did, Noah. Make sure they pay for the soldiers in Afghanistan as well as Chris and Paul."

"We have to," Noah whispered as water from his hair dripped down his face and Rowe's. "I feel like I can't get clean enough. We delivered the goods right into their hands."

"You can't take that guilt on. You did your job."

"Maybe if we'd stuck around longer, we could have helped."

"Or you could have ended up dead, too." Rowe shuddered and tightened his arms. "I can't stand to think of it."

"Well, I didn't. I'm here with you now. And for always."

Rowe pulled back, his green eyes full of affection.

"You have too many clothes on," Noah said, running his hands down Rowe's back. Sex, sex would ground him. He kissed his jaw, then his neck, tugging on his hair to get him to tilt his head. He opened his lips over Rowe's pulse, lightly biting down.

A low, rumbling growl spilled from Rowe's throat. "I know a way to make you feel better."

"I bet you do," Noah murmured, kissing down to his collarbone. He tugged on his shirt. "Off."

Rowe stepped away and yanked his shirt over his head. Noah's hand immediately went to his shoulder tattoo and he traced along the black lines with one finger, down to where the design circled one nipple. He tweaked that sexy nipple, then bent to take it into his mouth. He licked it. Another sound of pleasure left Rowe, and he pulled Noah up and slanted his mouth over his. They moved into a kiss, Rowe's tongue plunging deep into his mouth. The man tasted of beer and that perfect flavor of Rowe that went to Noah's head faster than booze. Rowe bit at his lips, sucking the lower one into his mouth.

Noah reached for Rowe's fly, but Rowe took him by surprise, dropping to his knees. He looked up at Noah and the passion on his face made Noah's belly tighten in anticipation. Rowe loved giving him head and half the time came just from doing that. Watching him revel in the pleasure was truly one of Noah's favorite things.

A warm hand grasped his cock and brought it to Rowe's mouth. His boyfriend licked along his shaft, swirling his tongue around the head. Soft lips enveloped him as Rowe pulled him into the hot cavern of his mouth. Noah nearly closed his eyes at the heady pleasure that filled him, but he wanted to watch Rowe. And as always, it was a true delight.

Between the tight sucking on his cock and the way Rowe obviously got off on it, he was soon counting in his head to make it last. Rowe had his eyes closed and every now and then, a small moan would vibrate in his throat. He ran his free hand up Noah's inner thigh, then brought his fingers to his mouth. He looked up at Noah as he sucked on his fingers.

He was so fucking hot, Noah couldn't believe how lucky he was to belong to this man.

Rowe brought his wet fingers to Noah's hole and pressed them up inside of him as he took his cock back into his mouth. He never once took his eyes off Noah's, and the stark intimacy of the moment wasn't lost on him. The warmth that filled his chest threatened to take him out at the knees. He loved this man so much.

Fingers hit his prostate and he sucked in a breath and began to pant as Rowe relentlessly massaged it as he ran his tongue over Noah's cock and sucked him deep into his throat.

"Oh babe," Noah growled, bending over Rowe's head. Hoarse cries escaped his throat as Rowe didn't let up with the dual attack. It felt so good, he couldn't believe he was still standing, and he longed for a bed so he could better focus on what Rowe was doing.

As if he read his mind, Rowe pulled off and said, "Walk to the bed in the other room."

Noah didn't hesitate. He hurried out of the bathroom, made sure the door was shut, pulled down the bedspread, and sprawled across the massive king-sized bed. Rowe strolled into the room slowly, his eyes at an intense half-mast, his dick hard and sticking straight out since he'd removed his pants.

Neither of them paid any attention to the window next to the bed. Anyone looking into this room would need binoculars. Instead, he enjoyed the moonlight streaming in through the floor-to-ceiling glass. It gave the room a dreamy, surreal feel that went with the mood.

Rowe licked him again, moaning as he loved on Noah's cock. He went right to sucking him down again, fingers going straight to his prostate. He pegged it over and over as he made love to Noah. Noah spread his legs, head tilting back as he panted and writhed. The sheets were sinfully soft under his skin and Rowe's mouth was sinfully hot around him. Rowe licked and sucked, bringing his mouth to Noah's tip, then sending it back down to the root. He tightened his suction.

Pleasure built and built inside Noah until he hovered right on the precipice, entire body tight; then his vision grayed out as he burst and spilled down Rowe's throat. Rowe groaned his pleasure and sat up on his knees, reaching for his dick, stroking it a few times before he aimed over Noah's chest. Hot splashes hit him as Rowe moaned and bucked above him. He fell on top of Noah, sprawling and breathing hard in his ear. "Fuck, I love you," Rowe breathed, nuzzling into the side of Noah's neck.

"Love you, too." He turned his head and pressed a soft kiss to Rowe's lips. "You've gotten so good at that, I may have to demand it daily."

"I'd happily do that daily. Love your dick. Love that silky skin in my mouth."

Noah could tell and again, he thought about how lucky he was. Not just that Rowe loved oral sex, but that the man loved him. There wasn't a doubt in his body over how Rowe felt about him, and Noah reveled in the knowledge that his longest running dream was still coming true. He ran his hand down Rowe's spine, loving the supple muscle and smooth skin under his palms. "We'll have to shower again. I got all sweaty."

"I like you sweaty. Smell so damn good." Rowe's nose was still buried in his neck. "Hope JB is good at fending for himself, because we may just stay in here and do that again."

Noah snorted. "Give me a few minutes."

"What's wrong, old man, need recovery time?"

Noah tightened his arms around Rowe. "You blew my mind. I need time to wallow in the afterglow. Besides, you feel good all sprawled on top of me like this."

"I'm heavy."

"It's all those muscles you've been building. But I like them and the way they feel on me, so that wasn't a complaint." He stroked his hand over those muscles and threaded their legs together. He enjoyed their after-sex snuggles as much as he enjoyed the sex itself. "You doing okay with JB around now?"

"Yeah. He's a pretty cool guy. I didn't want to like him, but it's hard not to."

"He's a good one."

"He still cares for you." Rowe lifted his head to look down at Noah.

"He always cared a little too much. It's why I didn't let us continue hooking up. He deserves someone who can give him his whole heart and not just a tiny corner of it. Mine was all taken up and still is." He stretched up to kiss Rowe.

"I'm the luckiest man in the world."

"We both are."

"We're also a pair of saps, and I wouldn't trade that. If Mel's death did anything, it taught me that love is precious and should be enjoyed every day that you have it. I cherish the day you decided to come back into my life and that you stuck with me while I was working things out. I gave you a hard time—I know."

Noah didn't bother to contradict that because Rowe *had* nearly broken his heart. "Totally worth it for what we have now."

Rowe kept staring at him and something in that gaze spoke to Noah's soul. They were a team, a perfect match, two sides of the same coin. He couldn't have come up with a better partner for him than if he'd made one.

Noah realized that lying there with Rowe, it was the perfect moment for one of them to propose. Sure they were messy, naked, and basking in the afterglow of a great orgasm while in the middle of a dangerous situation, but Noah couldn't think of a moment that better encapsulated who they were. But he didn't want to do it. Didn't want those words to cross Rowe's mouth.

Why didn't he want the same things as the rest of their family? Was there something wrong with him? Was he letting Rowe's previous marriage taint his idea of marriage?

What if Rowe was waiting for him to ask and he never did? Would it crush the man he loved so much?

"You okay?" Rowe asked. "Am I crushing you?"

Noah forced a smile when he realized his worries were starting to show on his face. "My mind drifted. I was trying to remember if we left enough dog food for the sitter."

Rowe grinned at him. "She's got them covered. Don't worry."

And with Rowe, he didn't want to worry. All he wanted was to spend his life with this man, and he didn't need a ceremony or fancy words.

He just needed Rowe.

⁓

*T*hey eventually went out into the kitchen to refuel on the leftover pizza. Rowe was feeling mellow from the sex and postcoital sweet nothings. Though he'd rather stay in bed with Noah, he felt rude leaving JB hanging out while they were busy getting their rocks off.

JB was sprawled in one of the chairs in the living room, back in a pair of shorts and another red T-shirt—he seemed to like the color. It looked good with his dark-blond hair. He had a small smile pulling up one corner of his lips, and Rowe realized they probably both looked well-fucked. He felt the puffiness in his lips and the nice, relaxed muscles from an incredible orgasm. *Nothing like a blowjob to take the edge off.* And damn, he loved giving those. Noah had the perfect dick with the softest skin.

He watched his boyfriend grab them beers and had to still the urge to cart him right back to the bedroom. But as he looked at JB, who watched them both, he couldn't help but feel bad for the guy. To have held Noah and lost him?

Rowe couldn't even contemplate what that would feel like.

All he knew was, he planned to hold on to Noah for the rest of his life.

Shoving their relationship in JB's face wasn't cool, though, so he stilled the urge to kiss Noah again when he brought him the beer and a leftover slice of pizza. It was hard though, after what they'd just shared. He wished they were home where they'd scarf down the food and run into their bedroom for a rowdy round two.

JB sat up straighter in his chair when Noah handed him a beer too. "Thanks," he said, twisting the top off. He took a long pull and sighed. "So, you both work at Ward Security? What's that like, seeing each other so much?"

"I go out on jobs often, so we get plenty of time apart. I also oversee a lot of the training of the other bodyguards. Rowe has been spending a lot more time in his office, meeting with his tech team and COO. Oh! And Carol from HR. She makes a visit to your office at least once a week."

"Hey!" Rowe said, reaching out to smack Noah's shoulder as he sat down on the couch next to him. "It's mostly for hiring now."

JB lifted his eyebrows and grinned. "She got a thing for you?"

Rowe groaned while Noah snickered hard enough that he thought the beer was going to come out of his nose. "The team can get a little rowdy," Rowe muttered.

"Like the time Dom chased you through the hall with his pants down around his ankles," Noah said with a laugh. "Or the time Quinn replaced all the coffee in the office with decaf. Thank God he's faster than he looks, because I'm pretty sure Garrett was going to murder him."

JB turned serious. "You don't fuck with a man's coffee."

"Lots of practical jokes and antics."

"Fewer recently," Rowe said softly. "We've just been too busy."

"I would have been out a few nights on a job this week if I hadn't gotten Sven to cover for me."

"How long have you been together?"

"Two and a half years," Rowe answered. "It's gone fast."

"I hear it's like that when it's good." JB took another drink of his beer and leaned over to set it on the coffee table.

Rowe put his hand on Noah's thigh. "You seeing anyone?"

"Nah. Like I told Noah the other night, my mom keeps trying to set me up. You can guess how that goes."

Rowe wouldn't know. He hardly had anything to do with his family, and it had been like that since before he'd left for the Army. They'd even sent him to live with his grandfather in Colorado. Granted, he'd given them a hell of a bad time, getting involved in drugs and other illegal activities after a friend of his was killed when he was sixteen.

His parents and siblings were all in Missouri, but the last time he'd seen them, Mel had still been alive. They'd attended that wedding, and she made an effort to drag him back to Missouri a couple of times just to keep the link alive, but Rowe had let that last tie mostly die with her.

They knew he now lived with Noah, but neither his mother nor father had anything to say about it. He barely existed for them. And he was fine with it. He had all the family he needed in Cincinnati.

"Noah said you work on your parents' ranch," Rowe said, pulling his thoughts from the dark quagmire that was his blood family. There was nothing to be gained by thinking about them.

"I do. Cattle and horses. I like it. More than I did when I was growing up. Since returning from the Army, I've been training to take it over. My sister was helping my parents while I was gone, but she married a man with his own ranch. I know she'd rather focus on that and her family. I like Texas. Love the land there."

Rowe leaned back on the couch, content with a belly full of beer and pizza. "I've never been to Texas. I hear everything is big there."

JB laughed. "You know it. After this is all over, you and Noah are welcome to come visit anytime. We've got a nice guest house, and I'll rustle up the biggest damn steak you've ever seen. The barbecue is out of this world. Nothing can touch it."

Rowe smirked at Noah and jerked his thumb toward JB. "Listen to this guy. It's like he knows me."

"The best way to convince you of anything is to talk to your stomach first," Noah agreed.

"Were you close to Chris and Paul?" Rowe asked.

"I was, though I hadn't seen either of them in some time. We kept in touch through email. I knew Chris was thinking of starting a family." He shook his head sadly. "I feel so sorry for Sally—it had to be hard losing him like that." He tightened his lips. "I want those guys to pay for what they've done."

"They will," Noah vowed. "They will all pay."

"I can't wrap my head around why our own men would turn on their own like that." JB scowled and shifted in his chair.

"Me neither." Noah threaded his fingers through Rowe's.

Rowe loved that he didn't hesitate to show affection, even in front of an ex. He stroked his thumb over Noah's knuckles. "Greed does bad things to people."

"You gotta be one cold motherfucker to pull something like that."

Rowe shrugged because in his experience, some bad guys were going to be bad no matter the circumstances. All he could do was remember that there was a lot of good in the world, and it wasn't hard when he thought of his friends and how they had his back. He thought of Noah, infinitely good and hurting over knowing he'd been a small part of what had happened in Afghanistan. He glanced at Noah to find him staring at his beer, the dejection on his face hard to swallow. He tightened his fingers and Noah glanced up at him and smiled, but those pretty blues held too much sadness.

He reminded himself that Noah had also lost two friends in Chris and Paul. Anger tightened his gut. They were going to get these guys and make sure they paid for what they'd done.

CHAPTER FOURTEEN

*R*owe tapped his fingers on the steering wheel as he glanced around the quiet neighborhood. Gidget managed to track down a last known address for Joseph Cates, now called Brent Wilder. They'd driven by the old-fashioned Cape Cod house with two little dormer windows on the second floor earlier in the day just to scope out the location. The pale-blue paint was faded and chipping in places. Bushes were growing wild and the flowerbeds were already choked with weeds despite it still being relatively early in the season.

A long crack wove down the center of the driveway, filled with more weeds, like nature was trying to reclaim this spot of the earth. A late-model Toyota was parked at the back of the driveway in front of a detached garage. They'd managed to get the license plate number, and Gidget confirmed that the car was registered to Cates. They had the right house.

Cates might live in the house, but he clearly wasn't interested in keeping up appearances. Rowe didn't know whether the man was simply lazy or just rarely home. Another option was that the house was a front for Erik's illegal activities.

He hated that they didn't have more time to scout the area and the house, but the longer Erik and his gang of murderous goons were on the loose, the higher the chances of someone getting in a lucky shot at Noah or JB.

Noah reached across the console and placed his hand over Rowe's fingers, stopping their tapping. Rowe looked over and could clearly see his grin in the faint light from the nearby streetlamp.

"Got a hinky feeling?" Noah asked.

"Something like that."

"Just so long as you're not going to say that the place looks haunted and we need to split up to investigate," JB said.

Noah chuckled and looked over his shoulder into the back seat. "Your parents let you watch way too much Scooby-Doo as a kid."

"Answer me this then," Rowe started. He lifted his eyes to look in the rearview mirror, catching JB's attention. "Which member are you?"

JB flashed Rowe the biggest grin he'd seen on the man's handsome face yet. "I'm totally Daphne. Definitely the hot one of our group."

"You mean danger-prone Daphne?" Rowe taunted.

JB winced, but his grin didn't fade. "Yeah, but when she got into danger, it usually led to a good clue."

"Ugh," Noah groaned but there was still smile lines framing his eyes and mouth. It was good to see him smiling when Rowe knew he was hurting so much on the inside.

"Who are we?" Rowe asked.

JB pointed at Noah. "He's totally Shaggy," he said, causing Noah to release Rowe's hand as he fell against the truck door laughing. "And you're Fred. Very bossy. Plus, everyone knows that Shaggy had a secret crush on Fred."

Rowe nodded. It made sense. "It was the ascot."

"I was thinking the pants. Tight across the ass and flared bellbottoms," JB murmured.

"You've both lost your minds," Noah declared.

"Maybe, but he's partially right. We do need to split up." It was time to get down to business. "I'll take the front door, ring the bell. See if we can get him to answer. You and JB will go around back. Take a peek in the garage windows if you can. While I'm making a racket in the front of the house, you break in from the rear."

"Are we worried about a security system?" JB asked. He shifted to the edge of his seat and dropped his forearms over the front seats between Rowe and Noah. "I mean, the guy does work for a security company. You would expect his place to be protected."

"That's where you're in luck," Noah said with a smirk. "You just happen to be with a guy who knows a thing or two about security systems because he works for a *real* security company. I know how to install them, and I know how to take them out."

"You've gotten scary," JB countered.

"Scary awesome."

"All right, you two," Rowe said sharply.

He didn't want to linger in this neighborhood for much longer. Something wasn't right about this entire setup, but he couldn't put his finger on what felt off. He couldn't see any sign of someone watching them. The cars on the street were empty. The other homes on the street looked a little better than their target, but not by a lot. The yards were a little neater and the homes were a little better kept, as if the occupants were trying to maintain their homes between long hours at work. Several places even had tiny signs in the yard proclaiming that they had one security system or another in place.

It was nearly two in the morning. No one had driven down the street since they'd parked more than ten minutes earlier. The lights in most of the homes were out as if the residents had gone to bed already. There were a couple of faint lights for the night owls, but overall, the neighborhood was quiet.

There was no more waiting. They needed to get their hands on Cates. From what Gidget could tell, David Johnson was in the wind. They couldn't find a residence, car, or even a driver's license record under his new name. Unless they caught him walking out of Clayborne Security, they were unlikely to spot him, and Rowe had no desire to camp outside Clayborne.

Cates was their key to getting the truth of what happened at the

Afghanistan ambush and exactly what Erik and his men got their hands on.

"How much time?" Noah asked.

"Two minutes and then I'm knocking on the front door," Rowe said.

Noah nodded. "See you in three, then." He reached for the door handle, but Rowe grabbed the back of his neck, pulling him across the console for a hard, soul-searing kiss that had Noah melting into him. Rowe never wanted to lose this. It didn't matter how much time passed, the heat between them never faded. He would never get enough of Noah. He didn't want to face a day where he couldn't reach across and pull him into his arms.

"Be careful," Rowe growled before releasing Noah. The younger man winked at him before he silently slid out of the car.

Rowe looked over his shoulder to find JB looking at him expectantly. "You got one of those for me?" he asked.

"Go!" Rowe barked, but the single word was strangled behind a surprised laugh.

JB snickered as he jumped out of the truck and silently closed the door behind him. *Fuck.* He was really starting to like the guy, and he didn't want to. It was so much easier to be swallowed up by irrational jealousy. But the more time he spent with the guy, the more obvious it became that JB was a good man with a soft heart and a weird sense of humor. No wonder he and Noah got along so well.

Looking down at his watch, Rowe started his mental countdown while watching Noah and JB walk down the sidewalk. They cut up Cates's driveway, their heads low so they wouldn't be seen easily out the first-floor windows. Noah paused and pulled something out of his pocket, handing it over to JB before directing him over to the garage. Noah then grabbed something else out of his pocket, and Rowe realized they were putting on black latex gloves. With a smirk, Rowe leaned over to the glove compartment and grabbed a pair for himself. There was no need to leave any prints behind for the cops to find if something did happen to go wrong.

Rowe hated the way his heart sped up when Noah disappeared

around the back of the house. Noah had years of experience as an Army Airborne Ranger and a couple of years' experience working at Ward Security. The man knew his shit. He knew how to handle a weapon, and he knew how to maneuver through a volatile situation. But the fast thump of his heart said that he only wanted to keep Noah safe and rational thought didn't fucking matter.

He looked down at his watch to find that his two minutes were nearly up. Grabbing the keys from the ignition, he shoved them into his pocket and quietly climbed out of the vehicle. He kept his hands loose at his sides as he slowly walked down the sidewalk and up to the front of the house. His steps slowed just a little bit as he looked over the old concrete stairs to the front porch. There were no signs of any kind of early warning systems or booby traps.

Lifting his gaze to the house, he could see that the front windows were covered by heavy curtains that blocked out the sun as well as the prying eyes of neighbors. It was a pretty safe guess that Joseph Cates wasn't close to his neighbors. The entire house had a very unwelcoming feel to it. But that didn't stop Rowe from climbing the stairs.

At the door, he paused again and looked around. He was a little stunned to find that there was no mini camera at the door or placed around the small front porch with protective roof. Those little cameras were relatively cheap and could be accessed through an app on your phone. Practically everyone had them now. His bad feeling kept getting worse.

With a deep breath, Rowe skipped the doorbell and pounded on the old wood door, rattling the glass in the frame. He felt like he hammered the door loud enough that the entire neighborhood heard him. At the very least, Noah and JB did from the backyard. He held his breath and waited, straining in the silence to hear any kind of movement within the house, but there was nothing. No creak of the floorboards or footsteps on the stairs. Rowe waited a few seconds and then repeated the knocking, but there was no answer. He waited a few more seconds and knocked on the door again.

His only warning was a soft click of the deadbolt sliding into its housing before the door swung soundlessly open. He reached for his gun out of instinct, but Noah was on the other side of the door.

"Hold. It's just me," Noah quickly said in a whisper.

"You're already inside?" Rowe asked.

He stepped out of the way, allowing Rowe to step inside. "No security system and the back door was unlocked."

"That's not a good sign."

"No, but you haven't seen the worst of it."

Rowe wanted to hit his head against the doorjamb at Noah's words. He wasn't in the mood for worse. He wanted something better. He wanted something to work out in their favor for once. Following Noah into the living room, he found JB standing in the center of the room, the flashlight on his phone directed toward the couch. And the dead body of Joseph Cates.

"Fuck," Rowe snarled. It looked like the man took several shots to the chest while he was sitting on the couch. The TV was still on, showing some infomercial offering a quick and tasty way to cut fat from your diet.

"There goes our chance to get some information," JB muttered.

"True, but he might still have some good info. You and Noah go upstairs. Look around for anything useful. You've got three minutes." Both men nodded and Rowe was grateful that they didn't argue. He wanted a moment to look over the scene.

As soon as they headed out of the room, Rowe flipped on a floor lamp and looked more closely at the living room. Cates's body was seated on the couch, the TV remote next to his right hand. Some fast-food wrappers littered the battered coffee table in front of him, as if he'd recently finished a meal. There was an open can of beer on the table as well. Rowe turned slowly, taking in the room. There was a large cushioned chair resting diagonally to the couch and an unopened can of beer on the little side table next to the chair. Interesting...

It looked like Joseph had returned home with some fast food. He turned on the TV and ate dinner. Then company arrived. Someone he knew. While the place wasn't exactly clean, it didn't look as if there had been a struggle. Nothing was overturned or torn. No, poor Joe sat and shared a beer with his guest before the asshole killed him. The murderer probably walked right out the back door.

Rowe was willing to put money on the likelihood that it had been Erik. If that man was the mastermind behind the plot to steal the Army weapons, then he was probably tying up some loose ends. Cates and his own brother could cause problems for him if someone started taking a closer look at the ambush.

But would Erik kill his little brother?

Signs were pointing toward yes on that one. The man had spearheaded an attack to kill his fellow countrymen. He likely killed one of his confederates. There was no way David Johnson was safe.

Rowe glanced back down at his watch and drew in a breath to shout for Noah and JB. Their three minutes of searching were up. But before he could even speak, he heard two sets of footsteps thundering down the stairs.

"We've got company," JB announced before he reached the first floor.

"Car just pulled into the driveway with the lights off," Noah added.

Rowe grabbed the gun from its holster on his hip and chambered a round. He couldn't say he was overly surprised. They might have been cautious entering the house, but there had to have been some hidden camera or sensor to tip off Erik. If Chris Perkins had spotted Dave, Erik had to figure it was only a matter of time that they'd locate Joseph. "How many?"

"Three got out. There's one still behind the wheel."

Rowe gave a quick nod. Johnson had lost at least three at the attack on the motel and Jeff had left town. He'd killed Joseph and would probably dispose of David. And now four more men. How many men did he have to throw at them? Such a fucking waste.

"Noah, back door. I'll cover the front. JB, check to make sure there isn't a side door or an entrance through the basement."

The two men didn't say a word as they darted off to their assignments. Rowe turned on one heel and jogged to the front door. He didn't bother to lock it again. That was silly. He wanted the fuckers to come inside. There were more hiding places and cover for him to use for protection. He had the advantage over the invaders.

Hanging at the edge of the living room, his shoulder leaning against the doorjamb leading to the hall, Rowe waited. Shots were fired through the front door, shattering the glass and pummeling the old wood. These assholes weren't interested in being sneaky in the least. A second later, a booted foot slammed into the door, kicking it open. Rowe smirked and dropped back a little, watching as the handgun entered the house first, followed by a large man in a black T-shirt and a ski mask. With a sigh, Rowe lifted his gun, took half a second to aim, and squeezed the trigger twice. He easily put two in the guy's chest, sending him sprawling backward into the door, pushing it farther from where it had sprung back after the initial kick.

"Idiot," he muttered. From the rear of the house, he could hear more breaking glass and bullets hitting wood. "One!" he called out toward Noah.

"Fuck you. I'm not playing," Noah shouted in a playful singsong voice.

"No entrance through the basement," JB announced when he jogged into the living room.

Rowe looked over his shoulder to find the man crouched down next to the big chair, using it as a bit of cover. He started to instruct JB to head to the back of the house and help Noah when the man raised his gun and fired off a few rounds. For a second, Rowe's heart jerked to a hard stop and then rushed forward again when he heard pained cries from behind him. He looked around to find another man falling face forward through the front door in the same T-shirt and ski mask getup. Rowe hadn't heard the guy's approach. His attention had been on JB and the gunfire coming from Noah's direction.

With a wide grin at Rowe, JB shouted, "One!"

"Fuck you both!" Noah sang out.

"Only one left, Noah," Rowe called back, teasing.

With only three targets, it wasn't much of a game. When he and Noah had been teamed up on missions, they'd played this game when their targets were well into the double digits. While he wasn't particularly proud of turning their missions into a game, it was a way of coping with ending the lives of multiple people. The fact that those same people would have happily killed them if given the chance wasn't always enough to let them sleep at night.

Rowe edged toward the front door, stepping over the outreached arm of the second dead man to look out the opening. The dark sedan with tinted windows still idled in the driveway. He couldn't see the driver, but he had a feeling that the man was starting to panic. There was no question that he could see that two of his companions were dead in the front of the house. He had to be waiting for the third guy. Rowe weighed the idea of walking out to the car. There would be no sneaking.

But as he tried to formulate a plan, Noah shouted, "Got 'im!" and the car peeled out of the driveway in reverse.

"Come on, kids!" Rowe said.

The police had likely been called by one or more neighbors woken by the sound of gunfire. There was no reason to wait around for the cops to respond and answer a lot of questions they didn't want to answer. They also didn't have the benefit of having Lucas's snazzy, sharklike lawyer on hand to smooth things over.

Dropping his gun to his thigh, Rowe led the way out of the house and across the lawn toward the Jeep. His head moved on a swivel, continuously swinging from side to side to make sure no one else was waiting in the shadows, but nothing moved. A quick glance at the houses surrounding Cate's place revealed only a couple had turned on their lights, but he was sure that more had heard the shots. Those poor people were probably just hiding under their blankets, praying that the shooters left their street. They didn't want to get involved, didn't want to risk getting shot.

By the time he reached the Jeep, he looked over to find JB and Noah jogging across the lawn, also looking around the area with the same alertness. But there was no one. Erik was sorely underestimating them, and it was going to come back and bite the fucker in the ass. Rowe was almost insulted.

Jumping into the car, he jammed the key into the ignition and the engine roared to life. Noah and JB joined him in the Jeep and they tore off down the street, away from the approaching sirens. He was glad they'd removed the license plate before heading to Cates's. It was unlikely anyone from the neighborhood would have written it down, but he wasn't taking any chances.

Before they returned to the penthouse, they would pull over at a twenty-four-hour fast-food joint to check over the truck for tracking devices. During the shooting, the driver could have placed a tracker on the truck. He didn't think it was likely, but Rowe wasn't going to risk giving away their hiding place just yet.

"Well, that wasn't as helpful as I'd been hoping for," JB said with an aggravated sigh. "I'm not saying that I feel bad for Cates. He deserved to die for what he did."

"Disappointed you weren't the one who put the bullets in his chest?" Noah asked.

Rowe looked into the rearview mirror to see JB give a little shrug as he continued to stare out the window at the blur of neon lights from the passing shopping plaza. "I don't know. Not sure I could have done that. But I would have liked to beat the shit out of him before handing him over to the cops."

"Yeah," Noah said, heaving his own sigh.

Rowe wanted to reach over and pull Noah into his lap, hold the man tight in his arms until the ache went away. Even if Noah didn't know the men who had died during the ambush that well, he respected them. They were fellow soldiers. Men and women who risked their lives to protect the rights and freedoms of others. They shouldn't have been killed because they were betrayed by one of their own.

Cates should have been forced to answer for that betrayal in front of the world. Instead, he was shot in a shitty little house, and it was unlikely the rest of the world would ever know his real name or what he did.

Extending his right hand, Rowe placed it on Noah's thigh and squeezed. It was the best he could do until they got back to the penthouse. Then he was going to wrap himself around his lover and not let go.

"I'm guessing you didn't find anything upstairs," Rowe said.

"Nothing," JB said. "Bathroom had the usual crap and the second bedroom was mostly empty. Just some boxes that looked like they had some clothes and stuff from when he was younger. Baseball trophies, hats, magazines. That kind of shit."

Noah shifted, pulling something from his back pocket. "The bedroom wasn't much. Couldn't find any useful paperwork. But I got his wallet off the dresser." He held up a worn brown leather wallet in the dim light from the streetlamps.

"We can take pictures of everything inside and send it off to the triplets. They can add it to all their info and see what they can turn up."

"God, you think your friend has any more alcohol stashed at that penthouse? I could use something to drink beyond a beer," JB asked. He scrubbed his hand over his face like he was trying to clear his head. "That blue ribbon stuff is nearly gone."

Rowe chuckled low. "Yeah, I'm pretty sure Lucas has some more good liquor stashed at the penthouse."

Oh, yeah. Lucas definitely had some whiskey or bourbon hidden somewhere, and they were going to burn through it.

CHAPTER FIFTEEN

*R*owe made sure to take a roundabout route to get to the penthouse, skirting Washington DC and driving along the Potomac River. He felt Lucas's condo was still fairly off the radar, but it was better to play it safe. Who knew, though? These guys seemed to be one step ahead, and that didn't sit well with him. They'd stopped at a fast-food restaurant to check for tracking devices and found nothing, so maybe they were still in the lead.

"Just one drink for me," Rowe said when Noah got down three glasses once they were in the condo. "One of us has to stay sober in case the baddies show."

"We all need to stay sober, so one shot each," Noah said as he broke the label on the bottle he'd found in the wet bar. City lights shone outside the floor-to-ceiling windows, sparkling in the dark of the early morning hour.

Noah poured for all three of them while Rowe turned on the television in the kitchen. He hadn't even realized it was there before because it was wall-mounted behind a set of cabinet doors. He'd only found it when he'd gotten curious and started opening all the cabinets that morning. *There were so many.* He turned the volume down low, wanting it more for the familiar noise to drown out the dark thoughts running rampant in his brain.

He hadn't expected Clayborne to take out Cates. The kind of evil they were dealing with was unfortunately all too familiar. It brought back memories of Jagger, the Cincinnati crime boss who had put them through hell. Brought back memories of his late wife and how one of Jagger's goons had taken her life when he'd meant to take Rowe's. He felt like punching something, but instead, he reached for his drink.

The alcohol burned when he took his shot. Scorched the adrenaline racing through him from their visit to Cates's house. He slammed the glass down and looked at Noah, who was watching him with a concerned expression. "They took out one of their own," he said, voice raspy from the bourbon.

"Have to say I'm surprised." Noah knocked back his own shot. "Makes me wonder who did it. Whether Erik did it himself or ordered one of his men to do it."

"I bet he did it himself, because what excuse would he have to order anyone to do that?" JB asked, cradling his own glass in his hands.

Noah shook his head. "We know there's more than just Erik taking folks out. How many men did Gidget say were working for this outfit?"

"Thirty-two," Rowe answered. "All with military records. I sincerely doubt all of these men would be willing to take out people like Chris, Paul, and Cates. Look at Jeff. He'd been more of an unwilling pawn."

"Well, we know some are involved. They would have needed enough for three teams to hit Chris, Paul, and us within a couple of days of each other."

"More likely four," Rowe corrected. He looked over at JB, who paled a little. "I think you got out just in time. The team sent to kill you missed seeing you in Texas."

"You think my family is safe? I talked to my dad and my sister earlier today. They haven't seen anything out of the ordinary."

Rowe nodded. "They might be asshole killers, but they are being precise. Sticking to their targets. They took out both Paul and Chris when they were alone."

"Erik has got to know you're here," Noah added. "He's going to keep coming after you."

"Strangely, that makes me feel better," JB said, giving them both a crooked smile.

"Between the hotel and Cates's house, we took down six. Seven if you count Jeff leaving town." Noah stared at the bottle, shrugged, and poured them all another shot. "One more can't hurt. We should have the triplets cross-reference the employees with prison records, dishonorable discharges, things like that."

"That's a good idea," Rowe said. "You think Dave is still alive?"

JB set his glass down, frowning. "Surely the guy wouldn't take out his own brother."

"That's the thing." Rowe picked up his second shot. "He ambushed his own people in Afghanistan and is now taking out anyone who can tie him to that ambush. I wouldn't be surprised if he's the type to sit down with you for a beer before putting one in your chest right across the table. That's what it looked like at Cates's house. Taking out his own brother would still surprise me, but not much. Not at this point."

"I don't know," JB said slowly. "Hard to imagine someone being that evil."

"We're all too familiar with that brand of evil." Rowe set his glass down without drinking the bourbon. "The thing that keeps nagging me in the back of my brain is how the fuck he's doing this without the feds or the NSA or at least the cops chomping down on his ass. I mean, he's in *DC*, where everything is supposed to be under higher security. Either he's got balls, or he has help."

Rowe frowned when his phone suddenly vibrated from an incoming text message. He wasn't sure if he should expect an annoying message from Lucas or from the office. He was only partially relieved to see that it was from Quinn. The guy must be working late because his private eye boyfriend was working a stakeout. It was kind of cute that Quinn worked late when Shane wasn't going to be home.

Quinn: *Police report: Travis Long was found murdered in his home in an apparent burglary attempt. Was this you?!?!?!??!*

"Shit," Rowe swore and quickly started typing out a response.

Rowe: *No! We were across town at Joseph Cates's house.*

Quinn: *Get anything?*

Rowe: *Dead when we got there. Noah got his wallet. Will send images later.*

Quinn: *Everyone safe?*

Rowe: *Everyone is safe.*

Quinn sent back an emoji of a little guy breathing a sigh of relief.

"What's up?" Noah asked. "That the office?"

"Yeah," Rowe said, putting his phone down on the counter. "Quinn found a police report that Dave Johnson, aka Travis Long, was found dead in his home from an apparent burglary attempt gone wrong."

Contemplating the depth of Erik's evil was one thing, but seeing it right there on his phone was another. He looked at Noah, heart frozen in his throat, and thought about how badly this Erik wanted to take out his man. Fury drove a spike through him. It was time they stepped up their game.

"This shit just got real," JB muttered. "His own fucking brother. I can't believe it."

"How is he getting away with this?" Noah asked. "Is there someone high up in the government shielding him? This makes no sense unless he has bigger hands in this mess."

"He's responsible for four deaths that we know of now and a massive hit on our hotel. I think you're right." Rowe frowned. "Someone is watching out for him. Covering for him. It's time I called in a favor. I know just the person, and he lives here. He's still got his fingers in things, so he'll be in the know."

"Cal?" Noah asked, following his train of thought.

Rowe nodded. Cal Hamilton was a retired general who'd worked with Noah and Rowe when they'd been in the service, and he'd been one of those who hired Rowe on occasion for a few outside missions.

"He's a good guy who has his nose in everything going on. He'll give us the scoop. I'll give him a call in the morning and see if he'll meet with me."

"You mean meet with us," Noah said.

"No, I meant me. We don't want to draw attention to the man. You and JB go check on Sally, make sure she's okay." Though it didn't sit right with him letting Noah out of his sight right then, he knew the man was more than capable of taking care of himself, and JB seemed to be pretty skilled as well. He would have had to have been as a ranger.

"Let's talk in the bedroom," Noah said, not waiting for an answer as he turned and headed that direction.

JB raised an eyebrow at him, amusement playing about the corner of his lips.

Rowe could tell Noah was annoyed with him and he understood. He'd feel the same in Noah's shoes, but he had no intention of taking Noah with him to meet with Cal. Yeah, Noah knew the man, too, but Rowe and Cal had kept up after he'd left the service. Rowe did jobs at Cal's request that he hadn't exactly discussed with Noah in the past. There was a long-built trust between them, and Rowe was afraid that Cal might not be as forthcoming with information if Noah was there.

When they got to the bedroom, Noah shut the door, flipped on the light, and crossed his arms. The scowl on his face told Rowe volumes about how he liked this new idea. "What's the deal, Rowan?"

He inwardly flinched. Noah only pulled out his full name when he was truly pissed. But for now, he thought it was safest to play dumb. "I don't know what you mean."

"Why the hell don't you want me meeting with Cal?"

"I told you that I want you to check on Sally. Plus, it's to protect Cal."

"Don't hand me that bullshit. I know you."

"That's not bullshit." It wasn't a lie, but it also wasn't the entire truth.

"Does this have to do with all that Black Ops shit you've done?" Noah walked over to Rowe, leaning close so that his nose was only an inch away from Rowe's. "Don't forget that I've seen your so-called storage warehouse in the middle of nowhere with all the toys you won't even share with your Ward Security boys. You've even mentioned your Black Ops missions in passing. You haven't taken on a secret mission since you've been with me, but I know you did them before. Are you trying to protect your own secrets here?"

Rowe was silent for several long moments. Was he? The truth was...no, he didn't want Noah to know about some of the questionable shit Cal and others had him do. And he'd pretty much stopped all that activity since he'd been with Noah. He'd pass along any intel if he had it. Offer advice on how to handle something. But he hadn't suited up and gone into the field since Noah came back into his life.

"You still don't trust me." The hurt in Noah's eyes speared through him.

"What?"

"You don't trust me. Not the way I want you to."

Rowe's mouth fell open and his stomach knotted. "Of course I trust you. I trust you more than anyone on this Earth."

"Did you tell Mel about your Black Ops shit? Did she know what you did?"

Rowe swallowed hard and slowly shook his head. "She knew I occasionally went out of town...for government work."

"But didn't know you were putting yourself in danger?"

"No."

"What about Lucas, Snow, and Ian? Did they know?"

"Fuck no," Rowe said in horror.

"Why? Why do you do it? And keep it a secret from everyone?"

Rowe shoved his hands through his hair. "It started years ago. When I first got out and was healed from the damn shot to my ticker. I was bored out of my mind. I was so used to being active, in the middle of things. Cal contacted me. Said he had a friend in the CIA who needed a favor. It was a quick job over in Eastern Europe, Croatia. I said sure. Anything to be active. The whole thing took three days and I was back home. No one knew and I felt useful again."

"But if you'd been killed, would anyone have known what happened to you?"

"There's always a handler. People would have been told a story. Not the truth, but they'd know I was dead."

Noah gave a little groan as he paced away. Guilt tore through Rowe at the sound. He didn't mean to hurt Noah with this. In truth, he hadn't given it much thought because he'd stopped a while ago. These little missions weren't a part of his life any longer.

"Why did you stop?" Noah turned back to him, eyes narrowed. "Was it because of me?"

Rowe winced, unsure of how Noah would react to this. "No. I made the decision to stop going into the field after Mel's last Thanksgiving. There had been that whole pregnancy scare thing, which got us thinking and talking about whether we wanted to have kids. I knew that if we were going to have kids, I couldn't go on these damn missions anymore. The risk was too big that she'd be left alone to raise our kid or kids. Couldn't do that to her."

Noah's shoulders slumped a little, and Rowe hated that he couldn't read his lover's mind. "Do you want to do the missions again? We don't have kids."

That was an easy answer. Rowe swiftly marched across the short distance separating him and Noah, placing both of his hands on his wide shoulders. "No. No, I don't. You and our family and Ward Security are all the action I need. I don't need it and I don't miss it."

Some of the tension and worry appeared to leave Noah's face and body, but he was far from happy.

"Then why would you keep me from going with you to see Cal? It's not like I don't know the man. It'll be good to see him, in fact."

"It's just what I said. We all go there and draw attention to the man and his wife. Want that on your conscience?"

"What I want is for us to not separate."

That took the wind out of his sails. "It won't take me much time to see him. We won't be separated for long. And it's not like I want you out of my sight right now either. But we can't risk putting Cal in danger. We owe the man a lot." He'd watched their backs on more than one occasion in the past.

"When are you going to tell me what he's had you doing?"

Rowe tried to give him his usual cocky smirk. "You know how that shit works, Noah."

"Do I? Right now, we've got some evil motherfucker gunning for my life. JB's too. You could easily end up in the crosshairs at this point, because I doubt this guy is willing to leave anyone alive. No, I know he isn't. He took out his own fucking brother, so there's no doubt about it. We're all three in the worst kind of danger and especially if we're right and he has bigger people in his pocket. It could even be Cal."

"You don't honestly believe that."

Noah shrugged. "No, I don't. But that's my point. We have no idea who we're up against here, and I don't want you out of my sight."

"I'll just do this one thing, then we won't separate again. Promise. I'll even have you drop me off there once I get in touch with him." Rowe tugged Noah into his arms. He held him close, enjoying the sound of his breaths in his ear. He wanted this man to continue breathing, so he was willing to take the risk of seeing Cal. Willing to separate just long enough to get some real fucking answers.

Noah pulled away to cup Rowe's face. He kissed him, staring hard at him. "Okay, but this will be the only thing we don't do together. Understand?"

Rowe grinned. "I do."

"And no heroics by yourself."

"That goes both ways."

Noah smirked and kissed him again. A peck of the lips, then he slanted his mouth over Rowe's and slid his tongue into his mouth. He tasted of the bourbon they drank. Rowe smoothed his hands up Noah's spine and tugged him as close as possible. Familiar desire sparked through him, and he vowed once again to get to the bottom of this. Noah was infinitely too precious to him and he wanted to keep him.

The kiss deepened and Noah backed him into the bed. They fell across it, the kisses wet and hot. Noah nipped his chin, down his neck, his mouth opening to suck, and Rowe's eyes closed as pleasure swamped him. He ran his hands down Noah's shoulders, feeling the taut muscles of his arms. Arms that held him so tight. Noah was intoxicating, and he pulled him back up to crush his mouth with his. Passion rose like a wave inside him as he rolled them and speared his fingers in Noah's soft hair. They kissed until his lips felt sensitive; then he sat up to pull Noah's shirt off. He paused to tug off his own, then returned, moaning at the feel of naked skin against him.

Noah's hands ran over his spine and down to his ass and he ground up against him. "I hope you brought lube."

"It's in my bag."

"You get it while I run into the bathroom. I want you to fuck me when I get back."

Rowe scrambled to his feet and tugged off his jeans and underwear, his dick slapping against his belly. Noah grinned as he got off the bed and strode slowly into the bathroom. Rowe watched his gorgeous, round ass the whole way.

He walked to his bag and remembered something else he'd thrown in—Noah's favorite prostate massager. Grinning, he grabbed it with the remote and the lube and returned to the bed, stuffing the toy under the pillow.

Noah came back to the bed and pushed him down on it. He straddled him and rubbed their dicks together. Rowe grasped his hips, feeling the ripple of muscles under his fingers. He squeezed before running his hands up Noah's wide chest. Hair teased his palms. He played with Noah's nipples, getting them nice and hard, watching as pleasure made Noah's lids lower. The man gazed at him with fire in his blue eyes.

Rowe pulled him down, slashing his lips across his, pressing until Noah opened for his tongue. He licked into his mouth and swallowed Noah's moan. Noah grasped their dicks together in one hand and started stroking. Pressing his head into the bedding, Rowe gasped and thrust into his hand.

Letting go of his own dick, Noah ran his fingers over Rowe's. "Want you to fuck me with this."

He stared up at him, at the heavy-lidded lust in his expression and felt that spark of excitement he always felt with Noah. Excitement tinged with a heady love that still had the power to awe him. He pulled the man down for another kiss and rolled them so Noah was on his back. Kissing down his body, he reveled in the taste of Noah. He kissed his abdomen, his dick, and kept going until he reached his balls. He nuzzled, inhaling the wonderful musky scent of Noah there, then lifted his leg until Noah wrapped one arm around it to hold it up. He dipped his head and licked, tasting freshly washed skin, his tongue sliding into the puckered hole. Noah cried out and clenched around his tongue and Rowe remembered his surprise. He reached for the massager and caught Noah's wide eyes.

Anticipation curled in Rowe's groin as he sat up and lubed the massager as Noah watched. He made a show of getting it nice and slick. He slowly rubbed it around Noah's hole, then slipped it in, moving it in and out. They had several of these things, and this was a favorite they shared because it hit just the right spot and had several settings—Noah's preference being the second one.

But Rowe was in the mood to tease.

He watched Noah's ass clasp around the toy as he pushed it into the right position. The man had begun to pant and when Rowe took the remote in hand, his mouth fell open as the vibration started. His eyes rolled back into his head, and he let out the sexiest long moan. Rowe had to grasp his own dick as he watched his lover writhe on the bed.

"I love the way you squirm on this thing," he muttered, tightening his fingers around himself. At the same time, he increased the vibration, grinning when Noah gasped and clenched his ass. He watched him work the toy in his body and Rowe knew what he was feeling— that clutching around it made it vibrate in just the right spot. They kept this one charged for good reason.

He hit the next level of vibration. Noah bucked up off the bed, his legs spreading wider. Pre-cum leaked from the tip of his dick onto his abs. He was so damn gorgeous like this, giving himself over to the pleasure, Rowe had to stroke himself harder. Blue eyes suddenly met his and Rowe came down over Noah, staring at him as he thrashed on the bed. Rowe scrolled through the vibrations until he got to Noah's favorite, a steady hum that tormented as much as it gave pleasure.

Noah's mouth was open, his eyes wide. His hands came up to clutch Rowe's arms before he reached for Rowe's cock. His callused palm felt fantastic on Rowe's dick.

"Feels good, doesn't it?" Rowe breathed, leaning down to bite at Noah's jaw. The man's panting had increased, and he still twisted on the bedding.

"Want you, Rowe," he gasped. "Come inside me."

Knowing Noah's prostate would be extra stimulated now, he came back up on his knees and played with the massager just a bit more, stroking it in and out of Noah's hole. He pressed it deep, then smirked and hit the button again until he could feel it giving out spurts of hard vibrations.

"Oh, you dirty fucker," Noah groaned, his hips coming up. "Agh!"

He was so fucking hot like this, completely at Rowe's mercy. "You're feeling it now, aren't you?"

Noah could only gasp and moan at this point. He'd reduced the man to monosyllables, and he couldn't have been happier about that. He flipped the remote to Noah's favorite steady vibration and watched as the man brought his legs up.

"You. Now."

Unable to resist, Rowe lubed himself up and pulled the toy out. He slid his cock into Noah's dilated hole, gritting his teeth when Noah tightened around him.

"Yeah," Noah breathed. "Fuck!"

Rowe pulled back, then pushed in deep again, his dick sliding over Noah's now highly sensitive prostate. He knew because Noah gasped and thrust his hips up. Fiery need raged through Rowe's body as he fucked into Noah over and over, propped up on his arms so he could watch the pleasure washing over Noah's face. Noah reached up and grasped hold of his hips, pulling him in deeper.

Rowe struggled to breathe, so turned-on he was seeing stars. "Christ, Noah!"

"So good. So. Damn. Good." Noah's ass clasped hard around Rowe.

Rowe shouted and sped up his hips, sinking deep inside Noah, the tight, clinging muscles so fucking good, he could barely think. Pleasure coiled in his gut, drew his balls up tight. He dropped down on Noah and kissed his chin, his neck. He sucked the skin into his mouth and moaned as Noah tightened his ass again. "You're killing me," he breathed.

"What a way to go." Noah's words came between pants. "Come for me, babe."

Rowe's orgasm exploded through him. He keened as he thrust his hips, spearing into Noah as deep as he could go. He came inside him, barely coherent enough to hear Noah shouting as he spurred him on.

"Yeah, yeah, feels so good."

Noah cried out and flung his head back. He reached down to jerk his dick. Rowe slowly pulled out of him, grabbed the toy and slid it home. He'd never turned the vibration off, and Noah gasped, then groaned. Rowe fucked him with the massager, watching him stroke his dick. Noah suddenly went still and let out a long, low moan, his entire body taut. Splashes hit his chest and stomach.

"Fuck yeah," Rowe breathed as he slowed down the thrusts of the toy. Damn, he loved the way Noah let himself go when they were like this. "I love you so damn much," Rowe whispered. "So damn hot."

"Love you too," Noah said, then hissed. "Too sensitive. Turn it off."

Chuckling, Rowe hunted for the remote.

He must have been taking too long, because Noah gave out a gasping sort of frustrated laugh as he lunged up and pulled the toy out of his ass.

"Shit, I can't find the remote."

Still laughing, Noah helped him search for it, and they finally found it on the floor next to the bed.

"How did it get there?" Rowe chuckled and flipped it off.

"I probably kicked it." Noah stared at him. "You know, I didn't bring you in here for sex, but I can't complain."

"No, you brought me in here to gripe at me."

"We both see how well that went." Noah smirked and walked toward the bathroom, carrying the massager. Rowe heard the water running. A few minutes later, Noah came back out, tossed the toy into Rowe's open bag, and sprawled on the bed next to him. One of his legs flopped over Rowe's.

Rowe ran his hand down the sweat on Noah's chest, the slick muscles feeling fantastic under his palm. He would never tire of touching Noah. Never tire of fucking him. In that moment, he felt alive. He rolled onto his side and cupped Noah's cheek. "We're going to get to the bottom of this mess, and then we're going to take that camping trip we've been talking about. Just you and me and a tent in the woods."

"Sounds perfect."

It did sound perfect. Everything about his life with Noah was perfect.

So why wasn't he rushing to marry this man? The moment he'd realized that Mel was the one and only for him for the rest of his life, he bought a ring and asked. No great deliberation. No crazy plans for a big moment. He wanted to snatch her up before she came to her senses and ran from him.

With Noah, he felt the same damn way. This was forever. He couldn't imagine being with another person and being this happy.

Not for the first time, he wished Mel was there to talk to. She had this amazing way of being able to sort through the crazy in his brain, make sense of it, and give him a logical answer to his problem. Noah could do that too, but he was afraid of hurting him with his dilemma.

So, what would she say now if he asked why he didn't want to marry Noah even if he loved him as much as he loved Mel?

Lying there with Noah pressed against him, his body sated and brain surprisingly clear, an answer came. He almost laughed. He could see Mel's smug, I-told-you-so smile as if she were standing right there.

Why didn't he want to marry Noah?

Because Noah wasn't Mel.

CHAPTER SIXTEEN

*R*owe hated the worried look in Noah's soft eyes, but it was better if they separated this one time. He and JB could check on Sally Perkins while Rowe met with former General Cal Hamilton. The anxiety that was drawing the muscles in Noah's shoulders into a tense, hard line was understandable. Washington DC was not known for being a town filled with trustworthy people, and living in the midst of them all was a mercenary who had killed American soldiers and stolen weapons. That couldn't happen unless someone was protecting them.

But Rowe knew Cal. Trusted the man. He was willing to stake his life on the fact that Cal wouldn't double-cross him.

That didn't mean he was showing up to the meeting unarmed. No, he wasn't naïve and stupid.

The old general had done well for himself in pseudo-retirement. He'd left a career in the Army to work for the Pentagon and sit on a variety of committees, though Rowe wasn't entirely sure where he had his fingers now. He was confident his friend would be able to pull information on the ambush and Clayborne Security.

After waving good-bye to Noah and JB, Rowe turned toward the house. The front looked like a quaint two-story home with white shutters and a dove-gray paint. The trees and bushes were neatly manicured, while flowers added bright pops of color to the bed. Everything about the place had a sweet, homey feel without being too ostentatious, but Rowe had little doubt that thanks to its McLean, Virginia address, the place was likely to be priced in the millions. Yeah, the general had done just fine for himself.

As he climbed the stairs and reached for the doorbell, the heavy wood door with the exquisite cut glass window opened, revealing an older man with stark white hair and a familiar scowl.

"Goddamn, I knew it'd be a dark day when Rowe Ward stood on my doorstep," Cal announced.

Rowe stuck out his hand and grinned at his old friend. "But we both know you've been looking forward to it, you old troublemaker."

"Hell yes, I have!" Cal grabbed his hand and pulled him in for a bear hug that nearly cracked one of his ribs. Cal slapped him on the back a couple of times before releasing him. The man might have added about fifteen years and twenty pounds since Rowe last saw him, but it certainly didn't feel like he was slowing down at all. "Get your ass in here."

Cal released him and stepped back, allowing Rowe to enter the home filled with shining hardwood floors and framed family photos on the wall. Footsteps echoed from another part of the house and a woman with short gray hair appeared in the hallway with smiling, curious expression.

"Cal? What's all this noise about?"

"Maggie, come meet Rowe. He was under my command, not that he was all that good at taking orders." Cal flashed Rowe a grin while pulling the woman close. "Rowe Ward, this is my patient wife, Maggie."

Rowe shook her hand and smiled. "A pleasure, ma'am."

"It's nice to meet you, Rowe. Cal is always happy to have visitors from his old Army days."

"Yeah, Army vets are better than the meatheads on the Hill," Cal grumbled.

"How about I get you both something to drink while you catch up? Tea? Lemonade?"

"Lemonade would be wonderful, Mrs. Hamilton. Thank you."

"Thank you, Maggie. We'll be in my office." With a small wave, Cal led Rowe through the lovely home filled with family memories to a beautiful wood-paneled office with shelves overflowing with books. Cal carefully shut the door behind Rowe and nodded for him to take a seat in one of the big leather chairs in front of the empty fireplace.

"I saw that you've started a security business in Cincinnati. Still running around with those two troublemakers, Frost and Vallois?"

"We're never far apart," Rowe said proudly. He hated being away from the men he saw as his brothers, and he had a feeling that Lucas and Snow were chomping at the bit to have him home again.

"And that one boy that I had you paired with. Keegan? You ever get in contact with him after you got out?"

"Noah," Rowe said and there was no keeping the warmth and love that came with saying his name. "We're actually living together. Dating," he tacked on at the end to make sure it was clear that they were lovers and not merely roommates. He was done with a life of denying and hiding.

Cal dropped into the seat opposite him with a big sigh, his expression clouded for a second. "Can't say that I understand, but it doesn't matter if I understand it all. It's none of my business." He paused for a second and a slow smile crossed his face. "My sixteen-year-old grandson told me he was gay last year. I've seen men facing certain death in battle who didn't look as terrified as that boy. Told him I just wanted him happy." Cal shook his head. "Met his boyfriend at Christmas. Good kid. Smart as all hell. Never seen my grandson so happy in all of his life. Guess telling me turned out to be a good thing."

"The good thing was you telling him that you only wanted his happiness."

Cal gave a little grunt and stared into the empty fireplace for a moment, lost in thoughts that Rowe could only guess at. He'd seen plenty of instances where family had nearly crushed the light and happiness inside of a person because of their intolerance.

"I should have known when you finally offered to visit me, it wouldn't be for some small thing. You had to go dig this up."

"You know I wouldn't have come to you if it wasn't important." Rowe leaned forward, placing his forearms on his knees so that he could look directly into Cal's tired eyes. "We have reason to believe someone is hunting down and killing people from Noah's team. It's got something to do with the Afghanistan ambush and Erik Johnson. I'm not letting anyone take Noah from me. I've already lost a wife. I can't lose him too."

"It's a hornets' nest you've stepped in, my friend," Cal warned.

"Tell me."

"It actually starts before the ambush. I never met Erik Johnson, but I've heard of him and I know his type. Hotheaded, stubborn, and sure he knows more than the smartest man in the room. He started out as a marine. Probably wanted to prove he was the toughest man on the planet. But he finally got into one too many fights. Nearly killed a man. Was dishonorably discharged after three years in and did some time in prison. After he was released, he pulled together a mercenary group of ex-military."

"He wouldn't be the first to go that route."

Cal nodded. "Nope. There's a lot of them out there, and the money can be damn good. Particularly if you've got connections, which Johnson did. His people were willing to take on some crazy missions. If you didn't mind high body counts, then he could get a job done for you. Moron didn't even mind putting his own people at risk. The CIA hired them for a number of missions. And from what I understand, so did a lot of groups."

"Where'd it all go wrong?"

"Syria. Bunch of civilians were killed in what should have been a low-key extraction. Images were blasted across the news, and a lot of people were made to look really bad who would have preferred to stay out of the limelight."

"He lost his contacts?"

"All of them. He became *persona non grata* in the global intelligence community. No one was willing to risk hiring them after that mess."

"How does the Afghanistan ambush figure in?"

Cal opened his mouth and started to answer but stopped at a soft knock on the door. A second later, Cal's wife walked in with a tray of lemonade and little finger sandwiches.

"I thought you might want a little snack as you talk," Maggie said with a smile.

Rowe instantly jumped to his feet and hurried across the room to take the tray from her. He thanked her and placed the drinks and food on the table between him and Cal. "I can see why Cal has been enjoying his retirement so much. You take too good of care of him," Rowe teased.

"Only because he promised to help me hang some curtains later. You boys have a nice visit," she said with a little wave before leaving the room again.

Rowe returned to his seat and picked up a sandwich of chicken salad. He hummed a little as he ate. "You are definitely spoiled," he murmured to Cal with a smile.

"I thank God every day for Maggie," Cal said. "I'm lucky to have her."

Rowe knew the feeling. He'd been lucky to have Mel for as long as he did. He was too damn lucky to have been given a second chance with Noah. He was going to do everything within his power to keep Noah safe.

"I would imagine being shut out from some of the most lucrative contracts was enough to finally push him over the edge. When the Afghanistan ambush happened, we were quick to blame it on the Taliban. But when we saw that one of the missing was Erik's brother, Dave, we knew it was likely that he hit the convoy. His brother could have easily provided him with inside information, and he'd done enough missions with us that he would have known all the procedures."

"And of course it was covered up because we couldn't let anyone know that American soldiers were killed, and weapons were stolen by an American mercenary that we'd used in the past for missions."

Cal glared at him for a moment and Rowe glared right back. The small sandwich he'd eaten was no longer sitting right in his stomach, and he wished he had something stronger to drink than lemonade.

"He should have been put down a long time ago," Rowe growled.

"I'm not arguing with you. He's dangerous. A loose cannon. But he also knows a hell of a lot of secrets and information that the intelligence community would rather not get out to the general public."

"So…what? You struck a deal with him."

Cal sighed again and stared down on his hands. "Of sorts. If he keeps our secrets—all of them—then we will continue to feed him contract work."

"And by all of them, you're including what happened with the Afghanistan ambush that killed American soldiers."

Cal nodded, still not looking at Rowe.

Swearing, Rowe shoved out of his chair and paced to the far side of the room. He ran his hands through his hair, tightening his fingers on the strands as thoughts zipped through his brain. None of them were good.

It all made sense as to why Erik was so hot to get rid of Chris and the rest of his team. Dave had been recognized once. In his mind, the only people left from the Army who might recognize Dave or even Joseph from that mission were the members of Noah's team. They were the last ones to interact with the fallen soldiers. They were the only ones left who might be able to figure out the truth because they were on the ground there and walked away.

A truth that Erik was desperate to keep buried if he wanted to retain his under-the-table contracts with the intelligence community.

"Johnson is out of control," Rowe grumbled. "His own brother turned up dead last night and so did Joseph Cates. The last two survivors of the Afghanistan ambush were murdered. I don't know if Erik pulled the trigger, but I'm willing to bet that he at least gave the order. He's not going to stop until Noah and JB Alexander, the last member of Noah's team, are dead."

"I agree," Cal said solemnly.

Rowe paced back to where Cal was sitting and stopped right in front of him, hands propped on his hips. "I'm not letting that happen."

His hard voice was barely above a whisper. "I don't give a shit if the CIA, FBI, and NSA are protecting this asshole. He's dead before he can lay a finger on Noah."

"Yeah, we figured you'd feel that way."

Rowe jerked a half-step backward and stared at his old friend, who just chuckled.

"What?" Cal said with a smirk. "You think you could breeze into this town and remain under the radar? Especially after that bullshit with the motel?"

"I didn't start that shit!"

"Never said you did." Cal shook his head and Rowe hated to admit that he was feeling off-balance. They'd been careful when they rolled into Alexandria. They kept a low profile, didn't leave behind prints, and avoided surveillance cameras. But apparently he was missing some of the cameras, and there were more people watching them than Clayborne. Of course, the men from Clayborne were so clumsy and obvious, he just stopped looking after he spotted them.

"But you have to remember that this close to DC, there are more eyes watching than in your little town of Cincinnati."

Rowe clenched his teeth at the mocking tone Cal used when he talked about Rowe's home. He loved his city. Sure, it wasn't as cosmopolitan as some of the bigger cities, and maybe she still harbored too many prejudices, but she was growing and learning and his. Cal had a point, though. Security was always going to be tighter around DC.

"Let's just say that there'd be a lot of people who would be very grateful if their Erik Johnson and Clayborne problem just...went away. *Quietly.* No questions asked."

"Fuck me," Rowe groaned and stomped away from Cal and his laughter. "I told you three years ago that I had no interest in doing any more little jobs for the intelligence community."

"And yet here you are...doing a job for us. Weren't even smart enough to arrange for payment either."

Rowe swung back, eyes narrowed on the old general. "Someone somewhere is gonna owe me a damn big favor when this is over."

Cal nodded. "I have a feeling that you're going to be able to call in a few if you need them. I'll even get you names and private numbers when this is over."

Lifting his hand, Rowe scratched his jaw as a plan started to form in his brain. *Oh, this is going to be fun.* "Can you get me a little C4?"

"Ward, I said quietly. C4 isn't quiet."

He rolled his eyes and flashed his most charming smile. "We'll make it look like an accident. And no one will get hurt."

"You're not making any sense."

"I don't have to. I'm going to take care of this little pest problem the military and intelligence community has developed."

Cal sighed and nodded. "Thank you, and I am sorry that you and Noah have gotten dragged into this. It shouldn't be your mess to clean up."

"No, it shouldn't, but I've made my fair share of messes in life. I've gotten pretty good at cleaning them up."

Reaching into his pocket, Rowe pulled out his cell phone. He shot a quick text to Noah, telling him to swing back to pick him up when he could. They needed to start making some plans to dismantle Clayborne and take down Erik Johnson.

CHAPTER SEVENTEEN

*I*t felt like a wave of humidity had swept into Virginia overnight. The sun beat down on the Jeep, turning it into a metal sauna. Noah flipped the air-conditioning on high as they left Rowe and headed to Sally Perkins's house. His mind was on his conversation with Rowe, and he tightened his fingers on the steering wheel when he thought of the other conversation they desperately needed to have. He just didn't know how to go about bringing it up. Rowe had hurt him when he'd decided not to include him in the conversation with Cal, but in a way, he understood. Rowe had known the man better, but he couldn't help but feel Rowe was still hiding parts of his life from him and he hated that.

"You seem really happy, Noah," JB said into the quiet of the car, the only noise the hum of the vents and the engine. They passed neighborhoods and lots of trees and got onto the George Washington Memorial Parkway. As expected…they hit traffic. "I'm happy for you, but I have to say, it's a little hard to see it sometimes."

He glanced at JB to find a contemplative expression on his face. "Why is that?"

The smile JB gave him then held a hint of melancholy. "I really cared about you. I knew what we were doing was just casual, but it ended up meaning more to me. To be honest, I felt like you could possibly be the one. My forever man."

Shock froze him for a moment as they stopped. He'd known the man had cared for him, but not quite that much. Regret tightened his lips as he regarded JB. "I hadn't realized. Fuck, I'm sorry, JB."

"Don't feel bad, though back then I wanted you to hurt like I did." JB shrugged. "But a part of me always knew I could never have that same level of caring from you, so it wasn't totally a surprise when you broke things off. At the time, I was devastated, but hopefully I hid that."

"You did. I didn't mean to make you feel I didn't care." He hit the gas when the car in front of them moved.

JB ran his hands down his jeans. "No, you did care. As much as you could. You aren't the type to really string someone along—you just didn't care the way I wanted you to. There was something in your voice when you talked about Rowe. I knew your feelings for him ran deep. I just hoped maybe I could change your mind. But now that I see you with him...well, it's obvious you two belong together. Not sure I've ever seen two people more suited to each other."

"I love him more than I thought it possible to love anyone." He didn't want to hurt JB and didn't think the man's feelings still ran deep, but he also wanted to be honest with him. Rowe was it for him and always would be.

"There's something off, though. I can sense you're holding back." He fiddled with one of the vents like he was suddenly uncomfortable. "I did get to know you quite well, and you were holding back even more with me." He paused. "You know you can talk to me if you need to. I'd like us to at least go back to being friends."

He was quiet as traffic picked up and they headed down the parkway, passing along the Potomac River. The sun sparkled on the water. He stayed that way all the way into Alexandria. When Noah pulled down Sally's street, he looked into the parked cars. Thankfully, they were all empty. He brought the Jeep to a stop outside her house and sighed.

It wasn't as if he could have this conversation with any of his friends in Cincinnati. He looked back at JB to find the man quietly watching him. He could only hope all those old feelings were a part of his past now. He did feel the need to spill his guts. They'd started out as good friends, and he'd like to think they were again.

"There are still some unresolved issues with us that have to do with the usual. Marriage and kids." He thought of Mel, of all the pictures he'd hung up of the woman because he hadn't wanted to erase such an important time in Rowe's life. But sometimes, he felt like he could never truly compare to the woman of Rowe's memories. His friends talked about her and she'd sounded so great. "Did you know Rowe used to be married to a woman?"

"He told me about that. I saw all the pictures at your house, too."

"From what I can tell, she was pretty damned perfect for him."

"And you think you aren't?"

He had to smile at the incredulity in JB's response. "No, it's not that. Well, maybe a little, but that's just my own insecurity. What we have is obviously different. I just wish I knew how he felt about marriage. Every time the subject comes up, he does this tensing thing and deflects. Makes a joke." He flexed his fingers on the steering wheel. A small black-and-gray bird lit onto the hood of the Jeep, then flew off. "Drives me nuts with worry."

"What do you want?" JB asked.

"I like what we have now. No, I *love* it. It feels right to me. I don't need to have some legal paper telling me it's real, and I'm sure I don't want kids. I like the freedom we have. I like being able to take off hiking or hell, skydiving, on a whim. Things like that. I know you can still do that with kids, it's just not something I really want. I like kids, don't get me wrong—"

"But it's not what you want," JB repeated. "So what? You're afraid to tell him that?"

He held his breath for a moment. "What if marriage and children are what he really wants?" Just voicing that aloud made his hands tremble. He clenched them and dropped them into his lap. Of course, if that was what Rowe wanted, he was all on board. But so much would change about their lives. Would they still have the fire and the laughter they had now?

"I think you should talk to him about this. Be honest. If he's your person in this world, who else are you going to share those kinds of worries with? Are you afraid you'll lose him if you want different things?"

Noah shook his head because he did feel secure that they would stay together. "No, I won't lose him. But I don't want him to just settle either, you know?"

And that was his biggest fear. Right there. In a nutshell. That Rowe would settle with what Noah wanted and not have everything he wanted for himself. He wanted Rowe to have everything he wanted out of life. *Everything*.

"I think the relationship can only grow stronger with pure honesty, and keeping such an important thing out of discussion can only damage it."

"Yeah, I think you're right."

JB cleared his throat. "Rowe strikes me as someone who'd want you to lay it all out for him. He's pretty damn straightforward."

"He is definitely that. In everything else, I know exactly where I stand. It's just this is a big thing, you know?"

"Yeah, it is."

"Come on, let's check on Sally." He started to get out of the Jeep and paused to look back at JB. "And thanks. I am really sorry I couldn't give you what you needed from me."

"There's someone out there for me and if I'm lucky, it'll be a lot like what you share with Rowe."

"I want that for you," Noah said, really meaning it.

They walked across Sally's yard and she opened the door before they could knock. "Do you have more information about what happened to my husband?" she demanded. She looked even less put-together than she had the other day, in sweat pants and a thick sweatshirt, her hair in tangles around her face. Dark circles shadowed her eyes.

"Just that we're sure your husband's accident was anything but."

Noah stood with his hands in his pockets, the smell of freshly cut grass teasing his nose. "But you don't want to know more than that. Isn't safe."

"But the cops—"

"The cops aren't going to figure this out," Noah broke in. "Not with who's behind it. We just wanted to check and make sure you're okay."

"You think I'm in danger?" She hugged her arms to herself.

"We do know you were being watched, but I don't think they are going to harm you. This guy is far more interested in JB and me right now, and we're going to keep him interested in us."

"Is there anything I can do to help you? I spent all those years with him gone, waiting for that bad call, and knowing there was nothing I could do about it. I don't want to sit on my hands and do nothing anymore."

JB smiled at her. "I wish there was, but we've got this. I swear. We want you to be safe."

She nodded. "Please. You two stay safe. Chris would have hated for anything to happen to either of you." She hugged JB and then hugged Noah.

They said good-bye and climbed back into the Jeep. Noah's phone buzzed and he picked it up to see that Rowe was ready. He sent a quick message that they were leaving Sally's and on their way to him.

He started the vehicle and headed north toward Cal's house in McLean. It wasn't that far, but with traffic, he knew it could take over half an hour again, so he settled in and tried to enjoy the scenery with the peeks of the glittering river.

JB told him about working on a ranch, sharing hilarious stories of mischievous horses and nosy neighbors. They got lucky and the trip didn't take longer than half an hour. Rowe was coming down the porch steps when they arrived, and he climbed into the back seat.

"Did he have any information?" JB asked, twisting in his seat to look in the back.

"And then some. It's just like we thought. Erik and his band of misfits have had a deal with all the government alphabet outfits, but guess what?"

Noah couldn't help but grin at the wicked gleam in Rowe's eyes in the rearview mirror. "What?"

"We've been given a job, and the payment is payback. But whatever we decide to do, the authorities will be looking the other way…within reason." He rubbed his hands together and leaned between the seats, his grin cheeky. "We're about to have some fun, boys."

CHAPTER EIGHTEEN

*L*ightning flashed, streaking across the black sky. Noah silently counted. Thunder rolled like a bulldozer slowly plowing through a junkyard. The storm was getting closer. It would come in handy, offering them added cover and possibly slowing down any response to alarms or a shout for help. That was assuming that he fucked up taking down the security system for Clayborne in the first place. He knew how to install security systems, and he also knew how to disable them.

Noah was the first to admit that this was one of Rowe's more insane and dangerous plans, but neither he nor JB could come up with a better alternative. The information Rowe had brought back from his meeting with the general made it clear that they needed to take down Erik Johnson and his mercenary team. But they also needed to make an effort to wipe out any information that he might have.

And if he was storing it anywhere, Noah was willing to bet that it was at the Clayborne offices.

From what they'd managed to pull together on the man, he wasn't a big long-term planner. He wasn't finesse or craft. He was brute force. Hell, Noah could think of half a dozen ways to conduct the Afghanistan ambush that wouldn't have resulted in the murder of so many American soldiers. But Johnson didn't care about protecting lives. He wanted his payday. Noah was also willing to bet that the man enjoyed the killing part. A perk of the job for him.

Noah had taken more than his fair share of lives while operating in war zones, and each one left a wound on his soul. They took a toll. But Johnson's life, he'd take that one and wouldn't lose a moment's sleep over it. The man needed to pay for his crimes, and Noah had no qualms over being the executioner.

Leaning against the side of a neighboring building, Noah glanced around the area. Clayborne Security was located outside the city proper in an old industrial warehouse district. For several blocks, the region had a strong blue-collar feel. The place was all about manufacturing goods and shipping products from one location to millions of others around the globe. Everywhere he looked were rows of shipping containers, forklifts, crates, and wooden skids. Too many places for other people to effectively hide and pick off targets. But it also meant that it was hard to effectively place surveillance cameras.

The three-story brick building holding Clayborne was right in the middle of this manufacturing and shipping chaos. It meant no one would give a second look at strange shipments or movements going on with the office building. There was too much other activity going on. Gidget had already run a check of the building when she was pulling plans on record with the city and found that Clayborne was the only one renting space within the building. That certainly made it easier on them.

"How are we looking, gang?" Noah asked softly, knowing the mic pressed to his throat was going to easily pick up anything he said and relay it to everyone listening.

"Security cameras are down, and I've got the front doors unlocked," Cole replied.

The IT specialist had volunteered to stay late and hack his way through Clayborne's security system remotely. Noah was more accustomed to hearing Quinn's excited and snarky voice in his ear when he worked, but he was overseeing an actual paying job at Ward Security, so Cole took over. The large, muscular man was serious at all times, which left Noah feeling like Cole would find himself at odds with his coworkers, but Quinn and Gidget raved about him. They found a way to make it work.

"I'm on the move," Noah said. He shoved away from the building wall and quickly crossed the open parking lot between the manufacturing warehouse and Clayborne Security. Cole had already reported in that the building was empty, but Noah wasn't taking any chances that he'd missed someone. After all their run-ins, Erik had to be expecting them to do something at this point.

As he reached the office building front door, a little smile grew on his lips. "You know, we totally forgot to come up with code names." Standing in front of the door, he pulled a spray-paint can from his small pack and wrote the word TRAITOR in big, bold letters across the double doors, careful to miss the door handles. He stuffed the paint can away but left the bag partially open so he could easily get into it again.

"Not this mission. The next one," Rowe immediately replied. Noah knew this little stunt was just the tip of the iceberg. Rowe had something much bigger and darker planned for Erik and his group of bullies.

"Code names? Really?" JB said, amusement clear in his voice.

"It's SOP," Rowe said in a know-it-all tone that had Noah rolling his eyes even though no one could see it. His lover was getting a little better around JB, but he couldn't stop himself from getting his digs in whenever he could. Yes, code names were definitely part of their standard operating procedure, but JB had no idea that this kind of insanity was normal for them.

"Well, when we do pick code names, I'm claiming Alpha One," JB declared, undeterred by Rowe's tone.

Both he and Rowe groaned at JB. Poor man. He had no idea what he was missing out on.

"And that just proves why you're not going to be picking the code names," Rowe stated with glee.

"What?" JB cried.

"We'll explain later," Noah said as he jerked open one of the doors.

Grabbing his gun from his side holster, Noah hurried inside the building. Rowe would be following on his heels within the next thirty seconds, followed by JB one minute after that. "I'm inside."

"Starting my timer," Rowe replied, all joking gone from his voice.

Noah cut through the main lobby, heading down a hallway lit only by a set of tiny emergency lights left on overnight. He'd memorized the first-floor layout of the building so that at a critical moment he wouldn't have to refer to the paper version he carried. The lobby didn't hold much, and it certainly wasn't inviting as you would expect if you were trying to get clients.

Sure, Ward Security's lobby wasn't much, but it had a high-class, polished feel to it that was so different from the back offices and the training area. But then, clients rarely saw the training facilities. There were several offices and fancy conference rooms where people could talk to customer-care representatives about their needs. Rowe had always grumbled that those were his suit and tie days.

And the moment Andrei had been moved up to COO, Rowe had shoved those client meetings off on the poor man. It really was best for the business. Rowe claimed it was because Andrei was sexier in a suit, but Noah was sure it came down to the fact that Andrei had a softer, gentler touch with the would-be clients than Rowe. Andrei innately knew when to push and when to coddle. Rowe was all growling and table-pounding. Great for bedroom fun, but bad for business.

But Clayborne only had a plain sign with the company logo, which was a simple sword clenched in a fist. A couple of basic, uncomfortable-looking chairs were off to one side, and there was a plain wooden desk that looked like it had been picked up from the side of the road, with a phone on it and a blank notepad. There wasn't even an area rug or a potted plant.

There was no doubt in Noah's mind; Erik Johnson had no interest in getting clients. Clayborne was just a front for its darker, mercenary activities.

"I see the target. The swipe pad light is on," Noah murmured. There were only a few doors off the hall, but the one at the end of the hall looked heavier and had a little card reader sensor pad to the left of the doorjamb. He'd barely finished speaking when the green light on the pad went out.

"You're clear," Cole replied.

The man might be quiet, but he was damn good at his job.

Noah pulled open the heavy door, muscles straining under the weight. Slipping inside, he squinted against the darkness. He could barely make out the towering stacks with an array of red, yellow, green, and blue lights flashing on and off along the servers. There weren't a lot of them, but enough to handle any computers within the office and the security system. He hurried down the narrow aisle, digging into his bag of tricks as he moved. His fingers brushed along a device barely larger than his fist and he grabbed it. Moving it to his other hand, he reached back in and grabbed a roll of duct tape. He couldn't see it in the dim light, but he knew he'd packed his favorite Abraham Lincoln rubber duckie roll.

When he reached what looked to be the middle of the room, he stepped up to one of the stacks and started taping the device directly to one of the servers. Cole had been clear that they should all have a thick shielding and ground that would protect from things like a lightning strike directly to the building, but not enough to take a direct blast from within the room. Rowe's homemade electromagnetic pulse bomb should wipe out their servers and take down the building's entire security system.

With the EMP in place, Noah set the timer and ran to the door. "Five seconds," he warned. He got the door open and slid out into the lobby hall, pulling the thick door closed behind him. The EMP didn't carry a blast that was particularly harmful to humans, just computers. However, Noah wasn't entirely sure how long it had been since Rowe had cooked up one of his special little devices, and he wasn't taking any chances in case his crazy boyfriend got it a bit wrong.

He'd barely reached the lobby when the emergency lights flickered, and there was an electrical sizzle in the air. The hairs on his arms stood up, and it felt like static cling had infused his clothes. At the very least, something had happened.

"Cole? You still there? Anyone hear me?" Noah asked, wondering if maybe the door hadn't shielded his earpiece and it was now fried along with the servers.

"Still here," Cole immediately replied.

"I'm here," Rowe answered.

"Ditto," JB chimed it.

"Looks like security has been completely taken down. I'm blind to the building," Cole continued. That was to be expected. With the security system taken out, the cameras Cole had hacked into were no longer working. "I'll be monitoring the police bands for any calls."

"Heading to the third floor," Rowe said. He would have ducked inside while Noah was taping down the EMP. He would be on the stairs, going straight for Erik's office.

"Moving on to the second," Noah said. He jogged across the lobby to a door marked STAIRS. He paused with the spray-paint in hand and wrote the same word as before across the wall in large letters.

"Moving inside in thirty," JB said.

Just as Noah was starting to relax a little because everything about their mission was going according to plan, Cole's voice unexpectedly came back across his earpiece. "Gidget wants me to tell you that she thinks the CIA is monitoring our conversation and would like to know who Rowe talked to in DC."

That was a damn good question. Cal was not CIA. At least, Noah was pretty sure the old general wasn't involved with the CIA. But he wouldn't have been surprised if the wily old man had connections to that government group. And Rowe obviously had connections to the agency, but not once had Noah ever heard a name.

"Tell Gidget not to worry about it," Rowe growled.

"Hey, Cole?" JB suddenly asked. "Can you ask Gidget if she can tap into the security camera on the exterior of the sheet-metal manufacturing company next to Clayborne or maybe the traffic cam on the main road turning into Clayborne? That might give us a better heads up since the office cams are down."

There was a moment of silence and then Cole replied, "She's on it now. We'll keep a close watch for you guys."

"Thanks," JB said, and Noah could hear the relief in his voice.

Very soon they were all going to be inside the building. There was a good chance Erik or one of his men were going to notice that the security system was down at the office. They were very unlikely to call the cops. They were more likely to come charging as one large group with guns blazing. It was not something they wanted to be surprised by.

When Noah reached the second floor, he leaned against the wall, his gun in his right hand while slowly opening the door with his left. When the crack was big enough to peer through, he glanced around the floor, his jaw dropping. He'd been expecting offices and maybe a ragtag grouping of desks. What he got was a boys' playroom.

Off to one side, there were some mats for sparring and a few punching bags. There were several weight machines and a couple of treadmills. And then it shifted to a couple of pool tables and a giant couch placed in front of one of the biggest TVs he'd ever seen.

He slowly crossed the giant open room, his gun still held at the ready. There were posters of half-naked women on the walls, and there was a lingering smell of stale beer and pizza in the air. It was like he'd walked into a frat house or a private clubhouse. Nowhere did he see a computer or a desk. There was nothing to indicate that this was a place of business.

No, this was where Erik's friends and mercenary buddies hung out between missions. There was no sign of where they did any training to hone their skills or work on improving their techniques for protecting people. This place wasn't about protection.

And somehow Chris had been drawn into this.

Noah shook his head and sighed. It had to have been the world's worst mistake. Erik had probably put out a call for people with military training to fill out their ranks after losing someone while on a mission. Chris naturally put in his application. The guy had a killer résumé after serving most of his life in the Army, and he was always looking for a way to protect and help people. Plus, a security company would have likely put him in contact with people of similar backgrounds. Whoever reviewed Chris's résumé didn't look close enough, didn't look to see where the former Ranger had served. Or they just didn't think there was anyone who would have recognized David Johnson from his time in the field.

Even if Chris hadn't recognized David, Noah had to wonder if Chris would have met with some accident later. Clayborne was not who Chris was. He wouldn't have joined a team that didn't value human life. He wouldn't have agreed to do some of the missions they likely accepted from the government. There had been some things Noah and his team had to do while in the Army that they didn't agree with, but there had been nothing they could do about it. They'd had to follow orders. Out of the Army, they finally had a choice. Chris would have chosen to walk away. But would Johnson have let him?

There were no answers to those questions, so Noah shoved them aside. He was there to do a job. To get justice for Chris and Paul.

Heading to the circular concrete pillar closest to the center of the room, Noah pulled out his roll of duct tape and another homemade device from Rowe. He did not ask how the man had gotten his hands on several pounds of C4. He truly didn't want to know. The knowledge of how to effectively create a bomb using the explosive material had undoubtedly come from his years in the military. Noah had learned how at one time, taught by the squirrely redhead, but he was sorely out of practice and hadn't wanted to help make the bombs. But he'd watched Rowe and it was slightly terrifying to see him working with such ease and confidence with the stuff.

It was painfully clear that even after living together for nearly three years, there was still a lot he didn't know about Rowe that happened between him leaving the Army and Noah's appearance in his life again.

Again, more questions without answers, but at least he felt like he could implement some kind of sexual torture at a later date and get the information out of Rowe. Okay, three years was definitely long enough to wait. He was going to start getting all the secrets out of Rowe, and they were both going to enjoy the process.

Once the C4 was attached to the column, Noah took a half-step backward. It would have been more effective to drill into the column and place the bomb inside the concrete, but they didn't have the time or the equipment for something so elaborate. They had enough explosive material to bring the building down or at least weaken it so that it would have to be condemned. Either way, Erik and his goons were going to find themselves homeless.

Lifting his hand, Noah gritted his teeth at the sight of his shaking fingers. Not much rattled him anymore. Between his time in the Army and working for Ward Security, he really felt like he'd seen it all, but he had to admit that it had been a while since he'd worked with a bomb.

He cleared his throat and said, "Setting the first timer on the second floor."

"Good to go," Rowe replied.

"Good to go," JB said.

Slowly releasing the breath he'd been holding, Noah pushed the button for the timer. His heart skipped a beat as he waited for the time to start its countdown from five minutes. Lifting his wrist, he synced his watch up to the bomb timer. They each had two charges to set, and then they had to escape the building, back to his Jeep. It didn't sound like a lot of time but in reality, it felt like too much time in which things could go so very wrong.

Once he saw three seconds tick off, confirming that the timer hadn't been damaged by the EMP, Noah walked across the floor to the second pillar that had been marked for a bomb. Using his duct tape, he attached it the column. When the timer on the first bomb was down to four minutes, he set the second charge. If they timed it just right, all six bombs would go off at exactly the same time, which should bring the building straight down.

Well, that was what they were hoping. Not a damn one of them knew anything about the exact science of imploding a building. Noah hoped it didn't matter too much. The other buildings close to the Clayborne office were several hundred yards away and empty at this hour. The bombs were attached to critical load-bearing columns. It was highly unlikely that innocent people were going to be hurt.

Rowe, JB, and Noah, on the other hand...well, that was a different matter.

As soon as the second bomb was set, Noah paused to write TRAITOR on the wall and ran for the stairs. He didn't know if anyone would ever see the spray-painted words, but he felt a cathartic joy in putting them there.

Above him, he could already hear the soft scrape of Rowe's boots as he quickly descended. His lover would be on his heels at any second. JB should also be finishing putting his last bomb in place. They just needed to get out of the building and to the Jeep.

"Incoming!" Cole practically shouted in his ear.

Noah winced and he nearly tripped as he came around the landing to head down the last flight of stairs.

"Gidget spotted two vehicles speeding toward the building. Not cops."

"Fuck! Seriously?" Rowe snarled.

"Apparently someone lives close to work, or they were watching for us to hit the building," JB said. "I'm heading for the front door now."

As Noah reached the door on the ground floor, he paused and looked over his shoulder to see Rowe rounding the last landing to hit the final set of stairs. Noah gave his lover a grim look. There was one major flaw in their plan that not one of them had been brave enough to voice. They didn't have nearly enough ammo or guns on them to hold off a sustained attack by multiple assailants. The attack on the building was only going to work if they could sneak in *and* out without being seen. They could not get pinned down inside the building, or this whole thing was for nothing.

"We got this," Rowe said firmly. If it was possible for a man to will the world to work exactly how he wanted, then Rowe would find a way. The odds might be stacked against them, but Noah trusted his life and JB's in Rowe's hands without question.

"Right there with you, babe," Noah said, not caring that both JB and Cole could hear him.

As Rowe reached the ground floor, Noah jerked open the door and ran down the hall with Rowe following behind him. JB was positioned next to the door, his back against the wall, cloaked in some of the shadows. His gun was raised and ready. *Fuck.* Next time he left town with Rowe, he was bringing a much bigger arsenal.

"No sign of the cars yet," JB said as they drew closer. "How much time do we have left?"

Noah glanced at his watch. "Just over three minutes. Do we want to wait until the last minute? Hold them off from coming inside?"

"Or let them walk into the building while we head to the car?" JB said.

Before Rowe could answer, headlights flared, lighting up the street before turning into the parking lot from a distant entrance. Tires squealed on the asphalt and two engines roared.

"Wait..." Rowe whispered.

Noah tensed and JB shifted his weight, one hand tightening on the handle of the front door.

When the outline of the two cars became clearer in the parking lot lamps, Rowe said, "Run for the Jeep!"

The race was on!

JB surged out the door but stopped just past the entrance, holding the door open with his left while pointing his gun at the approaching cars with his right. Noah didn't question it. He just led the way across the front of the building and toward the steel mill. They'd cut a hole in the chain link fence close to the Clayborne building and another hole at the back of the fence near where they'd parked the Jeep. It might take a few seconds longer to get to the Jeep by cutting through the steel mill yard, but it increased their chances of losing the people on their heels.

He'd barely cleared the building when gunfire broke out around him. There was more squealing of tires and the smell of burned rubber as the cars came to a halt closer to the buildings. While keeping his body pointed toward the steel mill, Noah reached back with his right hand and lined up his shot toward the men throwing open car doors and pointing at Rowe and JB. A quick glance revealed three potential shooters.

As they opened fire, Noah stopped worrying about them going into the building before it blew up. He knew Rowe had them wait in the building until he was sure they would be seen. He wanted the men to follow them, get their attackers away from the building, but as the threat of someone putting a bullet into Rowe increased, Noah found himself caring a whole lot less about his attackers' safety. Fuck them.

Squeezing the trigger, he quickly fired off three shots. His aim was off because he was on the run, but it was enough to get the other men to duck behind their cars for cover. Noah paused in his shooting long enough to slip through the opening in the fence. He held one end of the metal fence, pulling the opening wider as Rowe got closer.

JB shouted and went down. Noah's heart stopped in his chest as he watched in what felt like slow motion as JB's left leg collapsed beneath him and he hit the ground hard. Noah shifted his weight, starting to come back through the fence, but Rowe stopped him. He tossed Noah his gun a second before pivoting on his planted foot. Noah caught the gun and stepped through the opening, laying down cover for Rowe as he went for JB.

To get through the next couple of moments, Noah turned all his emotions off as easily as flipping a switch. He hadn't had to do it since leaving the Army, had been glad that such a thing was no longer part of his life. But at that moment, he couldn't risk looking at Rowe, wondering if his lover or his friend was about to take a bullet in the back of the head. He had to protect them.

Out of the corner of his eye, he could see Rowe pulling JB's arm over his shoulders and helping the man to his feet.

"JB is hit. Right thigh. Not near the femoral artery. Nothing major," Rowe said in a calm and even voice for both Noah and Cole.

"Fuck you. Still hurts like hell," JB snarled.

"Gidget is calling Frost. Where do you want him to meet you?"

"Just tell him to get his ass on the road heading east," Rowe said. There was a little more strain in his voice as he carried some of JB's weight while getting him moving toward Noah and the fence opening. "We'll work out details later. Tell him I can get the bullet out, but I'd rather he clean up and close."

Noah's gun clicked empty and he shifted it to his left hand while lifting Rowe's gun in his right. With the first round, he dropped a guy and something in his brain said that it had been a head shot. He was dead. The remaining two ducked down lower. Their returning fire became more infrequent and less accurate.

A part of Noah relaxed when Rowe and JB slipped past him. He slowly backed up, dipping through the opening in the fence. He chanced a glance down at his watch.

"Ten seconds," he said. They needed to get a little more distance in case the debris flew in every direction. Noah followed behind Rowe and JB, protecting their backs. He could no longer clearly see the cars, but it looked like the two men were following behind them.

A loud, concussive blast rumbled out from the Clayborne building, blowing out the windows and sending glass in every direction. The two men shouted in surprise and dropped to the ground. Rowe helped JB behind a shipping container and Noah stepped up close to him, putting JB's other arm over his shoulder. The earth shook beneath their feet, and a cloud of dust whooshed over the steel mill.

The moment the dust started to settle and the earth stopped shaking, Noah leaned JB against the container and peered around the edge. There was no sign of the men from Clayborne. The building was hard to spot, but it did look like huge chunks of it were now missing.

"Babe," Noah said with a huge grin. "I think you might have a future in demolition if you ever get bored with security."

Rowe chuckled. "Good to know."

"As fun as this has been, can we get me somewhere with drugs and a doctor?" JB said.

"Come on, Daphne. I think I might have some morphine stashed in Noah's Jeep, left over from a special occasion."

"I don't want to know," JB groaned and Rowe helped him limp to the Jeep.

Noah continued to bring up the rear, protecting them as they worked their way to the vehicle as quickly as JB could move. The cops were definitely being called now, and it was best if they escaped before anyone else spotted them. They really shouldn't be able to bring a building down without the cops being called, no matter who the hell Rowe was friends with.

"Are you sure they're going to follow us to Cincy?" Noah asked.

"When they can't find us in the area?" Rowe replied. "Yeah, they'll come to Cincy. Erik Johnson isn't going to just let this go."

"Are you sure that's smart? Leading them back to your home?" JB's voice was rough and thick with pain. Noah had suffered his fair share of gunshot wounds, and there hadn't been a single one of them that didn't hurt like hell. It didn't matter where he was hit.

"Smart? Nope," Rowe admitted. "But it's going to be a hell of a lot more fun."

CHAPTER NINETEEN

*W*hen they walked into Rowe's office at Ward Security the next afternoon, Rowe knew he was in for an ass-chewing when he saw Lucas waiting for him, hands on hips, a dark glower in his green-gray eyes. Rowe glared at Snow, who lounged on the large, black sofa against the far wall. "Tattletale."

Snow smirked and shrugged, leaning into the corner of the couch. He was wearing a pair of loose jeans and a light-blue T-shirt that matched his eyes. He'd met them on the road in the middle of the night and didn't even look like he'd lost a minute of sleep.

Lucas, on the other hand, also casual in jeans, looked like he hadn't slept in a couple of days. Dark circles shadowed his eyes, and there was a deep frown line between his dark brows. Andrei stood, leaning against the wall, his shoulder-length hair pulled back in a tail. He was the only one dressed for work, in a pair of black slacks and the Ward Security collared shirt.

"Lucas, Andrei, this is JB," Noah said as he settled in next to Snow.

Rowe pulled out a chair for JB, whose thigh had a huge bandage around it under another pair of khaki shorts. Andrei came forward to shake his hand after he settled.

"You didn't call me and fill me in," Lucas said after nodding

179

politely to JB. He turned the full force of his frown on Rowe. "Then I get a call from Snow telling me he drove out to fix a bullet wound in the middle of the night. A bullet wound, Rowe! What the hell?"

"You could have kept that part to yourself," Rowe growled to Snow.

"And ruin my fun? Never." Snow winked.

"I didn't have a chance to call. We had all kinds of craziness happening over the last few days and it's not over with." He filled them in on what had happened—from the first shooting at Noah, to last night and the Clayborne office. Even Snow blinked in shock.

"You blew up his building? Blew it up?" Snow chuckled and shook his head. "Damn, Ward."

"And pulled it off. You see any police here?" He blew on his knuckles and brushed them over his shirt.

Lucas frowned harder. "Next time, call me even if it's two in the morning. Wasn't sleeping for worrying anyway."

His heart just turned over. Lucas sometimes acted like his father, but he knew the man came from a place of love. He was also just nosy as hell.

"I'm hurt that you didn't involve us in your little party," Snow said. "I've never had the chance to blow up an entire building."

Lucas made a noise in the back of his throat and glared at Snow. "We blew up a fracking oil field in Oklahoma," he reminded him.

"Yeah, but we didn't do it on purpose," Snow replied.

Rowe gave a sad little sigh. "It would have been so much cooler if we did."

JB reached out and tapped on Rowe's shoulder. "I want to hear *that* story later."

"You know he's going to come after you three here now," Snow said, crossing an ankle over his knee. "I would if I was him."

"I brought him onto our turf on purpose. I've got a plan." He couldn't stop his grin, and he knew it was wicked when Lucas shook his head.

"Plan to share it?" Lucas asked.

"Soon. I'm still working out the kinks in my head."

"Well, whatever you do, don't take long. Like Snow, I doubt this Erik is going to put off coming here."

"And whatever it is, I'm in," Andrei said.

Lucas started to open his mouth, and Andrei held up a hand. Neither said a word but plenty passed between them before Lucas nodded, a small smile turning up one corner of his lips. He only stayed long enough to berate Rowe a little more, then left to get his daughter. Apparently, one of the bodyguards had her downstairs. Snow followed him, always up for a little Daciana time. Quinn came by and called Noah into the tech room.

Andrei stayed to fill him in on what had happened while they were gone. He'd interviewed another person for the bodyguard position and found someone he liked. Because Rowe trusted his judgment, he told him to go ahead and hire him. Turned out, it was a woman.

"Hot damn, that's good news." They'd had a few requests for female bodyguards, so this was fantastic. "What's her specialty?"

"Kicking ass. She's into MMA. Took down Garrett."

Rowe whistled because Garrett was hard to beat with his kick-boxing skills and long, lethal legs.

Once Andrei returned to his office to call her, Rowe was left with only JB in the office. It was the first time they'd been left alone since the first night. "How's your leg?"

"Hurts like a motherfucker." He knew Snow had offered good painkillers, but he understood that JB wanted to remain sharp right now. Far as he knew, the guy was working on only Tylenol.

"You handled yourself well out there. Ever thought about working security? We have job openings, and I'd be happy to have you on board."

"Nah, I like it on the ranch. And I'm glad to have left the chaos and explosions behind. This was enough of a taste to remind me of that."

Rowe nodded, understanding. He stared at the man, once again remembering that this had been someone who'd been intimate with his man. The jealousy had toned down some, thank goodness, but he still felt there were a few things he needed to say. He glanced out the window of his office to see Noah still down the hall.

"You were in love with him, weren't you?" Rowe asked, watching JB's face. The man looked away from him a moment, then shrugged.

"Yes. But I wouldn't step on your toes, and it wouldn't matter even if I tried. Noah loves you. Always did."

"You still are." This time it wasn't a question because he could tell just by the way the man had looked at Noah. By the way he spoke.

JB stared at him for several long moments. "It's not like those kinds of feelings just disappear. But what I feel for him now is more… nostalgic. Yes, there is regret I couldn't make him care for me in the same way, and there probably always will be, but even then I knew I didn't have all of him. He talked about you all the time, and it was in his voice." He shrugged. "I came to terms with it."

Rowe thought of how much he loved Noah and tried to imagine if those feelings weren't returned. The pain this caused him made him catch his breath. He realized he had respect for JB. He didn't think he could just stand back if he were in his shoes. No, he *knew* he couldn't. Noah was everything to him, and he was selfish enough to want to keep that. To fight for him. He suddenly felt sorry for JB, though he was sure the man would hate knowing that.

"You guys have something really nice here. Together and with all those people you've introduced me to." JB pointed toward the door. "It's a great family and I'm happy for Noah, because he needed something like this. I can tell all those men care for him."

"They do." He leaned against his desk, deciding to let the love talk go. There was no reason to grill the man anymore. He knew where he stood. "How about a tour? An easy one in deference to your leg? I won't even take you down to the basement to show off my toys. Those stairs are a pain in the ass. But I'd like you to meet some of our employees. Who knows? Maybe you'll change your mind."

"I won't do that. My heart is set on the ranch. But I'd like to meet more of Noah's friends."

He led him out to the landing overlooking the first floor. "It's not usually this quiet. Normally, we have self-defense classes running but we're shorthanded right now, so we've postponed them." He walked him down the hall toward the triplets' room and introduced him to

Quinn, Gidget, and Cole. Quinn's boyfriend, Shane, was also there and they were all laughing as Noah regaled them with the story of blowing up that building.

"Only you, Rowe," Quinn said, his lips twisted in a half smile. He was in his normal silly T-shirt and jeans. Shane stood next to him, with his hand on his lower back.

"Hey, I had help!"

"Yeah, you need help and I'm talking a completely different kind of help." Quinn's grin broke through. "But that had to be fun."

"It was," Noah agreed. "All except for JB getting shot."

"I'm okay," JB said, leaning against the doorjamb. "But I could do with this not happening again."

"You want out on the plans, then?" Noah asked.

"Hell, no. I just don't plan to get shot again."

"Come on, I'll show you around downstairs." Rowe turned and headed for the stairs, taking them slowly so JB could keep up. They reached the first floor where he had exercise mats and different kinds of training equipment. It resembled a gym, but his cleaning crew had obviously been working, because it didn't smell like one. "Like I said, we normally have classes going on in here. Classes or training exercises. We have people skilled in different fighting styles, including mixed martial arts and kickboxing. We have a shooting range for target practice downstairs, but I won't make you take any more stairs."

"This is impressive."

"Thanks. I didn't plan for it to grow quite as much as it has, but I'm proud of what we've built here. And it's a group effort. I hire only the best."

Royce, one of his shorter bodyguards, walked into the room and Rowe grinned at him. The man might not be as big as some of the other men here, but he was lethal. He had a sort of raw, restrained presence that put people on edge. Made them watch him. "Just the man I wanted to see."

"Uh, oh, what did I do now?"

Rowe walked to him and threw an arm over his shoulder. "I'm going to need to borrow your house."

"I'm assuming you mean the empty one in Morning View and not the one I share with Marc."

"Of course!" Rowe said, sounding offended.

"Hey, I'm just checking. I heard you've already blown up a building this week."

"Wow! Word really travels fast here," JB breathed in surprise.

Rowe glowered at JB for a moment. "You have no idea." He then turned his attention to Royce. "Yes, the Morning View house, and no, I'm not going to blow it up."

"Sure thing. Wish I could be involved but I'm just here to get my next assignment. Got a gig watching some celebrity chef coming into town. He's had some threatening letters. Someone must have gotten food poisoning."

"You might not be so happy with me when I'm done," Rowe warned.

Royce lifted one black eyebrow. "Sounds like my kind of fun. Damn. Sorry I'm going to miss it."

"Yeah, you won't be saying that when I have to get Lucas to float me a loan to buy the place."

CHAPTER TWENTY

*R*owe leaned against the wall in the quaint ranch house in Morning View, Kentucky, with his arms folded over his chest. It was a struggle not to pace. Muscles twitched and ached, demanding movement. He hated waiting. He was so bad at it. At his age, he thought he'd be much better, but he felt like he was getting worse with each passing year.

He glanced around the house, admiring the work Royce had gotten done. The bodyguard had inherited it from his aunt, and he'd allowed Rowe to use it as a safe house a couple of times while he updated the old farmhouse. Royce talked about selling it since the place was way too far out in the country to try to rent out. The commute to just about any job would be at least an hour, and who the hell wanted to start the day like that?

Of course, the house had some appeal. The closest neighbors on either side were nearly a quarter of a mile away. Just lots of open space, trees, and freaking quiet. They left a few windows open to allow in a breeze. Music from crickets and frogs rose up, making it feel like a peaceful summer night.

And the stars.

When he lifted his face to the sky, he found so many stars

shining overhead, it was humbling. The last time he'd enjoyed stars like that had been on his trip to Colorado to clear his head. The trips down to Red River Gorge for camping with Noah hadn't given him so many stars. Those nights had been overcast. Plus, he'd been more concerned with what was happening in their tent after the sun set.

Swallowing down a sigh, Rowe looked over at Noah as he sat at the old folding table that served as a planning center and makeshift dining room table. Quinn had printed out a map of the house and surrounding area. They'd marked possible entrances to the house. There was a lot of open land and trees to the east, but it all ended at the Licking River. And thanks to some heavy rains that spring, the river was running fast and high. It was highly unlikely that Erik would choose to come from that direction without having a chance to properly scout it first.

That left the main road. And considering how infrequently traffic came down the road after dark, he felt pretty confident that they'd be able to spot him.

Then why was anxiety clawing at his stomach like a trapped rat trying to gnaw its way out of his chest?

It had to be because of the man scowling at the map, his loose curls hanging around his face, threatening to get in front of his eyes. Rowe almost smiled at those ridiculous curls that gave Noah a relaxed surfer vibe. Rowe had given Andrei and Lucas so much shit over Lucas's desire to keep Andrei's hair long. But after spending the past few years with Noah, he totally got it, and it was even a little embarrassing. He loved running his fingers through Noah's soft hair when Noah fell asleep after sex with his head on Rowe's chest. Or the way he could wrap his fingers in that hair when they were fucking. He loved just reaching out and touching Noah whenever he wanted, those silken strands sliding through his fingers.

"Do I want to know what you're thinking?" Noah asked, pulling Rowe out of his thoughts.

Rowe blinked and he found Noah smiling up at him. "Later," Rowe promised. He let his voice dip a little, becoming rough and husky.

Now? was not the time to discuss all the ways he was absolutely addicted to the man.

"Thank you! I really don't want to know," Quinn chimed in, reminding them all that there was a larger audience listening in.

"Pfft…" Garrett made a scoffing noise. "You're not old enough to hear the wicked things rattling around in his brain. But I'm happy to take some notes from the seduction master."

Rowe rolled his eyes and huffed while several people, including Noah, laughed loudly.

And then Noah's cell phone started ringing. The laughter stopped and Noah held up the screen toward Rowe. It was a Virginia area code.

"Get ready," Rowe murmured and nodded for Noah to answer.

Putting the phone in the middle of the table, Noah answered and immediately put it on speaker. "Hello."

"Noah? It's Sally. Sally Perkins."

"Hey, Sally!" Noah said in a friendly voice, but he shot Rowe a worried look.

They hadn't been expecting to hear from her. They'd been confident that Erik and his goons would leave Sally alone as soon as Rowe, Noah, and JB left town. It was clear that she didn't know anything about Erik's operation and wasn't a threat. Now Rowe was kicking himself for not sending a couple of bodyguards to keep an eye on her until Erik was taken care of.

"Have you seen JB recently? I tried calling him, but he hasn't answered his phone."

"Yeah, JB is here with me. He's been having some trouble with his phone. He just stepped out with Rowe to get some food, but I'll tell him to give you a call when he gets back. Is there anything I can do for you?"

"Are you still in Virginia?"

Noah glanced up at Rowe, who shook his head. "Nope. We returned to Cincinnati. Emergency at work. Do you need us to come back?"

"I…umm…no, I don't think so. I…I was hoping to say good-bye to both you and JB before you left. Chris talked so highly of both of you. I was hoping we could talk again, but I understand emergencies." Her voice cracked on the mention of her husband, but that wasn't the only thing in her voice. It wavered with fear. Rowe had a feeling that she was being forced to keep Noah on the line so that his phone could be traced. He was willing to put money on the fact that someone was holding that sweet woman at gunpoint.

Rowe silently stepped out of the kitchen and into the living room so his voice wouldn't be picked up on the speakerphone. "I want Dom or Sven at that woman's house tonight. I don't care if we have to charter a private plane. She will be safe *tonight*."

"I'm calling our pilot now," Andrei said. "Tell whoever is sent to go to Lunken immediately. He can be with her in less than three hours."

"Sven is here. He's grabbing his bag and heading to the airport now," Quinn replied.

"Thanks, everyone." Rowe gave a relieved sigh. He still smirked a little at Andrei's "our pilot." That boy was blue-collar Kentucky through and through, but he'd also quickly adapted to being married to a billionaire. He was very good at using his new resources to help others.

Rowe walked back into the kitchen where Noah was reassuring Sally that he and JB would return to Virginia for a much longer visit and plan something to celebrate the lives of both Chris and Paul.

"It's been nearly two minutes. That's plenty of time to trace Noah's location," Quinn whispered.

"We're in the middle of fucking nowhere. Maybe it takes longer out here," Rowe said.

"It doesn't work like that," the tech genius muttered, and Rowe shrugged it off. Technology was not his forte. He was better with his fists and weapons, and he couldn't wait to prove it.

Before Quinn could elaborate, Sally said her good-byes and ended the call. She'd sounded both relieved and worried, closing with an admonishment for Noah, JB, and Rowe to stay safe.

"I want everyone to check in," Rowe said as he paced toward the front door. He knew that Erik could have been tracing that call while on the move. They'd left Virginia two days ago. That was plenty of time for the bastard to realize they were no longer in the state and follow them to Cincinnati.

"Tony Tiger, view from the back door is clear," Noah immediately replied.

"Cap'n Crunch in the basement. Everything is quiet," Andrei said.

"Sugar Bear has the garage covered," Garrett said in a low voice. "And I think I've found a new toy." There was a gleeful purr to the bodyguard's voice that had Rowe shaking his head. He could only imagine what Garrett found in the garage. They'd stashed all manner of things in there over the past year.

"Snap in the fucking field," JB bitched.

Rowe couldn't blame the guy. The gunshot to the thigh was going to heal just fine, but it meant that he moved far too slowly to be right in the middle of the action. Of course, Noah immediately volunteered the fact that JB was an excellent sniper. So, the guy was stuffed into a ghillie suit and dropped at the edge of the field so he could take out anyone who might approach from the rear or the side of the house. Even if it wasn't pitch-black out there, no one would be able to spot him as he blended so perfectly with the tall grasses and scraggly bushes.

"Crackle on the road. No one is approaching," Jackson murmured. "And can I go on record as saying that we've forever warped cereal for me?"

"Pop in the command center," Quinn said, his voice cheerful and excited, matching his codename perfectly. "All is quiet. Couldn't get anything interesting off the call. It did originate from Virginia, but she could have easily had someone with her. We're monitoring the police bands. There are zero cameras within the area of the house that we can tap. Sorry."

"Don't worry, Pop. We've got the house covered and eyes peeled. Just get our boy in the air for Virginia," Rowe said.

He walked into the empty living room. Royce had spent time ripping up the old shag carpet, patching holes, and painting the walls white. Rowe started paying him to rent it out so Andrei or Noah could run the bodyguards through training sessions. And then Rowe had to pay to fix anything they inevitably broke during those training sessions.

He'd been thinking about raiding the local thrift stores for some old furniture. It was one thing to train in an empty house where you didn't have to worry about tripping over a chair or coffee table—but he needed to make sure his guys had real-world experience. Maybe after this was all over...

The only domestic touch to the house was the black-out curtains hanging over the front windows. He carefully pushed one edge aside with a finger and looked out the window. The front porch light was on, and there was a second light on at the end of the long gravel drive-way. Rowe wasn't expecting Erik and his minions to drive straight up to the house, but he would be the first to admit that nothing should be put past this fucker.

But for now, nothing moved.

Rowe let the curtain fall into place and walked to the kitchen where Noah was doing a weapons check for the second time. It was a nervous tic that they both fell back on when they were forced to wait.

Looking up, Noah met his eyes and frowned. There was the same worry in his eyes. Too often they were up against inept criminals, jealous exes, or even overconfident executives dabbling in violence for the first time. With the trained team at Ward Security, those threats were easy to contain and counter. Erik Johnson and his former military mercs were an entirely different beast. They knew how to infiltrate a location and how to use a wide array of weapons. It wasn't that Noah questioned the abilities of their people, but just that they lacked the same real-world experience as the mercs. Rowe wanted to reassure him that they could handle it, but he didn't want to say anything that would make it sound like Noah was worried.

"I've got two SUVs," Jackson suddenly whispered into their earpieces. "Parked north of the house about five hundred yards. Looks empty."

"How many do you estimate on the ground?" Rowe asked.

Rowe stood tense on the edge of the kitchen, waiting in the silence for Jackson to come in with an estimate as he crept closer to the cars through what was likely thick brush and grasses. If Rowe remembered correctly, five hundred yards to the north was the other entrance to the short street where it crossed the railroad tracks. There were a couple of houses in the area, but the one at the end of the block was empty.

"Single back row in each vehicle. Max likely of ten men."

"Kill the tires," Noah said. "They're not leaving here."

"Got it." The line went silent and Rowe took a breath to give more orders, when Jackson came back on the line. "Fuck! Train!"

The warning came only a second before a loud whistle split the night. Rowe swore to himself as well as he hurried into the living room. The trains through Morning View were incredibly fast and noisy. With the houses and crossings spread out, the train engineers were able to open the throttle up and run them much faster than they could through cities. The train would be passing in front of the house for less than two minutes, but the noise would act as fantastic coverage for any kind of attack.

"Everyone get ready!" Rowe directed. He knew Erik wouldn't pass up the opportunity to attack during the train noise.

"Snap has movement," JB announced in a low voice. "Two coming up the front. At least another three from the north...and two more approaching at the rear of the house. I've got a clear shot of at least five of the seven."

"Hold," Noah immediately replied. "Don't want you to scare off our new playmates."

The train engine blew its whistle sharp and loud again even as the house started to tremble and shake. Rowe's heart sped up and he tightened his grip on the gun he'd pulled from its holster on his hip. A second later there was a soft snap and the power was cut, sending the house into complete darkness.

"Fucking amateurs," Garrett muttered. They'd expected this.

No orders needed to be given. Night-vision goggles were slipped into place, and the world glowed an eerie green.

"Solo breaking off for the south side of the house," JB said.

"Get him, Snap," Rowe growled.

They waited. There was no sound but the approaching train.

"Snap got one."

"Oh, Snap!" Quinn called with a chuckle. Rowe could have sworn he heard someone snicker softly on the line.

One down. Six to go.

The train charged past the house. Everything shook and rumbled under the weight of the engine and freight cars.

And then the world exploded into chaos.

Windows were broken and gunfire lit up the night. Rowe braced his back in a corner against the front door and the wall, gun pointed at the window. A large body sailed through the opening and he opened fire, unloading several bullets into the man's chest. He landed hard on the floor and didn't move again.

"Count Chocula got one." And in an instant, Rowe was in his element.

~

*a*nxiety prickled up Noah's spine and along his neck. A little voice screamed in his head to go to Rowe and cover his back, but he remained exactly where he was with his shoulder pressed to a doorjamb as he stared out into the darkness of the backyard. Rowe was a fucking professional. He had the front of the house covered. But that knowledge didn't chase away the teeth-grinding need to keep his lover safe.

Through the night-vision goggles, Noah stared out at a green world, waiting for their attackers to get close enough for him to put a bullet or two in someone's forehead. After the murder of Chris and Paul, Noah needed this. He needed to finally put things right for his teammates.

"Cap'n, you've got one approaching the basement stairs," JB warned.

"Let him come," Andrei said in a low, ominous voice that replaced Noah's anxiety with chills along his skin. He had no idea the

Romanian had a dark side, but the man sounded like he was tapping into it.

"Another one coming your way, Tony. Oh! Wait! Got him too," JB said playfully. "I believe that's two for Snap."

Noah couldn't stop his smirk. JB was making the best of being wounded and stuck in the field. He was a good man to have covering a person's back. When Rowe had been forced to leave the Army, Noah had felt lost. JB helped him find his purpose again and kept him from getting shot. He appreciated it more than he probably ever revealed to him.

A loud crash from the basement echoed through the house followed by a man's pained screams. And then it all went terrifyingly silent. Noah's heart skipped a beat and he held his breath, waiting. Andrei was alone in the basement. He'd said he was going to booby trap the stairs, and he was hoping the noise he heard was Erik's man triggering it. *Fuck...if something happened to Andrei...*

"That's one for Cap'n Crunch," Andrei drawled in a low, confident voice that got Noah's heart started again. He'd become close friends with Andrei over the past few years. They both had that same view of being a newcomer to a very close-knit group of men. Andrei kept him from feeling awkward and unwanted.

"And I think we're gonna have to buy Royce some new stairs," Andrei continued after a second.

"Can you get out?" Rowe demanded.

"Through the rear door if Snap can promise not to shoot me."

"I got your back if you want to do a sweep around the side of the house. My view of the north and detached garage isn't good."

"I've got you, Snap," Andrei replied.

From Noah's count, that was four down. Possibly only three left. Though, he had no idea where Erik Johnson was in this mess.

Outside a thunderous roar rose up, and the night sky suddenly seemed lighter. A man screamed in terror, followed by Garrett's deep chuckle. Gunfire picked up again, but Noah couldn't tell where it was directed. None of the bullets were hitting the house near him.

"Where you goin', boy? Come here and give Sugar Bear a hug!" Garrett shouted.

"Who the fuck gave Sugar Bear a flamethrower?" JB cried out.

"What?" Quinn squeaked in disbelief.

"Shit," Rowe muttered. "He found that, huh?"

Noah laughed. Rowe had mentioned finding a new toy that he was going to let the boys try out at the next training retreat. Apparently he'd stashed it at Royce's house to keep it hidden from the bodyguards, but Garrett had stumbled across it when poking around the garage.

Noah would have been the first to argue that they had zero use for a flamethrower, but Garrett was following behind a guy as he ran across the open backyard. Flames roared out of the nozzle a good three yards in front of him, and Garrett's cackle could just barely be heard above it. At the very least, it was good at scaring the shit out of an attacker.

Lifting his gun, Noah sighted his target and squeezed off a couple of rounds. The man went down hard and didn't get up again. "Tony got one."

"Awwww..." Garrett moaned. "I was still playing with him."

"And making yourself an easy target," Rowe admonished. "Put the toy away and go scout the area."

"Yes, sir," Garrett said quickly, turning back toward the garage.

"What's the count?" Noah asked.

"I've got five," Quinn immediately replied.

"Anyone got eyes on targets? We're missing at least two," Noah said.

Before anyone could speak, shots echoed from the front of the house. Noah's heart froze in his chest, and he stood rooted to the spot for a second. Those shots either came from Rowe or were aimed at him. He wanted to go help but was afraid of leaving their backs vulnerable.

"Snap?" Noah said.

"Nothing here."

Rowe still hadn't said a word. Noah couldn't wait. "I'm going to the front."

"Got you covered," JB said, and it helped to remove a little of the weight from Noah's shoulders.

Moving as quietly as possible, Noah hurried across the kitchen to the living room entrance. He placed his shoulder against the door-frame and slowly looked across the room. There were two dead bodies on the floor, blood pooling around them. Rowe stood stiffly in the center of the room, a large knife pressed to his throat, held in place by an even larger man with a shaved head and a wicked leer.

"There you are, Keegan," the man said in a low voice.

He struggled to pull his eyes from Rowe's pissed expression. The man holding his lover hostage was undoubtedly Erik Johnson. The man looked leaner and harder than the picture that Gidget had supplied. He'd also had a head of black hair, but shaving it either saved his vanity or worked as a disguise. Didn't matter. This man was not getting out of here alive, and he wasn't going to harm a single red hair on Rowe's head.

"Johnson," Noah said. He stepped away from the doorframe, his gun raised and pointed just over Rowe's shoulder. The larger man was doing the best he could to use Rowe's wide frame as a shield, but Erik easily had six inches on Rowe, making it an awkward fit. "Looks like we've wiped out your team."

"Also blew up your building," Rowe added smugly. He winked at Noah and gave a little smirk even as Erik tilted the knife up, digging it a little deeper into Rowe's throat. A trickle of blood spilled down his neck, soaking into the collar of his black T-shirt.

Noah swallowed hard against the lump that had grown in his throat. He wanted this man dead. He wanted to put bullet after bullet into Erik Johnson for ever laying a hand on Rowe. He knew he should want the man dead for being behind the deaths of Chris and Paul, but at that moment, he couldn't see past the threat he was leveling on Rowe.

"Let's not forget that you're the reason my brother is dead," Erik snarled.

"No, that was your doing. You killed your brother and Joseph Cates. You killed Paul Grimes and Chris Perkins too. How many more people have you killed to get what you want?"

"I'll kill anyone who gets in my way! I was willing to devote my life to the military, but they chucked me into prison because of one little scuffle. Of course, those same fuckers don't mind using me and my men for their dirty jobs. They thought we were expendable." He paused and chuckled. "Proved them wrong. We were willing to do the things they weren't, but we expected to get paid."

"And you didn't get paid as much as you wanted so, what? You staged the Afghanistan ambush?"

"Had to be done. They had to know not to fuck with us."

"They were your fucking comrades!" Rowe barked. He struggled for a second, but Erik dug the knife in deeper and Rowe settled again.

Noah shifted a little to the left. He didn't lower his gun, but he didn't have a good shot. Not yet. He just had to be patient. Erik had to know he was not getting out of there alive. And there was no way in hell that Noah was going to allow him to take Rowe from him.

"They were expendable. That's how all those government hacks saw us. Expendable. Just fodder to throw at one military group or terrorist cell after another. Does it really matter why they died?"

"Yeah, it does," Noah grumbled.

"I've got a shot," JB whispered in his ear. Noah struggled not to react. He couldn't allow his eyes to shift focus from Erik or it would give away JB's location. His friend had likely moved around to the front of the house and had lined up a shot through the front window. It was the only way he had an angle on Erik. Noah hesitated. Even with a headshot, Noah was afraid that Erik would jerk and press the blade straight into Rowe's throat.

He needed to keep Erik talking while he thought, but he didn't care about his wild reasonings. Noah knew his thoughts. Chris, Paul, and JB were all a threat to his dark secret. He kept the government contracts coming so long as the secrets stayed buried. They could have unearthed everything about the Afghanistan ambush, so they had to be silenced. Since Noah was the head of that team, he had to go too.

The secrets, lies, and Erik's trail of murders stopped now.

Taking a deep calming breath, Noah held it for a second and met Rowe's eyes. He doubted Rowe could guess what he was planning, but he smiled and winked all the same, trusting his lover completely. Rowe's stocky frame relaxed as he waited.

Noah shifted the sight of the gun slightly and squeezed the trigger. The bullet slammed straight into Erik's elbow, pulling the knife away from Rowe's throat. The man didn't have a chance to scream before blood and brains splattered across the nearest wall as JB sent a shot through Erik's head, killing the man before his body even collapsed to the ground.

Noah dropped his gun and rushed to Rowe's side, pressing his hand over Rowe's neck to staunch the bleeding. Air entered his body in broken pants, and trembling wracked his entire body. Oh God, he could have lost Rowe. It had been so close. He could have—

"I'm okay. I swear, I'm okay," Rowe repeated over and over again as he wrapped his left arm around Noah's waist while pressing his right hand to the long cut on his throat.

"Blood. You're bleeding. We need a doctor. Snow—" *Fuck.* He wasn't making any sense, but he was so grateful that Quinn was still listening to everything.

"The doc is already on his way. Should be there in about two minutes," Quinn interrupted.

"Ah...hell. It's not that bad," Rowe mumbled.

"Shut up. You need stitches or at least some bandages," Noah snapped. He wasn't taking any chances. He didn't know if Rowe was losing too much blood or if the cut was even bad. Didn't care. He wouldn't feel better until Snow declared him okay.

"Snow left for Morning View before the chaos even started. He figured someone was going to get shot and would need stitching up," Quinn said.

Noah closed his eyes and pressed his forehead against Rowe's, willing the shaking to finally stop. When he'd stepped into the living room and saw Rowe being held by Erik, his entire world had been placed on the edge of that blade. Everything he wanted, his future, could have come to a screaming halt. He didn't want anything or anyone but Rowe. The man was his soul and he didn't want to live without his soul.

Soft lips brushed the corner of his mouth, dragging a shaky smile from him. "You saved my life," Rowe murmured.

Noah opened his eyes and lifted his head. "Well, I did have some help."

Rowe turned toward the broken window and grinned at JB, who was standing there in the ghillie suit, looking like a giant pile of weeds had wandered onto the porch. "Thank you, Jolly Green Giant, for saving my life."

"Fuck you, Count Chocula," JB said, but it was with a wide smile. He stood there for a second and shook his head. "You two definitely deserve each other." He limped back across the porch, moving toward where Noah could see Garrett and Jackson talking.

"He's right," Rowe said, drawing Noah's gaze back to his face. "We deserve each other. No one fits me like you."

"So true." Noah leaned in and kissed him. He wanted to let his whole body sink into Rowe, but the damn wound on his neck needed attention first. Then he could spend some much-needed time wallowing in the strength and feel of Rowe. He reluctantly broke off the kiss and smiled. "But we've got to talk about this flamethrower."

Rowe flashed him his best innocent look. "What? It was supposed to be an early Christmas present for the boys."

Noah laughed. They still had a hell of a mess to clean up. Rowe needed medical attention. And they were waiting on word that Sally was safe. But for now, it didn't matter. Rowe was safe. JB was safe. The men who killed Chris and Paul were dead. It wasn't pretty, but justice was done.

CHAPTER TWENTY-ONE

Two days later, Noah woke to the memory of JB going home and that everything was once again right in their world. He rolled over to find Rowe propped up on his hand and watching him sleep. The cut on his neck hadn't been that bad and was now covered in a small bandage. Rowe's hair was damp and he smelled freshly showered. Surprised he hadn't woken up during all that activity, Noah gave him a sleepy smile and reached for him, but Rowe put a hand on his chest.

"We need to talk," he said.

All sleepiness disappeared as he took in the serious expression on Rowe's face. "What is it?"

Rowe sighed and stroked his hand down Noah's chest. "There's been something bothering me for a while. What would you say—and I want complete honesty here—if I said I didn't want to get married?"

Noah held his breath, finally feeling like he was ready for this conversation. He didn't know if the talk with JB had helped or if he was just tired of wondering. He slid one leg over Rowe's. "With complete honesty, I say I agree."

One red eyebrow went up. "Even though I was married to Mel? I worry you'll think my feelings for you aren't as strong." He curled his fingers in the hair on Noah's chest.

"I know you love me, Rowe."

"I do. So fucking much. I just don't feel like that's us. When I was with Mel, it was such a natural thing with her. It fit her. It fit who we were together. But when I'm with you, the whole idea of marriage feels wrong. My brain and heart kept arguing. I loved Mel and married Mel. I love you just as much, but don't want to get married. It took me a while to figure out that you aren't Mel."

Noah smirked. "Well, we do look pretty similar."

"What I'm saying is that it took me a while to figure out that I was trying to fit you into a mold that wasn't made for you. What we have is who we are and it's perfect."

"What about kids?" Noah asked.

"If you really wanted them, then I would...think about it. That's not something I want either, though. I like it just us. Like our freedom and all the adventures we can have together. Kids really don't fit into my plans. The business is enough of a responsibility for me, you know? But I don't want to feel like I'm being selfish if it's something you really want. You'd make a great dad."

"Rowe, I don't really want to be a dad. I like being an uncle just fine. We agree." Noah felt something give in his chest. "You have no idea how much I was worrying about this. I hoped we were on the same page, but I didn't want you to think I don't love you enough to marry you."

"Looks like we need to work on our communication." Rowe gave him a sweet smile. "So, it's you and me, huh?"

"For always, Rowe, and I don't need a piece of paper or a fancy ceremony to feel that way. I like what we have now and want it to stay that way. Who knows? We may someday change our minds, but it'll be nice not to worry about this anymore."

"I didn't realize you were worrying. I'm sorry I'm so clueless."

Noah pulled him on top of him and wrapped his arms around him. "Not clueless. This is a big deal. All our friends are getting married, and so it seems natural that should be our next move, but I truly don't need it. All I need is you."

"I need you, too. So much." He leaned down to kiss him, and Noah realized he'd brushed his teeth. Hoping his morning breath wasn't too bad, Noah kissed him.

Surprisingly, Rowe pulled back before it could go too far. "There is one more thing."

"Really?"

"After Mel and I had that pregnancy scare, we sat down and had a long talk about what we wanted, where we wanted to go, goals, things like that. It made us both realize that we both tended to get in a rut, put off things because we always thought there'd be more time."

Noah reached up and gently smoothed his fingers across Rowe's handsome face. The man knew all too well how quickly time could suddenly run out.

"There's one thing I've always wanted, but it wasn't a good fit for me and Mel, and I just kind of wanted to throw it out there. See if it would be something you'd be interested in."

"Sure," Noah said, his heart speeding up a little. It wasn't often that Rowe talked about his dreams, and it was a little exciting to have him share something new.

"I've always wanted a big house with a whole lot of land. Acres and acres. Just a lot of space. Maybe a pond for some fishing. A place where you can open the back door and let the dogs run without worrying about them bothering the neighbors. A space where we have a vegetable garden."

"And a couple of those ATVs for riding around the land," Noah suggested.

"Yeah!" Rowe's face lit up and Noah's heart stopped.

"Babe, that sounds like heaven to me."

"Seriously? You're not just saying that?"

"Nope. Let's do it. Let's find a place that's ours."

Rowe's lips crashed into Noah's in a searing kiss. It didn't take long for fire to spark along Noah's spine. God, Rowe felt good on top of him, heavy and warm. And he smelled so good, like peppermint shampoo and soap. He slid his tongue deep into Rowe's mouth and Rowe moaned, kissing him back just as deeply.

"Want you," Noah whispered, rolling them over so he was on top of Rowe. All those muscles felt fantastic underneath him. "Want inside you."

"Oh yeah," Rowe breathed. "I was hoping you were up for that, so I took a nice, thorough shower."

"I love a man who's prepared. Up for some toys today?"

Rowe spread his legs and rutted up against him. He shook his head. "Just wanna feel you. Only you. So fucking much."

They kissed and rubbed against each other, legs tangled together. One kiss bled into another until Noah was dizzy with desire. The lust Rowe sparked in him still stunned him because nothing had ever felt like this. The all-consuming need that rose in him with Rowe's touch awed him.

Noah kissed down Rowe's neck and chest. He took a nipple into his mouth and sucked, loving the way Rowe bowed up off the bed. He bit and licked, then lavished attention on the other nipple. Rowe's nipples were so responsive, hardening with the first touch of his tongue.

He licked down his stomach, enjoying the ripple of his abs as he tensed and writhed under him. He kept licking, following his red happy trail, kissing around his cock. He scooted down and took one fuzzy ball into his mouth, getting it nice and slick. Rowe cried out above him, his thighs shaking. God, the need racing through Noah's body had it humming, and he took in Rowe's other ball, giving it the same treatment. He nuzzled, licked and kissed all around his dick before taking it into his mouth. He went down to the root and swallowed around the soft head.

Rowe's fingers speared into his hair. "So good at that."

He loved going down on Rowe as much as the man loved doing that to him. But right then, he wanted inside him. He gave the head of his cock a kiss and came back up to reach for the lube off the bedside table. They didn't even bother putting it away these days.

He got his fingers slick and rubbed around Rowe's pucker. He pushed a finger inside him and groaned at the tight, hot clasp. "Yeah," he breathed, moving that finger in and out.

Rowe spread his legs more, his hips coming up off the bed as he fucked himself on Noah's finger. He was velvety smooth inside and Noah gritted his teeth at the thought of putting his cock in there. Green eyes locked with his, and he saw the love and need Rowe had for him in those eyes. He shuddered and added a second finger, watching Rowe's mouth fall open on a gasp.

"So good," he murmured, leaning down to kiss him.

"More," Rowe begged.

There was nothing hotter than reducing Rowe to a puddle of need, and he crooked his fingers and rubbed Rowe's prostate, smiling when the man came up off the bed again.

"If you don't get in there, it's going to be too late. I'm gonna come."

"You want me like this? On your back?"

"Yeah, wanna watch you. You're so hot when you're fucking me."

Noah got the lube and slicked himself up, then brought Rowe's legs up. He held them high and pressed the tip of his cock to Rowe's hole. Pushing slowly, he eased inside the man, his eyes rolling back at the unbelievable pleasure of Rowe's body swallowing him. Rowe clenched his ass around him, and Noah had to count in his head so he didn't spill. "Too turned-on."

"Good, because I'm not going to last long."

Wanting it to last, Noah didn't move much at first. He just held himself still once all the way inside his man. He stared down at him, taking in the glittering green eyes, the lust clouding Rowe's gorgeous face. "Love you," he whispered. "Love being inside you."

"Love you, too." Rowe's voice broke and he chuckled. "You gotta move."

He slowly started sliding out until just the tip remained inside Rowe, then pushed back in. Rowe groaned and lifted his hips into the thrust. He began to press in and out, never pulling himself all the way out, but teasing with the tip of his cock. Rowe made a strangled sound in his throat, a sound of amused frustration.

"Harder," he breathed.

Noah let his hips pick up strength and speed and he knew he got the angle just right when Rowe's mouth fell open and stayed that way. His head went back, his eyes closed, and he looked so beautiful, he took Noah's breath away. He loved him so damn much. Rowe's eyes opened and locked with his, and the love that passed between them made his hips stutter. He leaned down to kiss him, moaning at the slide of Rowe's tongue. He sucked his bottom lip into his mouth and nipped it.

Rowe reached between them and began stroking his dick and panting. Noah came up on his hands to watch. "Yeah," he breathed. Rowe's dick was flushed red, and he loved watching as Rowe pleasured himself. He ramped up his hip speed and Rowe yelled, his body tensing as he spilled all over his stomach.

"Fuck yeah," Noah cried out, his hips moving faster and faster, the sound of flesh hitting flesh loud in the room.

"That's it, babe. Come for me." Rowe grabbed his ass and shoved him in deeper, and that was all it took. Lightning speared through Noah's body, his eyes shutting as the orgasm tore out of him and he pumped inside Rowe's body. He slid in his own semen and it was so hot, he couldn't stop thrusting inside the man until he felt too sensitive and had to stop. He collapsed on top of him, panting into Rowe's neck.

"Damn," he muttered.

"Yeah," Rowe agreed, tightening his arms around Noah hard.

They caught their breaths, lying there and recovering. Noah's entire body felt lax as he sprawled on Rowe, feeling his heart beating against his own chest. Rowe stroked his hands up and down Noah's back, and he turned his head to kiss the corner of his lips. "Love you," he whispered.

"Love you, too."

"I'm so glad we're on the same page when it comes to what we want together."

"We just have to learn to talk about things sooner. Not let them fester."

"You sure you won't think I love you any less without marriage?"

Noah lifted his head to stare down at Rowe. "If there is one thing I'm sure of, it's your feelings for me. You show me in everything you do, in how you touch me, look at me. I've never felt more loved in my life."

Rowe's brows furrowed. "You do know JB was in love with you. I think he still is."

"I knew his feelings were growing, but no, I didn't know. Not until he told me a few days ago. I didn't know what to say. There's no chance of anything ever happening between us again. I've got what I want in my life. Exactly what I want. You."

"You say the sweetest things."

Noah rolled his eyes and pushed off to lie next to Rowe. He slid one thigh over Rowe's leg and tugged him close, ignoring the mess that had smeared all over the both of them. They could shower and wash the sheets. Connecting with Rowe felt more important right then. He wrapped one arm around him and kissed his shoulder. "Let's make a pact to talk about the things we're worried about from here on out. No wondering or stewing. If you're concerned, you talk to me. If you're angry, you talk to me. Even if you're just happy—tell me. As long as we're being up-front with each other, this is going to be exactly what we both want."

"Already is," Rowe said softly. He rolled onto his side, keeping their legs tangled together, and kissed Noah again. It was a soft, sweet kiss that made butterflies flutter in Noah's belly. Two and a half years and he still got them. He imagined he always would. He smiled against Rowe's lips.

"What?" Rowe whispered.

"Just imagining Ian's face when we tell him there won't be another wedding to plan."

Rowe laughed. "Eh, he'll get over it."

"Think our friends will understand our feelings?"

"They'll have to. This relationship belongs to you and me and nobody else. I know they like to get involved in well…everything, but this is none of their business. We'll tell them and that will be it. Ian still has Snow's wedding to plan, and he can turn that into something that will drive the man crazy."

It was Noah's turn to laugh. "I still can't believe those two are tying the knot."

"Yeah, I was pretty damn surprised myself, but they are happy and that's all that matters to me."

Noah pulled back to look at him. "And what about you? Are you happy?"

Rowe rolled on top of him and cupped both sides of his face. His green eyes were filled with emotion and honesty. "So happy. I've got all I need right here. Right now."

CHAPTER TWENTY-TWO

"*H*ey, Rowe!" Snow called. "Get over here and tell Hollis about the time we cornered a perp in the bathroom, and you threatened him with something warm and wet."

Rowe's shoulders shook with laughter at the memory of the time they were trying to track down the fucker who was threatening Lucas's life, and they'd grabbed a guy while he was reporting to his boss. He shut the cooler and walked back to the long patio table, putting one of the beers in his hand in front of Noah.

Noah looked up at him with a wide grin. "Why don't I know about this story?"

Leaning down, he pressed a kiss to the middle of Noah's forehead. "It was about a year before we got together, and I don't remember the story too well because we got totally wasted at Lucas's afterward. I woke up on the floor of the penthouse, halfway between the living room and the kitchen, with the mother of all hangovers. The freaking doc and Ian were hogging the couch."

"Ian was all warm and snuggly," Snow said as if that answered all of life's questions.

Ian perked his head up and smiled. "I am snuggly."

Rowe shook his head. That night, Snow had fallen asleep wrapped around Ian's smaller frame like he meant to shield the young man from any and all threats. Or maybe Ian had been the shield Snow needed to protect him from the demons that battered his mind and soul each day.

Their lives had changed so much over the past few years, it was more than a little shocking.

Lucas Vallois, billionaire philanthropist, was married...to a *man*. They'd all thought he'd get married, but Rowe, Snow, and Ian had all worried that it would be some sham marriage to a woman purely because she offered him connections and completion to his image. But Andrei had changed his life, and now they had a perfect little girl who was currently asleep on Jude's chest.

Snow was never supposed to get married. Hell, the way he was living, they weren't entirely sure the man would see forty. But Jude was the one to perfectly take the grumpy doctor in hand and heal all the wounded parts of Snow they couldn't reach. Now they had plans to marry and grow their family through adoption.

If anyone deserved their happily ever after, it was Ian. The young man had an enormous heart and a strong spirit. He loved everyone he met and wanted them all to be happy. His own dark past never dimmed or crushed his capacity for love. And he found the perfect person to love in Hollis Banner. The former cop might be a little rough around the edges, but he completed Ian.

They'd been back from their honeymoon for only a few weeks when Rowe and Noah invited everyone over for a backyard cookout. They kept it simple. Just fired up the grill, set up a cooler filled with beer, and lit some candles to keep the mosquitos away.

Now with their bellies full and the sun setting behind the trees, they relaxed in cushioned chairs as they told so many ridiculous stories of their youth. Rowe dropped down in his chair next to Noah and took a sip of his beer. As he set it on the table, he looked around at the men gathered and released a happy little sigh. His family. These were the people he lived and died for. Something inside of him relaxed to see them all safe and happy.

"That was a very contented sigh," Lucas observed. "Feeling pleased with yourself?"

"Yes, I am."

"It was just hamburgers and chicken on the grill," Snow teased.

Ian reached over and smacked Snow on the shoulder. "Hey! It was good. And some of us appreciate having a night off from cooking every once in a while."

Rowe's smile grew when Noah reached over and threaded his fingers through Rowe's. The food was not what Rowe was feeling so contented about and Noah knew it. After their long talk, he felt more settled and secure in the life that he was building with this family, and most importantly, with the man at his side.

"I know that look," Andrei said softly, catching everyone's attention. "You've made a decision about something."

Fucking Andrei. It was like the man had a sixth sense about these things. Rowe had no idea how the hell he read people so well, but he did. There really was no getting anything by him.

"Really?" Ian gasped. Rowe looked over to find the smaller man practically vibrating in his chair, and Rowe wanted to groan. "What is it?"

Rowe looked over at Noah, who grinned and shrugged at him, seemingly amused by Ian's excitement. Yeah, he could guess what they were all thinking, and it was time to lay that all to rest once and for all. No more jokes or evasions.

"You've got the floor, babe," Noah said.

Grabbing up his beer, he took a quick drink and cleared his throat. He hoped this was something they could understand. It was what he and Noah needed. What they wanted for their happiness.

"Noah and I have done a lot of talking recently. About what we wanted and needed individually. Also, what we needed and wanted as a couple," Rowe started. He glanced down at the fingers twined with his, and he knew he wanted to see that for the rest of his life. "And we've decided that we're not getting married."

"What?" Ian cried. His wide eyes darted from Rowe to Noah with worry. Rowe knew in Ian's mind that love and forever equaled marriage, and if they weren't getting married, it spelled trouble.

"We're not separating," Noah said quickly with his trademark warmth and smile.

"I love Noah. Love him just as much as I ever loved Mel. I want to spend the rest of my life with him doing weird and crazy shit. And even the boring stuff."

"Like laundry?" Noah teased.

"Fuck the laundry." Rowe turned serious when he looked back at Ian. "But I don't need or want to get married. It's not who I am."

"And it's not who I am," Noah added. "Or who we are together."

"But you married Mel," Hollis said. He reached over and placed a hand on Ian's shoulder, pulling his husband closer as if he was worried he needed comforting. "I don't mean to sound like a dick."

Rowe shrugged. "Mel and I got together and married almost ten years ago. We were young and relatively bright-eyed. We were still sure we could conquer the world. We both saw marriage as the logical next step for us." He paused and looked over at Noah. His smile had dimmed a little in the face of the sadness that now lingered in his beautiful eyes.

"Not going anywhere," Noah said, and Rowe knew it was true. The old worry that he was going to lose Noah like he lost Mel would probably dog him for the rest of his life, but Noah didn't mind reminding him every time that he was going to be right there by his side no matter what.

"But in the past ten years, we lost Mel. Lost friends. Made new friends and family. I got a second chance—"

"We got a second chance," Noah corrected.

Rowe smiled. "When we didn't think we'd get one. Marriage doesn't feel like the logical choice, that imperative need, for completion that it once did. We look around this table, and we know that we already have everything that we could ever want. Marriage isn't for us. We're perfectly happy the way things are."

"Things change," Snow said. Rowe looked over at the doctor. He was leaning to his side so that his right shoulder was touching Jude's, while his left hand rubbed up and down Daciana's back as she slept on Jude's chest. Yeah, Snow was a poster child for things changing. Rowe would never have expected the man to want marriage and kids, but so many things changed for Snow when he met Jude.

Rowe gave Snow a matching smirk. "True. Things change. And if things change for us, we'll talk about it. But for as far into the future as we can see, we don't see this changing for us."

"What about kids? Do you plan to have any?" Jude asked in a low voice so as not to disturb the little girl.

"We already have our kids," Noah said. "We've got three dogs that keep us busy at home."

"And Ward Security is our other family," Rowe added. He glanced over at Andrei to see the man smile and nod. He had a feeling that Andrei was developing a similar view of the company, as its COO.

"But even though we're not planning to have kids of our own, we are looking forward to being the awesome uncles of the family," Noah said. "Lucas and Andrei have already kicked things off with little Daci, and you know they're not going to stop until they add a little prince to the Vallois family." He then motioned over to Snow and Jude. "You're going to be adding to your family and keeping Grandma Anna busy," he said, mentioning Jude's energetic mother.

"And we all know that Ian's going to have a huge brood." Rowe pinned Ian with a knowing look. Ian rolled his eyes dramatically but didn't deny it. Rowe knew in his heart that Ian wanted several children, filling his home with the love and laughter he never got to experience growing up. He and Hollis were going to be amazing dads.

"We're looking forward to taking them camping and boating."

"Teaching them how to shoot a bow and arrow," Noah said.

"Self-defense and martial arts training at Ward Security."

"Oh! How to disable a security system."

"Code names!"

"Weapons maintenance."

"Explosives."

"No!" their friends shouted in unison.

Noah and Rowe looked at each other and started laughing. Their friends said "no" now, but they would come to realize it was better if their kids learned those important things from their Uncle Rowe and Uncle Noah.

Daciana popped her head up and gave a little whimper as she looked around. The moment she spotted her Daddy Lucas, she stretched out her arms. Lucas leaned forward and scooped her up, cradling her against his chest, and murmured soft words in her ear that sounded a lot like Romanian. He did it all as if he'd been doing things like that his entire life.

And yeah, the sight warmed something deep in Rowe's chest, but he didn't need one of those for himself. No, if he needed to cuddle a baby, he only had to reach out for Daciana or any of the other nieces and nephews that were undoubtedly heading his way.

Clearing his throat, Rowe said, "The point is that the life we want, that we dream about, we've already got."

Jude sat forward in his chair and picked up his glass of iced tea. He lifted into the air, smiling at Rowe and Noah. "To family."

A lump formed in Rowe's throat as they all picked up their glasses and repeated Jude's toast. Yes. To family. He was so damned lucky to have them all.

"Okay," Hollis said as they lowered their glasses again. "Tell me this 'warm and wet' bathroom story. It's probably just more proof of why I should have hauled all your asses in when I was a cop."

Noah's laughter brushed against Rowe, wrapping him up tight. Rowe was right where he was supposed to be. It hadn't been easy getting there, but he was finally happy and complete again.

~

Want to keep up with all the action? Jump into the chaos that is the Ward Security series.
Check out *Psycho Romeo*, book 1 of Ward Security series.

Geoffrey Ralse is known for being the life of the party. He loves the club scene, hanging with his friends, and flirting with whomever catches his eye. He certainly isn't going to stop living his life just because some would-be stalker starts sending him threats.

But it all changes when Geoffrey is drugged and wakes up half naked in his own home with a new message from his stalker.

He needs help and there's only one person he trusts...

Protective Agent Sven Larsen has been fighting Geoffrey's flirtatious advances for months, even though he's impossibly drawn to the man. There's no way he can be around him twenty-four/seven and not finally crack. But one look at Geoffrey's haunted eyes, and he knows there's no way he's letting Geoffrey walk out of Ward Security without him.

Even if it means breaking his own rules, he will keep Geoffrey safe.

Grab it now on Amazon.

Keep up with all our new books by signing up for our newsletter at **http://drakeandelliott.com/newsletter/**.

AUTHOR'S NOTE

Thanks so much for reading *Ignite* and going on another adventure with the Unbreakable Bonds boys. We still have one more adventure to write focusing on Ian and Hollis.

But first, we are taking a bit of a vacation by returning to the Pineapple Grove series. Wesley Blake has a B and B to protect from a ruthless property developer. We're aiming to have the new book out in September. If you haven't jumped into our Pineapple Grove series, grab up *Something About Jace* now.

Happy reading!

Jocelynn Drake

Rinda Elliott

ABOUT THE AUTHOR

Jocelynn Drake

It started with a battered notebook. Jocelynn Drake wrote her first story when she was 12 years old. It was a retelling of Robin Hood that now included a kickass female who could keep up with all the boys and be more than just a sad little love interest. From there, she explored space, talked to dragons, and fell in love again and again and again.

This former Kentucky girl has moved up, down, and across the U.S. with her patient husband. They've settled near the Rockies…for now. She spends the majority of her time lost in the strong embrace of a good book.

When she's not hammering away at her keyboard or curled up with a book, she can usually be found cuddling with her cat Demona, walking her dog Ace, or flinging curses at the TV while playing a video game. Outside of books, furry babies, and video games, she is completely enamored of Bruce Wayne, Ezio Auditore, travel, tattoos, explosions, and fast cars.

She is the author of the urban fantasy series: The Dark Days series and the Asylum Tales. She is also working on a gay romantic suspense series called The Exit Strategy. She has also co-authored with Rinda Elliot the following series: Unbreakable Bonds, Ward Security, and Pineapple Grove. She can be found at JocelynnDrake.com.

Rinda Elliott

Rinda loves unusual stories and credits growing up in a family of curious life-lovers who moved all over the country. Books and movies full of fantasy, science fiction and romance kept them amused, especially in some of the stranger places.

For years, she tried to separate her darker side with her humorous and romantic one. She published short fiction, but things really started happening when she gave in and mixed it up. When not lost in fiction, she loves collecting music, gaming and spending time with her husband and two children.

She is the author of the Beri O'Dell urban fantasy series, the YA Sister of Fate Trilogy with Harlequin Teen, and the paranormal romance Brothers Bernaux Trilogy. She also writes erotic ménage fiction. These days, she's concentrating on her first love, MM romance. She can also be found at RindaElliott.com.

Keep up with all our new books by signing up for our newsletter at **http://drakeandelliott.com/newsletter/**.

ALSO BY THE AUTHORS

The Unbreakable Bonds Series

Shiver

Shatter

Torch

Devour

Blaze

Fracture

Ignite

Unbreakable Bonds Short Story Collection

Unbreakable Stories: Lucas

Unbreakable Stories: Snow

Unbreakable Stories: Rowe

Unbreakable Stories: Ian

Ward Security Series

Psycho Romeo

Dantès Unglued

Deadly Dorian

Jackson (a novella)

Sadistic Sherlock

King of Romance (short story collection)

Killer Bond

Pineapple Grove

Something About Jace

Drew & Mr. Grumpy (a novella)

46582428R00141

Made in the USA
Lexington, KY
28 July 2019